MYTHICA RISING

A. L. D'ALONZO

First published in Australia 2026 by Dash Publishing

Illustrated and typeset by Dash Publishing
1st Edition 2026
ISBN: 978-1-7640654-2-9
E-Book: ISBN: 978-1-7640654-3-6

Also by A. L. D'Alonzo
The Nihilist Approach to Time Travel

For the rebels…

THE TROLL AND THE THOROUGHBRED

"You are by far one of the most grotesque creatures I've ever come across," Roan announced to the cigar-smoking troll.

It may have only been eight-thirty in the evening, but there was enough cigar smoke to choke a small cat and leave a dog with emphysema. The living room windows were bolted, and the small fan in the corner was only circulating gullies of ash instead of fresh air. The lime-green, corduroy couch lay flattened like a mashed potato. A hand the size of a softball mitt tapped the cigar onto the armrest and returned it to his slug-like lips.

That was Troll.

Troll just grunted and puffed smoke. You would be correct in describing Troll as grotesque. He was, in fact, a troll, although he could have passed as an eight-foot-nine professional wrestler that had been repeatedly hit by a train. Sparse tufts of black hair decorated his head, and his skin had the look of a rotten fish. He smoked at least two packets of cigarettes a day and as many cigars as he could get. His drinking habits weren't much better, and his personality was comparable to the aforementioned fish.

"You ain't exactly a thoroughbred either," Troll replied.

"If I don't get out of here soon, I'm going to need a lung transplant."

"Human or horse?" A wet burp escaped Troll as he chuckled at his own wit.

Roan impatiently hoofed the carpet again. He got the worst end of the deal. Stabled in this apartment all day did nothing for his health. It was not as if he could just take a stroll whenever he felt like it. He was half horse, for goodness' sake! The rangers would be on him in an instant, asking for his permits, his address, if he was up to date with his Mythica registration, which he certainly wasn't. They would capture him and send him to a zoo or force him to give pony rides at children's birthdays. If he had one more sticky child gripping his mane…

"Zack, stop buying Troll cigars. He's making the air unbreathable."

Zack was the pasty kid in the corner with his laptop screen glowing into his broody eyes.

"Last time I did that, he punched a hole in the wall."

"I don't care."

"You didn't have to deal with the landlord." Of the three of them, Zack was the most human, and so he was lumped with doing all those dumb human tasks. The joys of being a vampire.

Roan clopped his hoof again and returned to the scrawl of papers that covered his desk. He had a very organised system. It went something like this: the left corner puddle was research, the right corner puddle was accounts and rent, the floor was puddled with newspaper clippings, and everywhere else was littered with pages from his memoirs.

He used his native centaur script so that no prying eyes could read them. Not even Zack could find the translation on the internet. The centaurs were a secretive bunch. Roan was no exception. Memories were important; Roan knew this, and he insisted on writing his life down.

Unlike Zack, though, he did not use a computer. He preferred the typewriter; one of the few human inventions he could stomach. Roan had told Zack once that he enjoyed the sound it made. Zack suspected that the click-clack sound of keys was the closest Roan would ever get to the rhythmic clop of a herd of centaur hooves.

"There's a Mythical Creatures exhibition at the museum. I'll take you there tonight, Roan. It'll get you out of the apartment. I've been told that if you bribe the minotaur, they will let you pass," Zack did not look up from his screen as he spoke. Roan deduced he was on one of those online dating sites again. Zack was just too dweeby to be a lady-killer, even for a vampire. Not to mention Zack's dire efforts to make vampires cool again, but vampires are just *so* last year.

That's what humans did; they had their favourites, and they had their fashions. They had their magazines telling them which creatures to make friends with, which to avoid, and which would make great pets. It sickened him.

"Thank you," Roan replied. Zack smiled a thin smile under his beaky nose and swished his unkempt fringe. And the boy wondered why he didn't have a girlfriend.

Roan busied himself cleaning up his papers before Spike returned from hunting. The chupacabra was notorious for using Roan's desk as a litter box. Spike was the pet of this odd little family. Well, rather, the child that nobody wanted.

If Roan had his way, both Troll and his little monster would be gone in an instant. Zack didn't mind Spike. Chupacabras fed off blood, and so Zack felt an attachment towards the thing. The problem was that chupacabras fed on the blood of cattle and sheep. Often, Roan would wake up in the night with a mangy dog gnawing on his flank. Right now, it was off on its subway walks where it caught rats and drank them dry.

Roan gathered his cloak and fedora in preparation. Roan loved his fedoras; they were one of the few human things he didn't mind. He thought it made him look menacing, like a mob boss from the last century. Zack thought it made him look like something he called a *neck-beard*.

“There are a couple more emails for you, Roan.” Zack hooked up his laptop and printed them out. Roan hated looking at computer screens; it hurt his eyes.

“Thank you,” Roan sighed. He was not having a good day. His head was pounding from the lack of fresh air. His current predicament frustrated him. He thought life would have improved after their escape.

“It’s something about dwarf-made gold being sold, which will magically return to the owner after three hours, so you never run out of money. They say it’s good for the likes of us because, you know, we fall under the heading of *unemployable*.”

“It’s a trap.” Roan flipped the laptop shut. “It’s leprechaun gold that does that. Honestly, if these kidnappers are going to do their job, you’d think they would have done their research.”

The internet was a great way for their kind to interact and help one another out, but there were also humans that pretended to be something they were not. They would lure creatures into their traps and then sell them to zoos or private collectors, or breeding programs.

Spike returned through the little door, which had been handcrafted by Troll (by kicking his boot through it). The chupacabra was the size of a small dog with the face of a toad and needle fangs rimming his squat mouth. He was overweight, very overweight.

“Zack, we’re leaving,” Roan demanded before Spike could climb up his fetlock for dessert.

Zack did the usual corridor check. No one was there except Larry. He was no threat. He had passed out in front of his ex-wife’s door.

“Hey Larry,” Zack whispered, as he always did when they passed him. A landlord, who had won the *I-don’t-give-a-crap* award for three years straight, ran the set of flats they lived in. It was a small building, only four storeys high. The elevator hadn’t worked for years and was now home to a rabid family of raccoons. Roan had first been cautious of the security cameras, but after a week he realised they were as harmless as pink, plush bunnies.

The centaur had become accustomed to stairs; they still gave him a little trouble, but they lived on the first floor. If he had wanted to, he could have leaped the gap, but he wasn't in the mood, and they had to be quiet in case the single mother of three woke up and started screaming at whoever disturbed her baby. A few streets down, you could hear the cries and hoots of a gang beating up some poor tourist who had the misfortune to get lost.

The night was not how Roan remembered it to be. There were no stars, and the smog had created an artificial atmosphere over the moon. The only light came from the flickering streetlamps. Steam from the subway lingered around their ankles from the vents beneath them. They passed down two streets and then turned the corner. Zack and Roan did not speak. Roan had little to say.

They saw a man in the distance edging towards an ankle-height light. Roan stopped to watch. It enticed the man, who followed it curiously as it brought him closer to the foggy mist. Roan flared his nostrils in anticipation. Zack watched too, only because Roan was not moving. The man staggered, his foot slipped, and then he yelped before something dragged him into an invisible pothole.

"Rather unfortunate, don't you think?" Zack sighed.

"Serves them right," Roan replied gruffly. The will-o'-the-wisp had been preying on humans for as long as they had existed; now, Roan was glad of it. He had never seen one up close; he didn't think anyone alive had. Roan always thought of them akin to those deep-sea fish with lights in their heads that lure in other stupid fish. The thought satisfied him. As pretentious and self-obsessed as humans were, they were just big, stupid fish.

"I'll go talk to the minotaur," Zack said. They had come to the white marble steps of the New York Museum of Natural History. Its stone arches and columns created an impressive presence. On either side of the large doors stood two blue minotaurs. Their horns were the thickness of Roan's thigh, and their bodies made Troll look like a fairy. They were the perfect bouncers, and they snorted steam into the chilly night air. Despite their menacing appearance, Zack strolled up to them as if they were old friends. He drew something out of his satchel, which Roan knew were caramel chews. He spoke for a while and then tossed one to each of them. Roan approached once Zack gave him the signal.

The minotaurs didn't like humans much either, and had no qualms about breaking the rules. Zack picked the lock on the door, and within two minutes they were inside. The museum guards were not as vigilant as before. Probably because they thought the minotaurs were enough of a deterrent. In all honesty, if you were going to break into a building, a museum isn't exactly what springs to mind. Roan saw the posters on the wall advertising the latest exhibit.

ANCIENT MYTHICAL ARTEFACTS
Come explore the forgotten worlds of the Celts, Romans, and Greeks.
Mysteries revealed through the accounts of the creatures themselves.

"Why did you bring me here?" Roan felt sick.

"What are you talking about? You agreed to come."

"I changed my mind. I forget how much I dislike seeing our kind on display."

They strolled through the echoing corridors. Roan's hoof clops echoed on the marble.

"Who wants to see a room full of dead things?" Roan continued despite Zack's silence. Rooms housed stuffed animals and skeletons. Dead Mythica were now amongst them. The world had become obsessed.

"Troll has left you in a poor mood today."

"As always."

"Worse than usual."

"I suppose. Spike was gnawing on my fetlock too today. I'm going to need a rabies shot."

"Maybe we can try for a midnight stroll around Central Park tomorrow?"

"I don't think the gnomes will be too happy with a centaur clopping over their burrows."

"Screw them, the humans cause way more damage than we ever would."

"Some days I wonder if I'm better off here or back at the circus." Roan sighed. Zack stopped him in his tracks, standing in front of him.

"Don't you say that. You were miserable there."

"I had enough room to canter."

"In a circle … while people fed you carrots."

"I hate carrots. Fine, you are right."

A tacky cardboard pillar decorated with printed vines and roses framed the entrance to the Mythica exhibit. The first exhibit greeted them at the door. The echo of Roan's hooves halted at the sight.

"He was an old friend," Roan said sadly, standing before a taxidermy centaur. His palomino flank was dusty, and his mane cut short like a common mule's. In real life, the man would never have worn his mane like that. Roan wondered why they had cut it.

The plaque said he had died of natural causes and had willingly donated his body to science. "Willingly donated my arse. Someone poisoned him. Look at the hooves. See the blue discolouration?"

"I see," said Zack sadly, wondering if it was a mistake to bring Roan here. "This way," Zack said. Roan had a tendency to dawdle, and he followed Zack to the new exhibit. The room contained neat rows of artefacts, each in its little glass box balancing on metal poles.

"How do you think they got all these?" Zack asked.

"How do you think?" Roan scoffed. Some of these artefacts were not that old; others were heirlooms taken without consent, perhaps bought at a ridiculously low price from a needy Mythica. Roan recognised a spear from a Celtic elf tribe. "My mother told us stories about the elves," Roan said.

"What did she say about them?"

"Never make a deal with an elf; it will always turn to poison."

They passed a shrunken vampire head, to which Zack passed across quickly.

A bottomless cauldron blazed with embers.

"Pandora's cauldron," Zack read. "Not quite what the myth says. I thought it was a box."

"Maybe the human myths got it wrong. They usually do. What are you doing?"

"Checking for any electronics or pyrotechnics to make it sparkle like that."

"You think it's a fake?"

"Wouldn't put it past the humans to do something like that."

"It's a museum, not a circus; there are no special effects here." Roan turned his head towards the lone centaur. They approached a colour-changing orb with something trapped fluttering like a moth. "The only part of a will-o'-the-wisp anyone alive has ever seen," Zack explained.

"Great, so they severed an innocent creature's head, or eyeball, or whatever this is." Posters with timelines and facts were present, but they were largely inaccurate.

"Oh, hey, look here, this is from a centaur," Zack called from somewhere to the right. "*Although little is known about the elusive half-human, half-horse crossbreeds...*" Roan snorted derisively as Zack read the plaque. "*They are known for their intricate and lightweight armour and metalwork. This artefact was not believed to have been used in battle, but as a decorative piece. Our resident seer believes this cuff is embedded with residual magic, although its purpose remains a mystery.*" Roan clopped over, wondering how they would have gained anything from a centaur. His kind kept their possessions in places no human could ever get to.

That was why, when Roan saw the dull gold engravings of his family crest upon that arm cuff, he froze. He froze and stared at the thick golden armband decorated with delicate filigree and a shield. Impulse took command. Roan reared up onto his hind legs and kicked right through the glass.

Alarms sounded like a tone-deaf banshee choir.

"What the hell are you doing!" Zack screamed. Roan snatched the arm cuff and swung Zack onto his back. The minotaurs were coming, and so were the human security guards, and they were far worse and would not accept bribes of candy. Zack squealed and grappled madly for Roan's mane, climbing onto his back.

Roan leapt over the lower exhibits, through the dead-things corridor, and back into the main entrance hall, where two Dobermans and two human guards met them. Roan drew a breath and braced himself. All he needed to do was get through those front doors. Not that far away, right? If Roan didn't move, he would be mauled to mincemeat. When the first dog came, Roan reared up and kicked. The dog yelped and fell back, unable to stand again. Then Roan charged; he charged as he remembered running through the moors of old England.

"Zack, need more caramel chews." He didn't know how the vampire managed it, but somehow, with both hands still clutching madly to Roan's mane, an entire pack of caramel chews went flying over Roan's head. The two minotaurs watched it rise and fall between them. They dived, head-butting each other with such force that they toppled back in shock, making a clean getaway for themselves.

The street was screaming with sirens. Blue and red lights pulsed violently across the street.

"Police. Halt!"

"Like hell." Roan leapt over the bonnet of a police car and broke into a bolt. Then the bullets came. They came, and they didn't stop. Roan prayed the family cuff still held its magic. Zack was screaming like a girl at a boy-band concert. Roan felt a bullet hit his shoulder. He didn't stop. Well, the cuff was sort of working, well, sort of; the bullets had hit nothing vital. This would make front-page news. The media loved anything to do with Mythica. Mythica this, Mythica that, it was never-ending.

Roan continued galloping, losing sight of the police cars and sirens down a series of back alleys. Zack had righted himself on Roan's back. His body was all wrong; his hands clutched Roan's mane too tight, and he was far too ridged, Zack would feel every jolt of Roan's hoof beats.

"In all your seventy-three years of immortal life, you've never ridden a horse before?" Roan grunted as they came to a stop outside their apartment.

"Forgive me if I don't feel like talking right now; I've got a couple of bullets in my skull." Zack slumped off Roan's back and jammed the key into the lock. Larry was still unconscious. His ex-wife had placed a green plastic bucket beside him for his usual morning hangover.

"You're immortal, so what does it matter?"

"It still hurts."

"Tell me about it. I think I've got one in my shoulder." They entered the smoky room and recoiled at the smell. Troll was not smoking cigars or cigarettes this time. He had moved on to something a bit more … herbal.

"Troll, get the hell out of here. Keep guard outside." Roan wasn't sure how efficient Troll would be at keeping guard, but Troll did as he was told. In truth, Roan just wanted him out of here. Zack did not bleed as much as a living human. Roan was grateful for that because with the number of bullets that were in him, he would have left a blood trail for the police to follow. Roan, on the other hand, was bleeding quite a lot, but he hoped that most of the blood had just run down his body rather than onto the street.

Spike spun around in mad circles, making snorting, squealing noises like a pig, and licked the blood from Roan's legs as Zack brought him the first aid kit. It was a pretty pathetic box, but it would have to do. The tweezers weren't large enough; they were just those shitty plastic ones, so Zack plunged his nimble fingers into Roan's wound. Roan hissed in pain.

"Well, it serves you right, that stunt you pulled back there. What the hell was that about?" Zack rarely swore, but when he was angry, he would take a leaf out of Troll's book. Roan looked at the cuff wrapped around his bicep. Though scratched, the family crest remained, just as Roan remembered it. The last time he had seen this, he had been a foal. His grandfather had worn it.

Roan took it off and examined it as Zack bandaged his wounds. The cuff was no thicker than the length of his fingers, and within its rims were the first letters of his tribal name. The writing combined Ogham and centaurian scripts. This showed which part of England he had come from. Cambridge. Only a small tribe, but one that commanded respect. Well, at least it used to.

He followed the carving with his fingers — two straight parallel lines, then a thatch-work square coming off the left side, like a flag. A large looping '*g*' shape came off the other. The rest of the space was filled with inscriptions — a spell. It had kept him from being shot any worse than he was now.

"It's a family heirloom. I wasn't thinking. I'm sorry." Roan put the cuff back onto his arm. He wanted to keep it close. Zack was busy with the tweezers, picking out bullets from his own skull. They would just dissolve or succumb to whatever vampiric immune defences Zack had. As a gesture of truce, Roan went to the bar fridge and pulled out a juice box for his friend.

"You owe me a new jacket," Zack muttered, examining the holes in his sleeves.

"Take this instead." Roan dumped his fedora on Zack's head. "Ew, no. Fedoras are dumb." Zack tossed the hat among the discarded bullets.

"So is your fringe."

Blue and red lights blared through their blacked-out windows. Roan froze. This was not good. Roan prayed

Troll had hidden himself and was not bounding up to a cop car. Zack abandoned his bullet removal and opened his laptop.

"What are you doing?" Roan hissed, the apartment feeling far smaller than usual. They shouldn't have come back here. What a stupid idea!

"Calling for help."

"On your laptop!"

"I know a guy."

"You know a guy? If this is anything like your internet dates, I may as well surrender now."

"This is the police," an authoritative voice bellowed through a megaphone. "We have surrounded you. Come out peacefully and we will not fire." Would it be better to hide the cuff or to wear it? If he wore it, he could at least try to make a getaway. He refused to be arrested and sent to the Mythica jail. Someone would poison, stuff, and put him in a museum with a plaque that stated he gave his body for the good of humankind or some bullshit like that. If the humans wanted his body, Roan would riddle it with bullet holes first.

"Come on," he said to Zack. "Pack what you need; we're leaving."

"But —"

"Now!"

At that moment there was a loud bang and a swirl of mist from the centre of the room. Zack let out a girlish yelp. They were screwed.

THE FAMILY HEIRLOOM

The source of the mist was a man with slicked-back black hair and an expensive black suit. His eyes were bright yellow, like a cat's.

"Who the hell are you?" Roan reached for the first thing he could use as a weapon. It was a desk lamp. Hardly a weapon.

"It's okay. I called for him," Zack explained.

"There's no way anyone could get here that fast."

"He's a genie; he runs an internet business and he—"

"*He* can get you out of here," the genie finished in a voice that could melt chocolate. He looked like an Armani advertisement, complete with a black-collared shirt and pointed shoes you could see your face in. Pushing his well-defined body off the door frame, he strolled into the room. His Roman nose crinkled at his surroundings. "For a price, of course." Then his eyes rested on Roan's golden cuff. They widened a little. "That should suffice."

"No deal," Roan growled defensively.

"But Roan," Zack pleaded.

"Who is this guy? Looks like a prick to me."

"Denin." The genie held out a gloved hand. Roan ignored it. Denin retracted his arm as Roan scrutinised him.

"You're not getting this," Roan repeated. Outside, the police arrested Troll. Troll's voice screamed something about pineapple sundaes, whatever that meant.

“Then I can’t help you,” Denin sighed. “It will be a matter of seconds before they enter. Tick-tock.”

“Isn’t there anything we can offer you?”

“Nope, I want that.”

“It’s mine.”

“I’ll be off then. I suppose I can collect it later once you’re arrested.”

“Fine.” He ripped the cuff from his arm. He tossed it over, and Denin caught it in one smooth movement.

“Alright, I want the two of you to stand against that wall and don’t move.” Zack ran to the wall so fast that he almost ran into it. Roan glowered.

“Trust me,” Denin sighed as he examined his new toy. “You’ve got two minutes until they come in. Stand against the wall and don’t move. They won’t see you.”

“What about Troll?”

“Hmm, not part of our deal.”

“I gave you that cuff.”

“And I thank you very much for it.” Denin smiled a cunning smile and pocketed the trinket. “The invisibility will last forty-eight hours. That will protect you if forensics comes back. You only need to be still while they are here, but if I were you, I would try hiding out somewhere else for a while.”

“Got any suggestions where to go?” Zack asked as the sound of a door wrenched from its hinges awoke the baby of the single mother downstairs. Denin took a seat on the corduroy couch and regretted it as dust and ash contaminated his suit.

“Not the sewers,” Denin replied. “They are wretched.”

“Big surprise there,” Roan snorted, his body leaning against the wall. They were breaking down the apartment door now, and Zack flinched at each thud.

“Don’t move, Zack,” Denin warned. The door crashed to the ground. Three police officers clad in full SWAT uniforms entered, prowling through on flexed knees. Then the police entered with guns poised in outstretched arms. The police swept the room, kicking at walls, trying to find hidden passageways. They did not see Denin lounging on the couch or Zack holding his breath against the wall.

"Send in the seers," one of them ordered. Roan could feel Zack tense.

"Relax," Denin sighed. "They only see fairy crap if they're not con-artists." Roan relaxed a little, but Zack was still not breathing.

The seer was a middle-aged woman wearing a bulletproof vest over her khaki-green ankle-length dress. She entered with her arms outstretched and her eyes closed. Immediately, she choked on the smoke. Roan refrained from chuckling. The woman opened her eyes, which had begun to water. It was clear she didn't like being in here, and she quickly skimmed the room, waving her fake nails and equally false bejewelled rings in all directions. Roan knew humans were dumb, but surely they didn't believe this crazy old biddy?

"I sense … I sense…."

Sense the weeks-old pizza box hidden somewhere behind the couch.

The garbage bin that hadn't been emptied in over two weeks?

A litter box containing a termite mound of chupacabra poo?

If she had bothered to open the fridge, she would have seen the stack of juice boxes, and if she had bothered to investigate any further, she would have noticed they were in fact filled with blood.

Of course, she didn't, because she didn't really care what the police found as long as she got paid.

"They are not here," she said in her mystic voice. All seers had the same voice. A bunch of frauds, all of them. "This place has long been abandoned."

"What about the troll?"

"Taking advantage of an empty house."

"But the blood trail led us here. We saw them."

"They are not here," she repeated.

Well, duh.

"Come on, boys, we'll take the troll into custody for questioning. He could have been an accomplice." The police and SWAT teams filed out. The last to leave was the seer, who took one last look around this garbage dump of an apartment.

"You can move now," Denin said, jumping off the couch and dusting himself off as if he were being swarmed by ants. "If you will excuse me, I am about to take a very long shower. Thanks for the cuff, by the way," he addressed Roan. "What does it do, exactly? I sense it's magic, but…"

Roan gave a satisfied twitch to his lip before replying, "Sorry, not part of the deal." Denin ignored him and turned to Zack, "And Zack, if you ever want a girlfriend…" Before Zack could reply, Denin had vanished as if he had never been there.

"I can find a girlfriend on my own, thank you very much." Zack muttered begrudgingly at the space where Denin had been.

#

Denin transported himself directly into his shower and let the steam burn his flawless skin. His body loved the heat. It ached for it, and his skin tingled with the memory of the ancient Egyptian sun. The genie took a deep breath and let the shower calm his mind. He rolled his angled shoulders and tipped his head back to feel the force of his high-powered, very expensive jet shower head. If he had paid for it, he would have said it was worth the money.

Of course, being a genie, he hadn't needed to. This entire top-storey penthouse had come free. A client had traded it to elope to the Canary Islands with his mistress without his wife ever finding out.

Humans proved stressful to handle. They just wanted this and that like greedy children, and they failed to grasp how magic functioned. Magic was not created. It was a resource in the world that could be contained in objects or Mythica. Some Mythica like dwarves, would mine the depths of the earth for ancient magic in rocks. Elves would harness the natural magic of nature. Each Mythica had their way of harnessing magic and using it. But humans couldn't tap into that magic resource.

Being a genie, Denin naturally absorbed magic from the tiny shreds in the surrounding air, which he could use to do basically anything. Magic was energy, and Denin had tons of it.

He had not been confined to his genie's lamp for over twenty years. It was more of an urn, not a lamp. The pottery was a lovely brown colour, with gold trim and a Sanskrit inscription, and it made a charming decorative item on his fireplace mantel.

"Denin?" a curious voice inquired from the door. Denin cursed softly and turned off the water. Who was in his bedroom again?

"Hello beautiful. Aren't I lucky that you waited for me to return," he said, opening the screen and coming face to face with the redhead he had brought back to his apartment earlier that night.

"Some things are worth waiting for," she purred back. She was quite a catch, Denin had to admit. He had caught this one without the use of magic, none at all, he swore on his life. She had lovely wide hips that sloped into shapely legs and a rebellious tattoo on her shoulder blade.

Something glittered on the tip of her finger. Little Miss Red had the cuff he had left beside the sink.

"That, my dear, is why I had to leave." He gracefully took it from her hand. "It's precious."

He slipped past her towards the safe concealed in the far corner of the bedroom wardrobe. Before she arrived, he entered the code and threw the cuff in. Just as her hands went to his hips, he sealed it once more.

From the window, which took up the entire wall, he could see the New York City sky. Morning would come in a few hours. Denin shivered at the touch of her hands before he turned around. With a coy tilt in his voice, he purred, “Now, where were we?”

THE BIRD GIRL

Iloa had never seen sunlight. It was something she had wanted to see for a long time now. She wondered again and again what it would feel like on her translucent skin. The UV lamp in her cage stung her eyes, so she never used it. It was not the same as sunlight; Iloa knew it. She just knew it was different.

She had her ordinary lamp too, just a little bare light bulb. It collected moths, and Iloa spent her nights watching the delicate creatures flutter and race around. She let her lithe fingers dance around their shadow forms. The light illuminated her slender face and turned her feathered hair a ghost white.

She did not know what she was. For years she had been down here. She still had the shell of the egg from which she had hatched. It sat on the shelf above her bed. She had given herself a name; she thought it sounded pretty, and she wondered if it meant anything in any language. Mav told her it was gibberish, but Iloa didn't believe him. It had to mean something.

Mav was not her real father; he was more like her owner. Mav was human, and as far as Iloa knew, he made a living selling black market Mythica. He did not sell Iloa though. She was his pride and joy. Iloa did not understand why. Mav had created a room for her, sealing off half the basement with a wall of metal bars. He had the key to the door. Iloa couldn't remember the last time he had opened it. He just pushed food through the bars. Iloa discovered last week that she could fit through them, but she did not escape.

Mav told her what the humans had done to her kind. They beat them, used them as slaves, ripped out their organs as they walked down the street and sold them to the next passerby. Iloa asked what Mav did with the creatures upstairs. Mav said he sold them as pets. He told her he only sold small creatures, the ones with no real brains. From the screams and shrieks she could hear sometimes, Iloa wasn't so sure.

One book rested on Iloa's shelf. Iloa, unable to read, studied the pictures, envisioning stories for hours. They were pictures of animals; some of them were photographs and others were hand-drawn. One fascinated her above all others. It had feathers like hers, with long brown wings extended. Its beak was bright yellow, and its head was white. Iloa had seen nothing more powerful or beautiful. She did not know what it was called, and she didn't want to ask Mav. Just as Mav kept her, she wanted to keep the creature. She imagined the creature in her dreams, and she would fall asleep smiling, watching its body move and fly in her fantasy. She gave it a name, and it would take her to all the other creatures in her book, and they would talk to her and keep her company.

Iloa's smile was like sunshine on her slender face; her eyes were close together, perfectly round, yellow and black, just like the bird in the book. Perhaps that's where she came from. Upon Iloa's gentle fingers, a tiny moth rested. She could feel the touch of every one of its hair-thin legs. She crouched on her bird legs, knees bent backwards, wondering if she could fly too.

That was when Mav raced in. Mav was a greying-haired man, and behind his fractured glasses were equally grey eyes. Mav's face was flat and broad, and his nose was crooked and crushed, but he never told Iloa how it happened. Jumping, Iloa knocked and smashed the light bulb with her hand. She let out a yelp.

“Iloa? Iloa get here now.” Mav unlocked her cage with shaking hands. She leapt to her feet and blindly waved her hand toward the door. A rough, calloused hand found her wrist and yanked her through.

“Why? What is wrong?”

“The bad people are here. The bad people, remember what I told you about them? They will pluck you raw?”

“Of course.”

“They will take you away from me. They will take us to jail, you don’t want that, do you?” He pulled her towards a brick wall.

“In here, don’t speak.” Iloa didn’t dare open her mouth. She would do anything Mav told her. The sound of grating metal signified a trapdoor opening. He shoved Iloa inside. The door closed behind her, crushing Iloa against the icy brick, and she shivered with cold. Mav must have been in trouble. Iloa crushed her big, bird - like eyes and held her breath.

She had never felt darkness like this; this was cold, and the fear strangled her. She could hear shouting; Mav screamed. Mav had told her to keep quiet, but she couldn’t. She cried, her voice breaking into sorrowful chirps.

“I think there is another one here, Sergeant.”

“Approach carefully. Could be dangerous.”

“In position!”

Something near her ear clicked, and the brick released, revealing her hiding place. Iloa’s nerves made her legs buckle, and she didn’t dare turn around. Torches shone on her body like floodlights. Iloa tried to make herself as small as possible as the voices assaulted her with commands. Iloa squeezed her eyes shut. Someone lifted her up. Someone else handcuffed her. Iloa could not see; she was crying. News reporters and helicopters swarmed the scene. Night had fallen, yet lights blazed. Daylight was nothing like she had imagined. This burned the back of her eyes. This filled her with a rush of fear.

Where was Mav?

What would happen to her?

Iloa cried and sobbed and covered her face with her mop of white feathers.

"Don't take me, don't take me."

Everyone was looking at her; everyone was asking her questions, commanding her what to do. A crushing weight settled in Iloa's chest, and her muscles slackened as if all strength had drained away. The burning light disappeared, and Iloa was sure she was dead.

#

As soon as her eyes opened, Iloa understood she was in jail. The metal bars weren't the reason, nor was it the police officer. It was the creamy light that hit her eyes. It came through a small, barred window high above the bed she was sitting on.

Iloa lifted herself into a crouching stance, holding up her palm to the light. She squinted against it, waiting to feel the heat. She didn't feel it at first, but then, slowly, her fingers touched warmth. Her eyes adjusted, and she saw colour. This was colour beyond what she thought colour could ever be. No shadow skewed the brightness. There were no dull overtones; it was just … amazing.

"Look at you; anyone would think you haven't seen the sun before," a gruff voice said behind her.

Without turning, Iloa replied, "I haven't." Her voice was light with awe. Even though tears still stained her cheeks, her voice was not rough from crying. Under her white skin, she saw her blood pulse blue. She never knew her skin was so white. She became mesmerised. It always seemed yellow in the glow of her lightbulb.

It was only after the creature behind her blew its nose that Iloa turned around. Beside her, in the cell, a troll sat; he was so large that his weight bent the bed frame beneath him. He was one heck of an ugly beast, with greenish, calloused skin and tufts of black hair on his head. His arms were thick with curly hair that covered his hands like gritty gloves. Iloa took a moment to observe the stranger. Where was she? As if the troll read her mind, he said.

"Mythica jail. In the city. No one knows what to do with you. You technically did nothing wrong. But you'll probably stay in here for a couple of months just because they don't know what you are and whether you're dangerous. What are you anyway?"

"I'm Iloa," Iloa said, creeping closer to the troll. Her limbs moved cautiously, like a spider. "Who are you?"

"Troll," the troll replied. "And that's not what I meant; I meant, *what* are you?"

"I'm Iloa. That's all I know. Where's Mav?"

"Mav? You mean your magician-captor-weirdo?"

"Don't call him that," Iloa said, offended. Troll raised a thick eyebrow. His eyes were black, a shining black, not like the darkness Iloa was used to. They were obsidian, and if Iloa stared hard, she could see herself reflected in them. "Where is he?"

"Human prison. Don't think he'll be out for a long while."

"Why? What has he done?"

Troll shrugged with a coarse grunt. Everything about the troll radiated an aura akin to sandpaper, but Iloa was sure he was kind underneath somewhere. He was kind enough to her. "How long have you been here?"

"'Bout a week."

"What did you do?"

"But all."

"Excuse me?"

"Means I don't know. Jesus, kid, didn't anyone teach you how to swear?"

"You're the first Mythica I've ever spoken to. I've never spoken to anyone besides Mav."

"You're kidding me?" Iloa shook her head, her feathered hair tossing side to side over her shoulders. It reached her waist and covered her slender body like a cloak. Troll stood. The bed let out a sick-sounding creak. He stretched out his arms, which touched the low ceiling.

"Right," Troll said with a yawn. Iloa could smell his smoke-fouled breath from here. "The first thing you need to know is that fucking humans suck."

The first thing Iloa actually learnt about Troll was that he swore a lot, and she meant *a lot*. It didn't bother Iloa that much; in fact, she found it rather colourful, amusing even, to see the humans turn their noses up every time Troll opened his mouth.

The second thing she learnt was that Troll was funny too. His brutish humour was something Iloa didn't always understand but laughed anyway. She liked the way he taunted the guards and made a scene. He would bend the jail bars. The guards warned him that if he didn't settle down, they would have to sedate him.

Troll calmed down once he got the cigarette he had been asking for. You weren't technically allowed to smoke in jail, but Iloa believed the guards would do anything to quiet the troll. And Troll was proud to be a troll. He took it in his stride. Said he was born and bred a brute and would be a brute till the day he died.

Then there was a commotion; it came from down the hall.

"Hello, we're from the…."

"Oh, crap, here we go," Troll yawned as the voices came closer.

"What?" Iloa asked, perched on her bedpost like a cat.

"Yell if you need any help." Troll leant back against his bed and rolled another cigarette. An entire news crew was combusting in the holding area. Big black cameras swooped across the bars and focused on her. Iloa's yellow eyes widened at the commotion. A female reporter jammed her microphone through the bars.

"What is your name?" she asked as bright camera lights flashed and blinded her.

"Um, Iloa." The second question came before Iloa had finished her first.

"And what are you, Iloa? Fey? Elf?"

"Um?"

"Don't worry, let's move on to the next question."

"I've got a question," Troll interrupted, coming toward the bars. A couple of cameras drew back. "How much is your news station paying Iloa for her interview?"

"We have not negotiated a price yet. We can do that later."

"Like hell you will."

"And who are you?"

"I'm Iloa's manager, and I want your ugly little troop of hairless monkeys gone until you come back with some cash. That's right — cash, big fat wads of it, upfront. We'll give only one interview; highest bidder wins tomorrow at twelve o'clock. Now get your asses out of here." Reporters and paparazzi shuffled away, disgruntled. Troll stepped back with a satisfied smirk.

"Thank you," Iloa smiled.

"No problem. Just give me twenty-five percent."

"You mean I still have to do the interview?"

"Only if you want the cash. You could always try to escape." He leaned in close to the bars so only Iloa could hear. "Between you and me, if you tried really hard, I reckon you could fit through these bars."

Humans were so stupid sometimes. Iloa grinned. She had always known she could fit through those prison bars; they were even further apart than the ones in her basement. She was simply too scared to try. But now that she had Troll, she could do anything.

The guards clocked off at nine o'clock. There were no real criminals being contained, and so security slackened off. Iloa slipped through the bars. Troll told her where the keys should be.

"Front desk, in a drawer or something." Iloa's nimble body edged around the corners carefully to the front room. A motion-sensor light flicked on. A beep followed. They hadn't considered there would be a motion sensor alarm. Iloa froze at the entrance to the police station. No one was there now, but she knew someone would be soon. Iloa raced back down the corridor and into her cell.

"Go to sleep," Troll hissed. The alarm echoed down the hall. Iloa tucked herself into her itchy bedsheets. What would happen to her now? Would they send her somewhere else?

"I think you've just driven up your interview costs by a good few hundred bucks," Troll whispered across the darkness.

Eventually, the guards returned. Iloa feigned sleep, and Troll smart-mouthed the guards until they locked up again. They said they would view the security tapes tomorrow. It was an empty threat. No one had escaped, and they had better things to do with their time.

Iloa was dreading the interview. She wished she could get out, get away from it all. From what Troll had told her, these humans didn't treat her kind well, not well at all. They were pushy and demanding, but hey, you had to live with them. You had to become one. You needed money to survive. There was so much more she needed to know, and she needed Troll to help her.

Iloa was not used to morning sunlight; it blared through the bars of her window. The small girl yawned wide, and her stomach rumbled. A bowl of soup slid under her cell bars. It was breakfast. She sniffed it and recoiled.

"Pass it this way, fussy." Troll had slurped his bowl in one mouthful. It looked like he was about to eat the bowl as well. Troll downed Iloa's portion and then explained what was going to happen at twelve.

"Just let me do the talking, alright?"

"Thank you."

"Just remember, fifty percent." Iloa was sure he had said twenty-five yesterday.

The interview was a nightmare. Come twelve, every news crew in the state had crammed into the holding area. Not even the police could keep them away. Someone had set off a tear gas bomb, but all that happened was everyone crouched and gagged until it dissipated. You were supposed to go to the hospital if you were exposed to that stuff, but no one budged. The police gave up.

Troll conducted the biddings. He managed to get the price up to one thousand and twenty-five dollars. When Iloa asked how much that was, he replied, "Allotta smokes."

Troll snatched the money through the bars after they found the highest bidder. He counted it meticulously with his enormous paws. Someone fired questions at Iloa, and she didn't know how to answer them. Troll stepped in now and then to make sure the small camera crew that remained did not get their money's worth.

"Your owner, where is he now?"

"Can't divulge that information," Troll said flatly before Iloa had time to open her mouth.

"Will you be pressing charges against him for the unlawful imprisonment of—"

"Can't answer that because of the current investigation."

"How long will it be until your release?" Troll grew angry at that question because he knew the justice system would want to keep freaks like Iloa and himself away from society for as long as possible.

"Well," Troll rose to his feet and stuck his ugly face through the bars. "Once you fucking assholes stop treating us like scum, taking what is ours and crossing the street every time we turn the corner, then maybe, maybe you'll stop throwing us in fucking prison every time we sneeze wrong." Troll's voice was so loud it silenced the entire place. Troll took a breath and attempted a calm smile. "Now, we have time for one more question?" It was something stupid, and Troll let Iloa answer it.

"What did you do during your time down in the basement?"

Iloa looked at pictures. "A picture book," she said. Troll was too busy counting his money again to pay attention. There was no way in hell he was going to let the guards confiscate this much cash. Because Mythica weren't allowed bank accounts, not strictly speaking, Troll would hide it somewhere, which worked for him.

"Alright, everyone outta here," Troll barked, and the camera crew packed up.

That was when Troll noticed the man in the back corner of the room. He had slicked black hair and wore a very expensive looking suit. He completed his ensemble with a red cravat and looked like a complete dick.

Probably the station manager, Troll thought with a sneer. *Who the hell wears cravats nowadays?* The man was the last to leave, and he only pushed himself off the wall once the last crew member had left.

"So," the man had a smooth voice and strode forward with a clop of his tiny man-heels. "You wanna get out of here?"

"Who are you?" Iloa asked before Troll could spit out an insult about that cravat.

"Denin, my dear Iloa. It is a pleasure to meet you." Denin strode over to her cell with an outstretched hand. Iloa beamed at such civil treatment and shook it. Troll rolled his eyes.

"I'll give you fifty to get us out, both of us," Troll grumbled. Denin snorted.

"I don't want your money."

"Oh, really?"

"No, I'll get you out if Iloa is willing to trade."

"Trade?"

"All I want from you, Iloa," Denin smiled, "is just three of your feathers. That's not too much, is it?"

"No, I mean, I don't know," Iloa said quickly. "What are you?"

"A genie."

"I've heard of your kind," said Troll, "genies that like to scam the less fortunate."

"I'm a businessman. It's your choice whether or not you engage with my services. I can take you wherever you want to go, just like that." He clicked his fingers.

"Twelve Glover Street?" Troll asked.

"No, you don't want to go there. They've left already."

"How do you know?"

"Your nerdy little vampire friend engaged my services for a quick escape."

"And they didn't think of me?"

"Must have slipped his mind. For an additional fee, I can curse him if you like."

"Where are they now?" "I don't know. That centaur refused to say."

Troll thought for a moment. "Take us to Glover. I've got to pick up my chupacabra."

And Denin did just that. One moment they were in a prison cell, next thing they knew, they were at the front steps of their apartment building watching Larry's ex-wife toss him out onto the street.

"Lovely neighbourhood," Denin commented. Iloa hesitated before plucking three long, wispy feathers from her head. They were as long as her arm and as soft as the inside of a pillow. Denin accepted them with elegance. "Thank you, Iloa. And here, take this; it's my number. If you find yourself in any trouble, anything you need, anything at all, all it will cost you is one of these." He held a feather between two slender fingers. "We got a deal?"

Iloa nodded. Her feathers always grew back, and she was in no short supply; she usually stuffed them in her pillow to give it a bit more fluffiness. Denin gave Iloa a dashing wink and disappeared.

"Twat," Troll muttered under his breath. Denin suddenly reappeared.

"That's rich, coming from a troll." Before Troll could throw a punch, Denin had disappeared again.

"He seems sweet," Iloa said innocently, picking at the holes in her grey jeans.

"Of course he does," Troll said dryly and led Iloa up the steps. "They are the ones you've got to watch out for.

Iloa, you've got to stick with me until you get your wits about you."

"And where's my money?"

"Oh, yeah, take that. Don't lose it; I'll give you the rest when we find a place to crash." Troll handed her a ten-dollar note. Iloa, ignorant of its worth, victoriously pocketed her earnings.

They spent little time in the apartment, just long enough to catch the thing that looked like a hairless dog with the face of a toad. In reality, its size matched a Staffordshire Terrier, but in Troll's arms, it seemed no bigger than a Chihuahua.

"Where are we going?" Iloa asked.

"Not far from here. We've got a secret hideout. Didn't want that *Denin* knowing where it was. We'll keep to the back alleys. You'll be safe soon." As he spoke, Troll expertly juggled the squirming chupacabra and lit a cigarette at the same time.

#

The unnatural glow of the TV was something the Vetali twins couldn't get used to. Their white-blond hair took on an eerie green glow, and their pale skin turned even whiter. It was an unnatural situation for them to be in the motel room, where they had been staying for the past two years. The motel manager stopped asking them for money, stating something like, "*I'm not going near those freaks.*" This suited the twins just fine. Their two-year search was over.

Positioned on the brink of their double bed, they fixed their gaze upon the six o'clock news without a single blink. The twins rarely watched television. They found it trivial. But on this occasion, it proved rewarding.

A girl with familiar white feathers and golden eyes appeared on the screen. Without a word, the twins clasped hands. They watched the interview unfold; the troll taking up most of the airtime, cussing about Mythica rights. Nothing the twins did not already know.

It was the bird girl, Iloa; they called her, that was who they were interested in. And the more she spoke, the more impossible it was that she could exist.

"She talks."

"She has changed."

"The mortal did this to her."

"Unnatural."

"Sickening."

"He can undo it."

"We will need to find him. Should not be too hard."

"And the girl?"

"Find the troll."

"Find the girl."

Their hands gripped one another tighter before the television turned to static and died.

#

"Why did you have to bring it here?" Roan sighed as they sat at the table in their new hideout. It was an abandoned factory where a few Mythica gangs hung out from time to time. Roan had secured the topmost floor, which meant the icy air blasted in through the broken windows right down onto them. It also meant Roan did not have a great time dealing with stairs or a sluggishly slow service elevator.

"That's not a very nice thing to say about Iloa," Troll retorted.

"I meant Spike," Roan replied with acid. The chupacabra squirmed out of Troll's arms and was off to catch rats.

Zack had done some shopping and had brought back a few bits and pieces: a loaf of bread, crackers, jam, peanut butter, honey, some apples for Roan, and dozens of sausages for Troll. He ate them raw.

Iloa was starving. She took the pot of honey and clenched it in her hands like a cup of cocoa. She dipped her tongue in it delicately as her eyes watched the conversation.

"This place is a shithole," Troll mumbled. "Why did you have to lead the cops back to the apartment?"

"Where else could we have gone? I can't exactly hide, can I?" Roan snapped. He liked this place about as much as he liked Spike. The factory had a flea-ridden mattress in one corner and a coffee table with crates for chairs in another. This is where Zack and Iloa sat.

Zack stared at Iloa, gawking like an idiot. Iloa did her best not to notice and sipped her honey pot. "And Zack, if you don't blink soon, your eyes will roll out of your head," Roan said before combusting the rest of his anger out at Troll. "Everyone will be looking for her; you should have stayed in prison."

"Oh, yeah, you would have loved that, wouldn't you?" Troll gathered Spike in his arms protectively. The chupacabra had a dead rat hanging out of his mouth, but Troll didn't seem to notice. "Ever since we escaped from that circus, all you've wanted to do is get rid of me."

"Well, maybe if you weren't such a foul-mouthed git!"

"Alright, alright!" Zack bellowed, breaking his gaze at Iloa. "Will you stop? Troll, why don't you go down to the pub, Roan, go… polish your hooves or something. And as for Spike, we need something to eat the rats around here. Give it a week, and we'll go back to our old place. By then, the cops will have something bigger and more important to investigate."

Roan succumbed to Zack's logic with a sigh. "I apologise, Troll," he said in his proper English accent. Troll gave him the finger and flunked down the stairs. Troll was never good at apologies.

Zack turned back to Iloa, who commented, "You are a colourful bunch, aren't you?" Zack gave a sheepish smile. Roan rolled his eyes behind him, trying to organise himself a desk out of an old conveyor belt.

"Troll told me you were a vampire." Iloa's brow furrowed; she had noticed Zack's teeth. They were perfectly human.

"Oh, um," Zack's usual pallid appearance flushed pink. "You see, when we were at the circus, I was, well…"

"De-vampired," Roan replied, pulling out his papers.

"Yes, you see, in order for me to be considered safe, they filed down my fangs and made me wear falsies. Rather humiliating, really." In fact, it was downright de-vampirilating, if that was even a word. Without fangs, a vampire was just a pale weirdo who didn't like the sun very much and had special dietary requirements. If it weren't for the immortality, they would have been the equivalent of the nerdy kid at school who kept losing his retainer. It has not always been this way. Zack still remembered the time when vampires were the fearsome, coffin-dwelling, cape-wearing monsters. The old black and white movies with Bela Lugosi — that was the good stuff.

"Is that all you eat?" Zack asked. Iloa had finished half the pot already, and her tongue wasn't long enough to reach the second bit. Iloa nodded.

"Let's just say I have special dietary requirements, too."

"You're like a honey-bird."

"Ahem," Iloa nodded adamantly. "Once Mav bought me some fairy floss and —"

"Wait, what did you say?" Roan interrupted.

"I said once Mav brought me —"

"Your owner — your owner's name was Mav?"

"Ahum." Roan shared a look with Zack but said nothing. After a pause, Iloa continued. "Anything but sugar gives me stomach cramps. Mav said that I couldn't digest other things … is that the same with vampires?"

"Sort of," Zack admitted. Research wasn't the best on the vampire front. They were more popular in brothels for men who had a biting fetish. Because of this, female vampires tended to do very well in society, the males, on the other hand, were rather superfluous.

"By the way, Iloa, did you get your money off Troll?"

"He gave me ten dollars," Iloa said proudly, as if that was her fair share and then some. Roan snorted.

"And you won't ever see the rest of it. Not unless Troll wins at poker tonight."

"How much did he have?" Zack asked.

"One thousand."

"That bastard!" Zack slammed his fist onto the table and almost broke through the rotting wood.

"Zack, don't work yourself up over it," Roan sighed.

"But he's a cheat and a lying schemer —"

"Three deep breaths," Roan sighed. Zack took a breath but couldn't bring himself to exhale. "You'll just embarrass yourself in front of the girl. Now let it go, recite your binary prayer or something."

"I do not have a binary prayer."

"Of course you do; I hear you reciting those funny numbers before you go into torpor every night."

"That's *pi*, you idiot, and it's an irrational number. I can remember over one hundred decimals now," Zack finished proudly, hoping that Iloa would find this impressive. Iloa blinked her wide, gold and black eyes in cluelessness. "You know what *pi* is, don't you?"

Iloa shook her head. "Mav never taught me numbers or words."

"You mean you don't know how to read?"

"Nope. Do you?" Zack stopped himself from saying that; of course he did. He didn't want Iloa to feel ostracised.

"I can teach you, if you want?" Zack would be more than happy to; in fact, he hoped Iloa would say yes. The girl with pure white feathers for hair beamed, revealing an unbroken row of white teeth. Almost like a beak behind her lips.

"Thank you." Iloa squished her honey pot to take a few more licks. Zack stole some of Roan's spare papers in an avid rush to impress the girl. That night, before his torpor or reciting *pi*, he taught her the beginnings of the alphabet.

The next morning, Zack took Iloa to an internet cafe. He needed to check his emails; he said. It was just an excuse to take Iloa out on a sort of date. He needed a place to chat with her without Roan making his snide comments all the time, and when Troll entered drunk into the factory at seven in the morning; it was the perfect excuse to leave. Zack ensured that Iloa disguised herself well. Iloa covered her insect-thin legs with a long brown, swaying skirt and wore a long woollen jumper. She wrapped her feathered hair up in a black headscarf. She looked as if she were being eaten alive by some ravenous op-shop clothes. Zack thought she looked very bohemian.

"Here," he said, putting a cup of water down on the rickety little coffee table. He dumped a handful of sugar packets and a stirring rod with it. Then he sat back down at his laptop as Iloa ripped open the packets one by one and stirred each slowly. She stared at everyone who walked past her, and they stared back. If they smiled, she would smile, and if they frowned, she would keep staring, making them feel more and more uneasy.

"Will you stop that?" Zack hissed, leaning back into his high-backed velveteen chair. "Stop drawing attention to yourself."

"Sorry," Iloa replied. "It's just that people are much more interesting than sugar packets."

"Oh, no." Zack clicked his mouse button a few times, his brow furrowing.

"What is it?"

"I've got a date request."

"You mean from that website Roan says you signed up for? Roan says—"

"I know what Roan says. He says quite a lot when he should probably just keep his mouth shut."

"I thought a date was a good thing."

"It is." Zack couldn't tell Iloa that he kind of fancied her. He just met her; it would be unwise to put all his eggs in one basket. Besides, she was new to this city, so it wouldn't be fair to her.

Zack quickly typed a reply saying that he would love to meet Vamplovrr376 at the Blue Juice bar. It was one of the few places that catered to both vampires and humans. Zack gave a little smile to himself. He had a date.

He answered a couple more emails and then turned his attention toward Iloa, who was staring at the inside of an empty sugar packet.

"I wonder if they count the crystals to make sure each packet has the same amount," she mused. Zack raised an eyebrow.

"No, they don't. Iloa, come, let's go. I'll show you around the city; there are some cool places I want you to see." Zack took Iloa by the hand and walked down the street.

"I bet there are lots of vampires around here," Iloa mused as the sidewalks became busy with the morning bustle. Zack knew which streets to avoid.

"Oh, there are. There was even a market for turning people into vampires. The government quickly outlawed it, ran all these campaigns to say why being a vampire is not as glorious as it sounds."

"Why isn't it?"

"Well," Zack shrugged, "it's just not the same. I mean, do you know how much sunscreen I need to wear? And you always feel kinda cold, then there's the dependence on blood. You can't eat anything else. And the whole not-aging thing is kinda a letdown. I've always wanted to grow a beard and see, look, nothing for seventy-three years." Zack pushed out his chin for emphasis. "And you lose lots of your rights, and people think you're really dangerous and all. To be honest, it's not all it's cracked up to be."

"Do you reckon there are many of me?" Iloa was trying not to step on the crack in the concrete. Zack hadn't found shoes for her; she had funny-looking toes that kind of splayed out from her tiny heels like a duck.

"No, Iloa, you're one of a kind."

"I wonder if that's a good thing or a bad thing." She was still dancing around the cracks, her eyes on her feet the whole time. Zack watched her. "I mean, at least you have other vampires to go on dates with." Zack wanted to say that he would go on a date with her in a heartbeat. But of course, he didn't. He didn't think Iloa understood what a date was.

Iloa gave homeless people sugar packets as they walked, and they would look at her as if she were crazy. Iloa believed she was doing them some good. Zack didn't have the heart to tell her otherwise.

Zack discovered Iloa had a funny way of looking at things. Because she had been apart from society for so long, she had never learned social conventions. The things she said surprised Zack, made him laugh, and after living with Roan and Troll for years on end, he needed a laugh.

She would dance wildly in the street whenever they passed a busker. Iloa had never heard music before, but she said it felt like the right thing to do. Zack stood back, watching her flop her arm around and spin to the slow, smooth jazz of a saxophone. That was until Iloa grabbed Zack by the hand and pulled him forward.

"Iloa, I haven't danced since nineteen-seventy-seven, and that was disco."

"Disco? Show me disco."

"To jazz music? In public?" The busker raised an eyebrow behind his black shades, listening in on their conversation. But Iloa had begged with such enthusiasm that Zack couldn't refuse. He slipped off his laptop carry case, took a step back and busted out a few quick moves that would have made John Travolta proud.

Iloa clapped and hooted and then turned to copy but stumbled on her own feet and fell flat on her arse. Zack laughed until he saw Iloa's headscarf had come loose. He looked around. People were staring.

"Hey!" someone called. Zack hauled Iloa to her feet, and they ran. One or two people followed; the rest got in their way, gawking stupidly as humans do. Zack could hear the footsteps chasing after him.

"This is fun," Iloa mused, her long legs easily keeping up, and in fact surpassing Zack's speed.

It was only once they had returned to their hideout that Zack patted down his body, groping for a bag strap that was no longer there. He had forgotten his laptop.

#

"You what?" Roan cried when Zack told him that he had lost his laptop.

"I went back there, but I couldn't find it. Someone must have picked it up," Zack said.

"Did you go to the police?"

"I doubt that whoever stole it would have handed it in."

Roan paced back and forth. All their information was on their email, their communication with other Mythica. If it got into the wrong hands… "I've got passwords on just about everything," Zack assured Roan. It did little good. Roan hoofed the ground with enough force to punch through the rotting wood.

Iloa was shivering in the far corner, believing this was all her fault. She had been the one to make Zack dance. Of course, no one was paying attention to her. They didn't care whose fault it was; they just wanted that laptop back.

"What's the worst they could do, Roan?" Zack pleaded. He didn't like it when Roan was angry with him.

"I'm not buying you a new laptop," Roan growled in defeat. "Go get yourself a job or something."

"He can have my money," Iloa offered. It was the least she could do. The two Mythica turned to her as if they had forgotten she was there.

"You will do no such thing Iloa, that's your money; if Zack takes it, he'll be no better than Troll." Roan eyed Zack as he said those words to make sure the message sunk through.

"I wasn't going to," Zack hissed and turned to his little suitcase that he had packed before they had left for the factory. Out came his blue collared shirt and black pants. Tonight, he had a date and wanted to look nice. He was dreading telling Roan, especially after losing his laptop. Despite being a seventy-three-year-old vampire, Roan still managed to ground him. He smoothed out his shirt with unnecessary force. Fleas infested the place; he hoped they wouldn't attach themselves to him. He didn't want to be itching like mad. It would give the wrong impression.

"Date, are we?" Roan mused with a raised eyebrow.

"Yup," Zack replied, not looking his way.

"Where about?"

"Blue Juice."

"Ahum. What time?"

"None of your business."

"You better answer my questions if you want spending money; it's not a good impression when the girl has to buy your Bloody Mary."

"I've got my own money!" Zack was fuming now. Just because he looked seventeen didn't mean that he was. He had a good few years to rack up a savings account. Yes, he had a savings account, because he made one before people realised there were vampires on this planet. The banks still hadn't caught on yet, and just to make sure, Zack had someone forge another birth certificate every second decade. They were less strict with vampires because they were one of the few Mythica that had become rather popular in society. Centaurs and trolls, on the other hand, weren't exactly inconspicuous.

Zack spent the next hour combing his hair so it wouldn't look so grungy. He wanted to look older than he was, and he regretted not being able to grow even just a little stubble. If only he had been turned just a few years later.

He opted for no tie; he didn't want to look too formal. He didn't have a mirror to see himself in, but Iloa said that he looked very dashing. Roan rolled his eyes, which in this instance, was a good sign. The final touch was putting in his false fangs. Call him shallow, but he didn't want to explain why he didn't have fangs on his first date. It wasn't something to be proud of.

"Alright, I'm off." Zack forced himself to smile. Iloa beamed back at him. This was one of the rare occasions where maybe Zack wouldn't have minded cancelling his date.

THE LUCKY AND LUCKLESS

If you had a little bit of luck, then you could do anything, which was why being a genie made your life pretty fantastic. After all, if Denin hadn't suggested to that human who Iloa was, he would never have caused a commotion, and he would never have been able to steal that nerd's laptop.

Denin leant back in his brown leather recliner chair and popped his Gucci heels onto the footrest. He had the laptop open on his lap, and it had taken less than ten seconds to muster the magic to break it.

He was flicking through the vampire's files looking for any clues as to where his cuff had gone to. Yes, that cuff he had stashed in his wardrobe safe had gone. Stolen, no doubt. Denin's money was on the vampire, stealing it back for his centaur friend.

Roan would not have been able to do it; someone would have seen a centaur cram himself into the elevator. Troll was equally conspicuous. Iloa? No, she was basically a baby bird, harmless.

That left Zack. It would have been easy enough to scale the building and break into the safe. He had heard stories of vampires with strange powers. Or perhaps the boy was just a genius; geniuses always had computers, right? He could have hacked the safe code. However

Zack did it; Denin needed to undo it, or at least, hold his laptop as ransom.

Riffling through Zack's emails, all he found was a stack of dating site registrations and a bunch of emails to some vampire called Keiren, which was even more pathetic than it sounded. Apparently, this vampire had a pet gremlin. That was the equivalent of a friend who has a pet axolotl at school, the nerd kid, the worst! Why didn't the boy just give up already?

After checking over and over again, Denin found no trace of the centaur cuff. No emails about selling it, no research about what it does. All he found was a diary, which had been downright difficult to find, let alone crack. The vampire had it hidden away in a plainly titled file, hidden in a couple of dozen more files and encrypted it, then typed it in code. It was a good thing too, because there was some embarrassing shit on there, like how his last date was actually with an undercover journalist who just wanted the gossip about being a vampire, and Zack didn't realise it until dessert. How he thought he could earn some extra cash at a circus, but they kidnapped and showed him around like a freak instead. There had been quite a few attempted stake attacks and burnings, and so amused was Denin with Zack's life, he copied the document onto his hard drive to read later.

Then he came across an email from Vamplovrr376. Zack would be on a date at the Blue Juice bar in an hour. Denin closed the laptop with a smile. Like he said, a little bit of luck.

#

Zack flexed his hands. If he were human, they would have been dripping with sweat by now. No matter how many times Zack did this, he was always nervous.

Then he spotted a tall redhead staring at him. She wore a halter-neck red dress that finished just above her knee and pushed her boobs together so much that Zack wondered if they were going to fall out as she walked. He wondered whether this was his date. Hah! As if he would be that lucky. She was probably just a stranger lingering outside the door. Then she stopped in front of him. Her straight red hair tousled gently over her angled shoulders.

"Zack?"

"Miss Vamplovrr376?"

"Call me Ava," she smiled shyly. She was young, in her mid-twenties, and judging by the heat of her skin, human too. She hadn't overdone the makeup; in fact, she was rather classical. Apart from the provocative dress (which seemed obligatory for humans on a first date) she seemed rather charming. Smiling, she said, "Thank you" as Zack helped her up the stairs. She didn't seem like the sort of person to internet date. She was too young for a start, and too amazingly gorgeous. As Zack followed her up the steps, he noted a tattoo along her left shoulder blade. Three vertical lines of faded black ink scrawled just off her spine.

"Interesting tattoo. Is it writing? What does it mean?"

"Oh, that silly thing? Nothing important." Ava brushed her hair over her shoulders to cover it. Her wrist bore another mark, a slight curve resembling a rune, though in red ink, or possibly an uncommon birthmark.

Blue Juice was a restaurant and bar. Downstairs was more of a club, but upstairs was a restaurant that boasted the widest selection of connoisseur bloods in the city. It wasn't cheap, but it was well worth the money. A mix of purple velvet lounges and high-backed black leather chairs filled the dining room. The bar curved against one corner of the room, and the bartender was throwing a few cocktail shakers.

The server led them to their seats, and Zack waited for Ava to sit first, like a gentleman. There were some benefits of growing up in an era where manners had been taught. A server shoved menus under their noses, and Ava took hers.

This was the awkward part of every date. Where to start the conversation? Zack learnt that talking about the food was a big no-no. Firstly, he didn't eat. Secondly, it was a very dull topic. Zack found it best to just make an observation, make a comment, or ask a question.

"You don't seem the type to internet date, Ava." Ava gave a little shrug as if embarrassed.

"Well, most guys are jerks, and I've had my bad run of boyfriends. They're just so immature, you know? Then one of my friends told me to try a vampire because, well, they're usually a lot older and more mature and.... well, you don't seem as old as I thought you would be." Ava played with a bullet pendant that dangled low from her neck.

"Seventy-three is just a bit young, is it?"

"Just a little." Ava smiled again, her cheeks making her blue eyes into half-moons. A server came to take their drinks. Ava ordered a green-coloured cocktail while Zack grabbed a calf-blood pina colada. They served human blood as entrees and mains. They mixed the cheap stuff with the alcohol.

"So, you're only seventy-three — that's young for a vampire, isn't it?" Zack didn't really know. He talked little to the other vampires; mostly, he just read internet blogs, but some of them said there were vampires over a thousand years old. He didn't know how true it was.

"I suppose I don't really have many vampire friends." Unless you counted his internet friend, Keiren, whom he had never met in person. "So, have you dated many vampires?" Zack asked.

Well, actually you're the first one, but I've heard that they dislike when people ask about how they turned.

"Oh, well, I suppose I don't mind. I mean, it was a rather traumatic experience, so I understand why most vampires don't want to." No one had ever asked Zack how he had become a vampire. It wasn't like nowadays, where you read in these magazines about how some mother of three is dying of a terminal illness. So, she saved her own life by going to some Central European country to get herself bitten. Zack's story was that he got mugged and woke up feeling terribly sick. He remained at the hospital overnight, fell asleep, woke up in the morgue, panicked and ran away.

He told this to Ava. Before she could ask anything more, the server came with their drinks. It was a different server, a male. He looked vaguely familiar, but Zack didn't recognise him. Ava's expression changed a little before she controlled it. Zack noticed, but thought little of it. He thought they had given her the wrong drink. Before he could ask, Ava spoke.

"It's a good thing you escaped the morgue; otherwise, there would have been some explaining to do." She picked up her margarita with a delicate hand and licked the salt from the sides with cat-like licks.

"It's always bothered me that suddenly the entire world found out about the Mythica when they had been around us before we even existed," Ava mused.

"Yeah, tell me about it. No one knows what went wrong. Just one day a troll was stumbling down the street and, hey presto, someone noticed him."

"I heard a farmer found a minotaur amongst his herd."

"There are stories everywhere. My friend, he's made it his life's mission to find out what changed, what caused the Revealing." That was the name for the day Mythicas' secrecy ended.

"Your friends, are they…?"

"One's a troll, the other's a centaur."

"A centaur, really?" Ava's painted eyes widened. "I thought they lived in the countryside, not the city."

"Yeah, he hates it here."

"There was something on the news about a centaur stealing something from the museum." Zack's face went slack. "Oh, don't worry, I won't dob you in," Ava gave a cheeky grin. "It was you, wasn't it?" Zack gave a shrug, playing the dashing daredevil.

"I'm not saying anything."

"I wonder what could be so interesting that a centaur would risk his freedom for some museum artefact," Ava said, prying a little further. Zack fidgeted. "But of course, who knows the ways of the centaur? Like you said, they are very secretive."

"Tell me more about yourself," Zack said, steering the conversation away from his alleged illegal activities.

"Oh, not much to say, really." She circled a lazy finger around her bread plate. "I was orphaned at a very young age and never knew my actual parents, but the most powerful woman you will ever meet adopted me."

"Powerful? Interesting way to describe your adoptive mother. Is she a businesswoman or a lawyer, or something else?"

"She is passionate about social justice, you could say that," Ava said with an air of evasiveness which reminded Zack of Roan when he avoids answering questions about his tribe. It was their first date, and Ava probably did not want to talk about a potentially uncomfortable topic. Yes, that must be it; it's what Zack told himself, at least.

#

The moment Denin spotted Little Miss Red striding up to little, unsuspecting Zack, he knew instantly he had the wrong guy. It wasn't Zack who had stolen the cuff from him. It was her. So Denin donned a disguise, used a bit of magic to get himself into the place, then stole a random server's outfit. He had left the poor guy in a state of euphoria in one of the cleaning cupboards. He made sure only Ava could see his real identity, and she disguised her surprise well, but not well enough; there was a bitter edge in her voice as she gave her order.

"The steak and mushroom, please," she said. Denin had his pen poised in hand.

"And how would you like that done?"

"Rare."

Denin wrote *well done* in big capital letters and underlined it.

"And for you?" He turned to Zack.

"Oh, ah, I'll try the boiled AB."

"An excellent choice; you'll be very pleased." Denin smiled and backed away, his eyes narrowing on Ava. Ava narrowed back.

"Oh, waiter," Ava called. Denin returned. "What are the wine specials today?" The specials! They weren't on the menu. Ava was playing this game just as Denin was.

"The specials, Miss, are a deep red…" Denin had to think fast; he couldn't use magic to get himself out of this one. "A deep red 1978 *Thei-vien-bich* and a delicate French *Your-gha-fraud* white." He emphasised the last name. Ava let a twinkle at the edge of her lip.

"The red, please." Denin walked away to grab the bottle of blood that looked the most like red wine. The decanted O+ would suit, and he poured a lovely, full glass and waltzed right back over.

"There you are, madam," he smiled genially. He waited for her to sip the blood. In the dull blue light of the room, it resembled wine. He stopped himself from snickering as she tried not to spit back into the glass. She swallowed and hid her scowl with a smile.

"It's perfect, thank you."

"Make sure you drink it all; it's a rare flavour." He could say that again.

Denin looked forward to serving their food. He slipped the well-done steak onto his tray and conjured a short curly hair in the mushroom sauce.

"Here you are." He set down the big, soupy bowl of blood in front of Zack, then turned to Ava with one of his dashing smiles. "The rare steak."

Denin could not for the life of him figure out what Ava was. The blood in her cup was still blood. She hadn't used magic to change it. She had not tried to trick him, which suggested that she couldn't use magic at all, unless he hadn't provoked her enough yet. Perhaps she was human, and collected these artefacts to sell on the black market. But that wouldn't explain how she got into that safe. She couldn't have seen the numbers from behind him, could she? That was the last time Denin would ever pick up a woman from a bar without a thorough background check first.

"Can I get you anything else?"

"No, we're quite fine," Zack replied, lifting his spoon. Denin edged back as Ava cut into her meat to find it very well cooked. She glanced up at him with a scowl. Denin winked and then made the piece of meat on her fork fall into her lap. This meant that Ava had to excuse herself to wash up. Denin let her pass around the corner and out of Zack's sight. He waited outside the bathroom. She was expecting him.

"What are you doing here?" The girlish innocence had gone from her voice, replaced with a threatening growl.

"Ah, Ava, my love, it's a pleasure to see you too."

"Oh, so you remember my name now? Good work, Denin." There was a wet stain on her thigh from where she had washed the sauce off. She was not a genie nor a sorceress. Or perhaps she was a sorceress? Whatever she was, Denin knew he would have to watch her. Dammit! This was impossible.

"What are you doing with the kid?"

"Not jealous now, are we, Denin?" Ava purred.

"Where did you put it?"

"Put what?"

"The cuff — I know you stole it." Ava's eyes widened once again in innocence. Denin saw right through it.

"Did I now?"

"What are you?"

"Wouldn't you like to know?"

"I can make your life hell."

"What? And use up all your magic on silly old me? Now, Denin, do you think that's wise?"

“I think I can afford to spend a little magic on a beautiful witch such as yourself.” He was fishing now; was she a witch? Denin could not tell.

“Oh, stop, Denin, you’re making me blush.” She rolled her shoulder forward a little, so her breasts pressed together a little more, barely held back by a flimsy spaghetti strap halter neck. Denin couldn’t help but look, which gave him an idea. Boy, Zack was going to have a good night tonight.

#

Roan scrutinised the newspaper clippings from 1992. If he stared any harder, the newsprint would peel away from the paper and latch onto his eyes. He had been searching for answers, and he had been searching for the past ten years. He stored the clippings in an overstuffed plastic file, which was now heavy enough to break a window. But Roan still kept the file and flipped through it when he was particularly troubled. All the articles documented some new Mythica discovered, or the accounts of a couple of crazies who believed they had seen a unicorn on their farm. Roan hoped other articles, which seemed unrelated, were also connected. Most were natural disasters — earthquakes, cyclones. Roan just couldn’t connect the pieces yet. Had it just been bad luck? Or had something changed?

“Roan, I need your help.” Roan looked up to find Denin standing on the other side of the desk, dressed in a fancy server’s outfit. He had what appeared to be wine or bloodstains down his front. He didn’t look happy. His hair, usually flawless, was dishevelled, and frustration twisted his lips.

“Bad night out?” Roan inquired dryly, hiding his surprise at the genie’s sudden appearance. Neither Mythica was fond of the other.

“I need to know what was so special about that cuff?”

“What? You mean the one you took from me?”

"No, the other one," he replied sarcastically.

"Why don't you just use your magic superpowers to find out?"

"Because someone stole it."

"Oh?" Roan looked up in interest, not trying to hide his smug little smirk.

"Yes, stolen by the bitch who is currently finishing her dessert with Zack." Roan's smile faded. His lips twisted tightly. He understood now why Denin was dressed as a server. He had been spying on them.

"You didn't tell him, did you?"

"No, I'll leave that up to you." Roan wasn't sure how to break it to the boy.

"Shame. He hadn't had a decent date in a long while."

"Listen, this girl, Ava, she's a con-artist. If she's interested in that cuff, she'll be interested in you. Keep your wits about you," Denin warned, leaning his hands on Roan's desk. "Tell Zack to do the same. Now, I want you to tell me about that cuff. What does it do?"

"Why would I tell you?"

"You want to protect your friend, right?" Roan nodded. "Well, I can watch over him." He could have easily told Zack to stay away from Ava, but if he didn't give an explanation, there was no way the boy would listen to him. He would probably throw a hissy fit and run away. "Do I need to make you swear? Or sign a contract like a human?"

"You have a genie's word. And no, I don't make Mythica sign contracts. Only humans." Denin's tone when he spoke the word 'human' made Roan inclined to trust him.

Reluctantly, he said, "It protects the wearer from attack. Its power has worn off over the years, but it will still divert a stray bullet or two. This Ava girl — is she human?"

"No idea, which is why I need you in on this too."

"What's in it for me?"

“Ava knows more than she’s letting on, Roan,” Denin said under his breath. “Just make sure Zack’s careful with what he tells her. She may be working for the humans, like a spy or an agent.”

“I understand.” Roan’s eyes moved past Denin to see Iloa fidget in her sleep. She was curled up on the smelly old mattress in the far corner of the room.

“You really shouldn’t be living in a place like this,” he sighed.

“Is that an offer to pack up and move into your fancy-pants apartment?”

“How about we compromise and I’ll de-flea this place for you?” and as soon as he said it, the itching around Roan’s fetlocks ceased.

“Thanks,” the centaur muttered. Denin was being unusually kind tonight. It seemed that his kindness was inversely proportional to how well he was dressed.

#

Denin reclined in his heated bed, rifling through Zack’s laptop again. He would return it, but there was no harm in waiting a few days. He flicked Iloa’s feather absentmindedly across his cheek. There was a lot of magic in this feather. There was a lot of magic in Iloa too; it radiated from her like perfume. Just a few days spent in her presence would be enough to power Denin’s magic for a month. He was absorbing the magic from the feather as he clicked open files and skimmed others.

It was like breathing in freshly brewed coffee; you could feel it in your blood. It energised you; tingled in your veins; made you think you could do anything, which, in fact, you just about could. Why hadn’t he brought Iloa back with him? It was rare for creatures to be made of magic; some could harness it like an energy, but this magic — it was just there, like skin, or nails, or hair, or teeth. Denin pondered this as he breathed in the musty scent of the fine feather spurs. If only Iloa had been awake when he visited, he could have invited her here. She deserved better than that grumpy old nanny goat and moody teenager.

Denin was reading about how the subway line had shutdown, which was why Zack had been late for his date. Dreary stuff, really. There had been quite a few subway shutdowns and reroutes over the past few decades, and somehow, they always coincided with one of Zack's important events. Denin couldn't have planned it better if he had all the magic in the world. He knew he should have given the laptop back when he saw Roan, but since when had Denin done anything he should do?

As for that Ava woman, Denin was going to have to be a lot nicer to Roan and Zack to get the information he needed. It wouldn't be all bad, he supposed; he'll be close to Iloa. It also meant putting his other clients on hold, and there were quite a few of them. He had his websites and contacts, you see, for business. Clients pleaded their case and offered their money. Denin took what he needed, often at a very inflated price. It was revenge for millennia of serving sultans, pharaohs, and the like.

Denin remembered when the sultan was the only one who knew the likes of him existed. They would use genies as their personal servants, bleed them dry of magic, and then execute them when they couldn't do anything more. Humans were stupid. No matter how many times Denin explained how magic worked, they wouldn't listen. They just wanted more and more. Selfish bastards. Of course, sultans would keep the existence of genies a secret. Secrets were power. Now the secret was out…

Denin put the empty feather on his bedside and shut the laptop. He had had enough for tonight. He fell asleep. And when his eyes opened the next morning, that lustrous cloud-coloured feather of Iloa's had disappeared.

THE REFUGE

It was front-page news. Mav Oceelerson had escaped. The middle-aged man's snarl was blasting from every TV station. Denin couldn't believe his luck. This was his chance; it was fate. The genie flicked to another station just to make sure it was true. This time, Mav was filmed being arrested and escorted from his home. This was old footage from the time they first found Iloa.

"... arrested for illegal possession, breeding of Mythica, and conducting experiments potentially dangerous to people..." the voice-over read. Potentially dangerous to humans? What the hell was that supposed to mean? What sort of experiments? It didn't matter anyhow; the point was, Denin now had a legitimate reason to take Iloa.

The genie raced to his wardrobe and donned his best suit. With it, he burrowed his eagerness behind a suave exterior of coolness. That was how he always felt when he put a suit on. It was like a sedative; it was confidence; it was sexy; it was well... Denin in a nutshell.

He opted for no tie today; he left a few top buttons undone on his blue shirt; he looked like a dream. This was exactly what you wanted if you were a genie. You had to seduce your clients with all the possibilities you could offer them: a new car, a trip around the world, that promotion they always wanted, that exam that they really needed to pass. Seduction was so much easier when you were oozing gorgeousness.

With one quick check in the mirror, Denin flashed out of his apartment and into that dingy old factory Roan called home. The stench of mould assaulted him. He spotted Iloa perched upon a crate and sipping a pot of honey. Roan was chewing unhappily on a mouldy apple as he mused over his memoirs. Zack was nowhere to be seen.

"I assume you've heard the news," Denin announced upon his arrival. Roan did not look impressed.

"Do you mean you finally got your acceptance letter from the Society of Suited Gits?" Roan replied with his sharp wit, like always.

"Har-har." Denin sat on the empty crate beside Iloa. "Mav has escaped." Roan's long face paled.

"Has he now?"

"Yes, which means Iloa is in danger." Denin turned to Iloa. She had stopped mid-sip. Denin could feel the rush of magic radiating from her. It was like swimming in a bottle of his favourite perfume. He could feel his skin bunch and prickle with magic. Roan's expression mellowed a bit, and he returned to his apple with dissatisfaction.

"What do you care?"

"I'm sure Iloa does." To both Roan's and Denin's surprise, Iloa's wide eyes mirrored fear, but not the fear they expected.

"Is Mav okay?" Denin and Roan shared a look.

"He won't get to you, Iloa," Roan replied, uncertain if he understood.

"No, I mean, well, I just don't want him hurt, that's all."

"We are talking about the Mav that locked you in his basement for the entirety of your life?" The centaur had to clarify. Iloa nodded.

"Mav raised me from a chick." This was her simple reply. Roan sighed and put down his apple. He strode close to Iloa and knelt down on his carpi, so they were eye to eye.

“Let me tell you something that I hope will put things into perspective for you, Iloa.” His voice was soft. It was genuine. This was a topic close to Roan’s heart.

“Our kind shouldn’t be owned by humans. Mav may have looked after you, but he did not consider you his equal. You were a pet, just like Spike is a pet to Troll. This is not a good thing.

“There’s something else about Mav, something I wasn’t going to tell you. I’ve seen his picture in the newspaper; in fact, I knew who he was from the moment you mentioned his name. That man is the reason I am here. Poachers took me from my home territory, Iloa. They shipped me from England because there are people like Mav who want me displayed in zoos and circuses. Mav owned the circus that bought me.

“Every morning, he would glue my mouth shut so I couldn’t talk back to the kids who paid ten dollars to ride me around the track. Then he shoved me into a stable and treated me no better than a horse. He is the one who cut Zack’s fangs. He made Troll lift cars and trucks above his head and throw them day after day until one day Troll broke his wrist. He still had to lift things. If you look at Troll’s wrist now, you’ll see it’s healed at an angle. Pixies would die within weeks, but Mav didn’t care because they kept breeding, so he always had some. He fed the dead ones to Spike.

“There were other Mythica too, so many, so many shot because they retaliated, because they bit a child, or tried to escape. Mav is not a friend, Iloa, trust me on that one.” Roan’s dark eyes pierced Iloa. The desperation in his voice made her thin limbs shiver. She had the feeling she was only scraping the surface of Roan’s heartache. There was so much more underneath there, so much more hurt, like poison in a healing wound. Iloa recoiled and turned to Denin.

“You’ll be safe with me,” the genie said. He looked to Roan to see the centaur give an approving nod. Denin reached out a hand. His long fingers reached for Iloa.

"Wait. How do we contact you? Where are you taking her?" Roan asked.

"Zack has my number. Don't worry, I'll find you." Denin's heart was racing, and it skipped a beat when he felt the electric touch of Iloa's fingers. Her nails had keratinised into little claws.

"Thank you, Roan," Iloa said in her meek voice. Roan kept eye contact with Denin. The two men nodded as a gesture of farewell.

It was easy for Denin to find the magic; it was like a jolt of static electricity; and instantly they were back in Denin's apartment. Iloa appeared dazed for a moment before breaking into a wide smile.

"This place is…" She wandered towards the window that spanned the entire wall. The entire city was in full view. A cloudy mist covered the tops of buildings, and the sky was a peachy pink. It was still early.

"Amazing? Breathtaking? Brilliant?" Denin offered.

"It's like … I want to jump." Denin was not expecting that response, and he wondered if he should bolt the windows. "I mean, it's like…" Iloa pressed her body up against the glass. If it hadn't been there, she would have fallen. "It makes your heart race, that's all." Denin copied her stance. It felt as though there was nothing beneath his feet.

"Would you like to fly, Iloa?" Iloa looked to Denin as if all her dreams had come true. Denin took it as a yes. The glass wall disappeared. Iloa screamed as she fell. Denin did the same and slowed them down a little until they were floating down like feathers.

"You know," Denin mused, laying back as if he were reclining in an invisible chair. Iloa was trying to swim, frog-kicking against nothing. Denin was guiding them forward now, above a busy street and between buildings. No one below noticed them. Humans didn't bother with anything that wasn't directly in front of their eyes.

"Humans, they always want this or want that; it's all about material objects to them. A middle-aged secretary or banker would never wish to fly, never, wouldn't cross their minds."

Iloa was flapping her arms now, even though she didn't need to. The magic that held them up felt like an air current around them. Denin watched as Iloa tumbled and swooped in the air.

"I think you're going to enjoy living with me," Denin said beside Iloa. "Anything you want, Iloa, it's yours." Iloa wasn't sure what to make of this, and it showed in her expression. They flew in a circle around the block and then returned to the apartment.

By the end of that day, Iloa had a brand-new puppy, a bunny rabbit, and the entire collection of every TV show you could imagine. Boxes of toffees and sugary sweets that filled the entire kitchen. The latest video games, books on how to read, picture folios of animals covered every inch of the living room. Iloa had everything — everything she could ever want. And Denin was there to teach her about the world. He had stories to tell; he told her of his past, how he had been an advisor to royalty, how his magic had won kingdoms and destroyed others.

"Then what happened? What changed? Roan's trying to work it out — why did everyone begin to see Mythica?" Iloa asked, chewing on her third packet of toffee. Denin had been contemplating this over the years too, and he flipped open his laptop and searched for a video.

"I have a theory. It's based on a mortal experiment I saw. I think this is the best way to explain it." He put the slim, silver computer onto her lap and pressed play. "Count how many times the players pass the basketball." On the screen, it showed a group of people passing the ball between them as they weaved around each other. The video was short, and when it finished, Iloa replied, "Seventeen times."

"Was there anything else you saw? Anything unusual?" Iloa shook her head.

"Alright, watch again and this time don't count, just watch ... Humans only see what they want to see; they see what affects them."

"Oh, how could I have missed that?" A man in a gorilla suit dawdled across the screen.

"Exactly, you were focused elsewhere. In the past, only a few humans saw Mythica, and most people considered them insane and ostracised them from society. Leprechauns and other Mythica lured seers to their deaths to maintain their safety and secrecy. But if I showed you the video again, Iloa, do you reckon you could not see the gorilla?"

"I know it's there."

"Exactly, you can't unsee what you know is there; you'll see it again. That's exactly what happened with the Mythica." He closed the laptop and put it aside. "Humans invented video phones, the internet; they could film us, send photos to masses and masses of humans. At first, they thought there was some scientific explanation, that it was all just a trick, but the idea was there. The word spread; humans began looking for things, and they found them. In the end, we had no choice but to reveal ourselves."

"Couldn't you use magic? You could blind them again, make them forget?"

"There's not enough magic, Iloa, it can't be done," Denin sighed; he leaned back in his chair.

"But that's not all of it, I think. Roan knows it too. If it were a simple case of seeing something that had always been there, we would have been found out long ago. Mythica always have a bit of magic in them, just enough to make them abnormal, to make them different from everything else. Twenty years ago, something went wrong; something changed the magic on a worldwide scale. I could feel it. I didn't realise what it was at first, but now that I look back, it was so obvious. It was like a crack within the very core of the Earth. Then came the legislation, the laws, and in some places, just outright violence. The humans always won. We have magic, but they have the numbers and the guns. Perhaps we should have done something more. Maybe things would have been different…"

#

The cuff glowed a dull copper in the shadows of the place called Refuge. This cuff, balanced delicately on one finger. That finger belonged to a narrow, flexed hand. Black veins raced up her arm, blending with the henna markings that were the source of the power flooding through her. Elegance radiated from her; she was regal. She could have been a queen. She could have the entire human population respect her in an instant. And so, this was why Rashali was so out of place in the dull stench of Refuge.

Rashali, with her hair dark and long around her cat-like face. No, regal wasn't the word. Goddess. Mythica had even fashioned her a throne out of old subway train remains. The rusting metal carved and arched like a temple. Mythica had placed their spells upon it, little etching here and there while others had welded small statues and tokens.

Their Rashali.

Their Queen.

Their Saviour.

She draped herself in red elfin silks trimmed with gold. Gifts from the Mythica down here, from those that refused to live with the monsters that destroyed their lives, who wanted revenge.

Rashali's voice was like the biblical land of milk and honey. She could start wars with that voice, and that is what she intended to do.

"The world trembled under the thundering limbs of those who sought to bring justice. And this army, made from the hellish mind of the Destructors, will rid the world of its vermin," Rashali recited. "The mist from the underworld shall rise and choke those unworthy." She spoke these words, which were centuries old, so ancient that the Earth had created them. They had always been there, but they flowed from her tongue as if they needed to escape. Words rose from her throat like fluid and smoked out in an intoxicating breath.

These were her words, and she recited them to one man, one man who lay naked, bound at her feet. This tall, gangly man had ruffled black hair, and Refuge grime covered his body. His body was twisted, and his ribs were bruised. His shoulders rose as he lifted himself up to meet Rashali's eyes.

Rashali would not allow it and used a pulse of magic to push him back down again. Her henna glowed and faded as the magic worked itself on her victim. They trailed up her slender arms and bare shoulders, then down her chest and disappeared.

"Do you know what that means?" Rashali cooed.

"N-n-n-o, no," the man stuttered, trying to draw his scraped knees up under his shivering body.

"It means you are going to make my army." Her voice was just a hissed whisper, but it was infinite. It could have circled the globe thrice before fading.

The man was not stupid; he knew his life would end if he did not obey. Hell, it would end soon, anyway. His body flinched at every word she spoke; he whimpered just quietly enough that he didn't think she could hear.

It lightened Rashali's heart to know her power over a mere mortal, over just one monster who was undeserving of the world he had. It fuelled her like a drug, and her henna glowed as she sent crippling pain through her victim.

Her bloodlust had not degenerated since her creation. If anything, it had grown stronger. She reached out her hand to the vermin human and let her finger rake just above his flesh. Blood wept along the trace of his muscles and down his spine. Rashali loved watching the blood, loved how deep red welled and dripped down the contour of his ribs. It was one of her guilty pleasures.

"Scared, are you, Mav?" Rashali hitched up her silks to crouch upon the gritty floor. She let the man lift his head this time.

"Yes." This made Rashali smile. It was the smile you give to a small child who fears a doctor's needle. Mocking.

"Would you like to see what you'll be making?" Rashali's eyes scooped the surrounding darkness. Refuge was a dreary place. She called the beast forward with the coil of her twisting wrist. The sound came from the darkness like spitting thunder. Mav wept and drew back on his heels. Rashali smiled a curved smile, her body crouched threateningly close to his.

"Isn't she beautiful?" In the darkness, the creature was barely visible. Its movements were like wisps of shadow. Its footsteps clicked, metal against cement. Mav stared at it in horror. Rashali stared with hungry eyes. This creature would give her the world. It moved forward, Rashali's magic restraining it like a harness. Two obsidian hooves gleamed in the dull light that radiated from Rashali. Mav saw now that it was a horse, at least it used to be.

Black hooves led up to even darker legs, legs that had enough power in them to crush bricks. Acidic spit steamed from the creature's nose as it pawed the ground restlessly. Its eyes were bloodshot red around a tiny central pupil. Its head was enormous, larger than a normal horse, and broad, with a thick neck and flank to support it. Rashali brought it closer, close enough for it to devour Mav if it so desired.

"Do you know what this is?" she asked. The creature's mouth foamed, and Rashali caught a large dollop before it fell. She didn't let it touch her hand; it wavered just above, held there by an invisible barrier. She presented it to Mav. "If you touch this, Mav, you will die. This here, this is a Mare of Diomedes. Only four remain. These are the only ones I could save. They have been with me since ancient times, waiting.

"I know what you have done to Mythica. I know that you have been experimenting with them, some even successfully. You have created strange creatures, creatures that did not exist before. You use the magic of one species and put that into another. With you, Mav, I can make more of these." She gestured to the mares of Diomedes.

"They are all female, so I cannot breed them, but you will, you will breed them. I know you understand how to create Mythica, if those mortal charges against you are correct. And you will make others more deadly than what you see before you." She wafted the saliva under Mav's nose. "Because, you see, if you don't, well, one touch of this, and you're a dead man."

Mav tried to wince away from the acrid smell that burnt his nose. He could feel it getting into him, feel it pulsing in the front of his brain. What was in that? What could make it so potent? Rashali closed her hand, and the foamy venom was gone in an instant. "You will be under constant supervision by me personally. I will restrain the mares, and if one of them dies, Mav, the rest of them will eat you." Mav shivered as the horse raised its lips to reveal canines the size of a lion's. "And I'll make sure they eat you very, very slowly." She smiled then and drew back, letting Mav crouch onto his knees.

"But how? I can't make more horses without a male. I may be able to wield magic and science together, but I cannot defy the laws of biology. This is madness, madness."

"Don't you worry about that." Rashali replied cryptically, spinning the cuff around her fingers.

The horse disappeared as if it had never been there; only the acrid scent still lingered. "You will stay in my quarters so I can monitor you. Consider it a small mercy, one that I will take away rather easily if you try to do anything. Refuge is not at all what its name suggests."

“What’s in it for me?” Mav had the nerve to ask. Rashali raised a perfectly sculpted eyebrow and resisted the urge to stop his heart then and there.

“You, my lovely little human,” she spat the words out slowly and bitterly, with enough venom to give the mare a run for its money, “will stay alive while the entire human race dies. Isn’t that enough?” Mav was silent. Rashali dissolved the floor underneath him and banished him to his quarters.

Despite centuries of planning and absorbing sufficient magic for her plans, it proved insufficient. She required more; much to her disgust, she required Mav. She was one of the Ancients, the great genies, the ones of old, and she was certain somewhere there was a statue built for her.

Of course, simpler methods existed to rid the world of humans. She could have tapped into North Korea’s nuclear weaponry system or caused some devastating earthquake; hell, she could have poisoned the water supply with Diomede’s Mare venom. But that wasn’t any fun. When people die, they should know the reason they died. That is why Rashali wanted the humans to know it was the Mythica that killed them.

The genie retreated to her quarters, which were draped in the silks of her old country, the country from which she had been born, a country that no longer existed.

Incense intoxicated you from the moment you set foot into the elaborate tunnel system that was Rashali’s home. Candles flickered just above their wicks. Colours of purple and magenta surrounded her; each room a different shade.

“Avalin.” The red-headed mortal surprised Rashali. She was not fully mortal; she was the offspring of Mythica and a human. Rashali had found her as a baby, her Mythica mother murdered and still warm as the blood pooled around her. Ava had been crying. Rashali had taken pity on the baby and raised her as her own. Despite this, Ava always called Rashali by her name, and despite her preference for Ava, Rashali always called her daughter Avalin.

"What is this one doing here?" Rashali looked across to find a thin boy with a heavy black fringe lying on Avalin's bed. He was either passed out or in a deep sleep. "You know I don't like strangers in my quarters."

"This one," Ava explained, sitting on the bed beside her vampire pet. She wore draping silks just like Rashali, only these were deep blue rather than Rashali's signature fiery red. "is the one who stole the cuff from the museum. He knows the centaur it belongs to. He also knows Denin. If we can convince a centaur and a genie to join our cause, well, I can't say we've done poorly."

"I'm impressed, Avalin." Rashali approached in long, gliding steps. "And here I was thinking you had brought home a scrawny vampire for your own amusement. What are you going to do with him now?"

"I was going to ask you that. We need him to trust us. We need him to get to the centaur. I need to discover what the cuff does. I can sense its magic, but I don't know what the magic does."

"It's centaur magic; it's foreign to both of us. Did the signage at the museum have any information?"

"No, nothing useful."

"What are you going to tell this one when he wakes up?" Rashali examined Zack, pulling back his thick fringe with her delicate nails. He couldn't be over eighteen years of age. He was not an ancient vampire either. Young ones had some humanity left in them. This one would be harder to convert. A centaur, on the other hand, there were the few creatures who despised humans more than centaurs; it was in their blood.

"Perhaps it's best if we tell him." Rashali was taking a colossal risk, but it was necessary. Zack did not appear to be the kind who would react well to being deceived. "I will leave it up to you. If he let you take him here, I'm assuming there's a moderate degree of trust." Ava raised an eyebrow.

"Rashali, you will never understand men." It hadn't taken Zack two heartbeats to get him back here, mind you; he had been stumbling drunk. Alcohol affected vampires profoundly because their bodies couldn't metabolise it properly. He had passed out for the past twenty-four hours. Clearly, Zack didn't know his limits. But Ava needed to sway Zack into talking, and what better way to do that than to make him think he had an excellent time last night?

"What happened here?" Rashali held up the torn fabric of Ava's halter neck. "Does this boy have a bit more fire in him than his appearance suggests?"

"No, that … was because of a certain genie from whom I stole the cuff. He thought it would be fun for me to expose myself in the middle of dessert."

"To be honest, everything was exposed already." Rashali said in a true motherly fashion as she examined the garment, trying to smooth it out over her long legs.

"Thanks, Rashali," Ava replied dryly.

"One last thing," her mother added, seeing Zack twitch and stretch a little with consciousness. "Did he see how to enter this place?"

"Yes, but he won't remember it."

"Good. Keep it like that," Rashali pulled the ribbon that held the curtain to the room. The lilac silk swayed into place, closing the room off to only Ava and Zack.

Motherhood had suited Rashali. It gave her humility; it gave her a sense of purpose, which was something power and magic had taken away. Rashali could have anything in the world. She could command armies, rule kingdoms, she could demand others to kneel before her feet, praise her, anything. But what Ava gave her was not magic, but it was just as powerful. It was purpose; it was love. Few people would believe that a creature such as Rashali would want or even need those things, but love was not creature-specific.

Rashali had brought Ava up as her own, nursed her, tended to her cries. She used little magic in raising Ava, and she did not spoil her. She educated her in both human and Mythica ways, teaching her Math, English, Science and the ancient legends the humans forgot. That was the thing with humans. They gained so much knowledge as a species, but as individuals, they were as dumb as rocks. They never practiced what they preached, forgot what they learnt, always wanted what was bad for them, and made excuses about everything.

Throughout Ava's upbringing, Rashali prayed her daughter would not succumb to the human blood in her veins. Ava could not absorb magic from the world but could only take what Rashali gave to her through an ancient set of tattoos. That way Rashali could control how much power a half-mortal could wield.

She could hear the vampire waking up now, and Ava's soothing tone drifting across the room. Rashali did not want to hurt the boy. Mythica was not her enemy; she was trying to protect them, but she would not let her plans be foiled. She needed that centaur; then perhaps he could tell her what the cuff was for. If she did, Rashali could navigate through its magic like plunging a hand into a box full of suspended strings. If she didn't know which ones to pull, she could break the cuff altogether.

The golden cuff was heavy on her arm, but it fit snugly. It had moulded to her skin over the days she had been wearing it. It was living. The strings were like nerves. Once Zack told her where to find the centaur, Rashali would confront him. She knew he would accept.

THE VALSHA CURSE

"I feel like shit," Zack's voice was rough with sleep. His mouth felt dry as he rubbed his eyes. He hadn't felt this bad, not since sleeping through 1969 to 1972. He opened his eyes to find Ava sitting beside him, dressed in a sapphire robe, in a room decorated like some high-end brothel. Shit, was Ava a prostitute? Zack knew she had been too good to be true. The vampire moaned in disappointment, propping himself up to hear Ava give her explanation.

"Good afternoon to you too," Ava replied with a smile. She handed him his shirt. Zack took it wearily. Zack would never sleep with someone on a first date, surely he hadn't … Did someone drug him? Why couldn't he remember anything?

"Ava, where am I?"

"My place, silly. You drank too much, and you wouldn't tell me where you lived, so I brought you back here. I couldn't let you wander the streets in your state. Don't worry, nothing happened."

"Oh, um, thanks."

"Don't mention it. You hungry?" Zack didn't feel like he could stomach anything, but the weakness in his body meant he needed blood. "Here." Before Zack could protest, Ava slipped a knife down the length of her arm and let the blood drip into a silver bowl by her bedside.

"Ava, you shouldn't. What if you bleed out and…"

"Relax. Listen, I haven't been completely honest with you." *Oh crap, here it comes*, Zack sighed internally. He tried to reassure himself that it couldn't be worse than that undercover journalist. It made him angry, how every time he tried to find someone, life just threw shit in his face. It was like one big *fuck you.* "I'm not entirely human."

"What?"

"I'm half Mythica, half elf. I have a touch of magic within me." She flicked her wrist a little and stemmed the blood with magic. She passed the bowl to Zack, who, despite himself, slurped hungrily and prayed he wouldn't be sick. It tasted like normal blood, warm on his lips. He put the bowl down, waiting for Ava's explanation. He didn't realise he had a blood moustache on his upper lip. Ava was too preoccupied with her explanations to tell him. "I didn't tell you before because I wasn't going to bring it up, but then you started talking about your centaur friends and that cuff."

"Yeah, what about it?"

"Well," Ava swallowed, building the suspense. This was the make-or-break moment, the moment when she would either gain Zack's trust or lose it. "Well, I know where it is."

#

"And you know what I did? You wanna know?" The slurred speech of a leprechaun filled the cigar-plumed air of the pub. Pub was a loose use of the word. It resembled a seedy brothel's back room. But it sold booze and you could smoke there, so Troll was well at home.

What made tonight better was that he still had Iloa's cash, and he had doubled it in poker. Troll put down another card. He was good at poker; his face was too ugly to read. The loan-shark con-man leprechaun, on the other hand, who had progressively become more animated the more he drank, didn't even realise the vampire next to him had been looking at his cards the past five hands. Two others occupied that table, joined intermittently by the barkeeper for service and play.

The vampire, who sat beside Troll, rarely spoke. His shifty eyes leered between his opponents while his pale skin glowed through the foggy haze. Troll didn't know a thing about him, not even his name. They just referred to him as the vampire. Cornan the leprechaun was not as short as myth would lead you to believe. He was just a stumpy, bald, fat man with an obsession with gold, which could have described any banker or car dealer.

The last two set Troll's teeth on edge. They were the latest editions. Troll had never seen them before, and to be honest, they were not the usual type Troll would see around here. They were twins, a man and a woman, no older than twenty, children really. Their skin was white, and not pale white, but bleach white, the sort of *light at the end of a tunnel* white. Their eyes were ice-grey, and their hair was the golden shine of spider silk. They both wore it long, and it framed their identical catlike faces. They did not blink; they just didn't. Their eyes were like impenetrable glass.

They were Kayn and Lath, and they were lovers; at least Troll was sure they were; they stroked each other's hair, kissed, and whispered into one another's ears. Sometimes Troll was sure they spoke through telepathy because they answered each other's unasked questions. They moved together, like dancers who have rehearsed their entire lives. Their bodies were fluid, a mirror of one another.

They may have been twins or lovers, but Troll didn't think that human morality could apply to these siblings. After all, they were not human. They were Vetali, bringers of the dead. They could resurrect the dead by momentarily possessing the body and extracting what memories and thoughts remained. Troll had never seen this done, nor did he particularly want to.

The Vetali spoke little about their profession, only that the police desperately sought them to investigate homicides. The Vetali twins did not offer their services to just anyone; no; they were cruel and vindictive; they made sure they were paid in years. In return for the resurrection, the one who sought it sacrificed years of their life. How many years depended on how long they wanted their loved one alive. They thrived off mortal conflict; perhaps that was why whenever they met a human they would emphasise their incest; to watch them squirm. After all, which was worse: incest, or a night with your recently deceased husband?

The vampire began, "Refuge, it's stronger now," he said in his slick voice like black oil. "What we've always wanted, our freedom, could become a reality soon."

"Frankly, I don't see the point." Troll took a swig from his litre of vodka and wiped his lips with his crooked wrist. "So, what if we don't have the same rights? We've got other shit, like booze and cigarettes and…" Troll burped.

"What is your name, Troll?" Lath asked in her wind-chime voice.

"No, your real name," Kayn insisted before Troll could reply sarcastically.

"Your tribe — you had a tribe, Troll."

"You don't remember them, do you?"

"They are dead."

"Yes, dead."

"What does it matter?" Troll huffed begrudgingly. He tried to hide his uneasiness. He didn't remember them; he hadn't seen another troll since he was just an ugly, cauliflower-coloured baby. But what did it matter? You couldn't change the past.

"You miss them."

"No, I don't. You can't miss something you don't know."

"Of course you can," Lath sang in her melodic voice. Kayn chimed in like a harmony.

"It happens all the time."

"Like something you forget to remember."

"Like something that seems insignificant, but if you had it —"

"Would change your life forever."

"Will you quit the twin speak? It freaks me out," Troll muttered. The Vetali twins only gave their identical, patronising smiles.

"What they are trying to get at," the vampire offered, "is that you should want revenge on the humans after what they have done to us. They've trapped us in their society and we can't get out."

"What do you care? You're a vampire; you've almost got the same rights as any other human."

"True, but I am old; I've known differently. I remember when there were covens, when we hunted as vampires were meant to do. They took this right away from us. We have lost respect. We are nothing but a novelty to humanity." Troll knew how that felt. He had spent years in that god-damned circus. The work wasn't awful, but people didn't exactly appreciate it. He had his cigarettes, a home, and a job, so respect was not important to him.

"Refuge will declare war."

"We will fight."

"The humans will fall."

"We will take the years they had left for our own."

"It will be … gratifying."

"We are fighting for you, Troll."

"Will you fight with us?"

"I'll have to check my calendar," Troll replied dryly. To be honest, he enjoyed tormenting the humans. He would light their cars on fire in the middle of the night and abuse random strangers on the street. What was he going to do with his time?

"You were with the girl, weren't you?" Lath asked, head cocked to the side. Troll's beady eyes narrowed.

Now he understood why creep-one and creep-two were here.

"We saw you on the news."

"Interesting interview."

"So, she does not know what she is?"

"What do you care?"

The twins shared a look with one another but did not answer.

Lath slipped a white filigree business card through the poker chips towards Troll.

ADAM & CO.
Funeral Parlour
Afterlife Communication Services

"Call us when you decide to tell her where she is."

"We will reward you generously."

"Lovely, I'm looking forward to it," Troll said sarcastically before he sculled his drink, swiped his winnings, including the business card, trudged to the door, flung it wide open and marched out. "Fucking poker," he muttered.

#

"Where have you been?" Roan scolded like a distressed parent. Zack stood in the doorway of their old apartment with Ava by his side. The redhead smiled sheepishly in her black slacks and grey top. She had made herself more presentable. "On a date," Zack replied with a roll of his eyes.

"Is this your date? Who is this?"

"Roan, I'm not a child. This is Ava. She has something to say to you."

"Your date? You brought her here? Do you aspire to be alone forever?" Roan gestured to the pigsty of an abandoned apartment. Roan had moved back this morning and had killed five mice. Without Spike, those blasted rodents thrived like flies.

Roan's eyes scrutinised the woman still standing in the doorway. So, this was Ava. Roan's narrow eyes narrowed further under his heavy brow. She looked so innocent, with that tousled auburn hair over her shoulder, the way she clasped her hands in front of her, and that dainty little smile. No wonder Zack fell for her. Boy, that kid was gullible. Ava stepped inside, and Zack closed the door behind her. Roan needed an excuse to get Zack out of the room. He didn't know how much the vampire knew, and he wanted to heed Denin's advice. But before Roan could plan an excuse, Zack commented.

"Hey, where's Iloa?"

"Gone."

"Where?" Zack leapt to his feet in sudden panic. Roan raised an eyebrow. "With Denin, at his apartment," Roan replied coolly.

"What!"

"With Denin," Roan replied with equal passivity, "to keep her safe."

"You left her alone with him?"

"Is there a problem, Zack?"

"I … I should go see her, make sure she's okay." The problem was that Zack did not know where Denin lived. Neither did Roan. Roan and Ava shared a look. Ava sighed with a roll of her eyes.

"Penthouse. Park Avenue apartments," Ava replied, her eyes focused on Roan. In his panicked state, Zack did not think it was odd that Ava knew the address. Roan raised an eyebrow. Had she been to Denin's apartment before? She must have been, to steal the cuff.

"I see Zack has a crush on someone," Ava mused once Zack had slammed the door behind him. "How rude."

"He does, he just doesn't know it yet," Roan replied. Ava strode across the apartment, examining its dusty interior. Roan had attempted to clean it in the few hours he had of peace, but it made no difference. The place still smelt like sweat and every inch of the place would be worthy of its very own Petri dish.

“Lovely place you’ve got here,” Ava lied.

“How do you know Denin? He warned me about you.”

“And so he should. I’m a very dangerous woman,” Ava flirted. Roan had never really appreciated a female with two legs, but by human standards it wasn’t hard to see why Zack was so attracted to her.

“You stole the cuff from Denin, now you don’t know what to do with it. You don’t know what it does.”

“Aren’t you a bright one?”

“Your flirtatious behaviour sickens me.”

“Oh, that’s cold.” Ava pouted her lips in hurt. “Have you ever heard of a place called Refuge?”

“What? A tent in the sewers? What do you care anyway, human?”

“Am I? And Roan, what would you do to me if I were human?” Roan huffed, unable to hide the instant hate that surfaced as flared nostrils and clenched fists. But that was enough for Ava to know his opinion. “Rashali was right.” Ava said, noticing the change in his expression, “Centaurs hate humans. Roan, what if I told you that one day humans would no longer rule this world?”

“I would tell you that you were downright balmy. Who is Rashali?” Roan’s voice was flat, with no emotion. He wasn’t interested in hypothetical wish-wash. Humanity was far too vast, far too advanced. Whatever Ava’s plans were, they would crumble within a week.

“I’m not the only one, Roan; there are hundreds all over the world.”

“And here I was thinking you just wanted to know what the cuff does.”

“We do, but we want you too. You’re one of us.”

“Who’s us?”

“How about I show you?”

“How do I know this isn’t a trap?”

"You don't. But why would we kill the Mythica we are working to protect?"

Suddenly, there was a loud crash. That apartment door flung wide.

"What's going on here?" Troll barged into the room. He asked his question, then his beady eyes caught on Ava and he gave a little whistle. "Hey sexy."

"Stop it, Troll," Roan sighed, knowing very well the man was about to embarrass himself. He knew enough about Troll to know he made the most cringe worthy pick up lines. Zack had explained to him many times why it was inappropriate; Troll just didn't care.

"I see you've gotten over your irrational fear of female humans." Troll continued to roll his eyes up and down Ava, who ignored him completely.

"Why don't you go do something useful, like donate your face to a Halloween mask shop."

"Come to Refuge, just see what we are doing, then decide," Ava interrupted.

"Oh God, not this again," Troll sighed. Roan shot him a look.

"You've known about this?" Roan did not know there was a war being prepared for. Surely there wasn't enough Mythica to launch a proper attack. The humans would stomp them out and create a bunch of new restrictions to make their lives even more miserable.

"The boys at poker tried to recruit me. I told them to suck balls."

"Hmm." Roan raised an eyebrow. They tried to recruit Troll. What could Troll possibly do to help their cause? If anything, he would probably stuff it up completely.

"I have enough magic to transport both of you, if you would like to meet Rashali."

"Transport me?"

"Yes. We try to keep our location secret in case of less than amicable friends."

"What makes you think I won't just waltz up to the humans and tell them of your plans?"

“You might not like me, but I can sure as hell tell you hate the humans more. You go tell them what we’re planning, you might as well cut off your back legs and pick up a briefcase because you’ll be just like one of them.”

Roan pondered this while Ava’s sharp eyes burrowed into him. He wasn’t used to being stared at as if the fate of the world rested with him. There had always been a part of Roan that wanted revenge. For centuries, it had nested inside him like a lost cause or an idle dream. To survive, his tribe fled their forest. Roan was at fault, and because of what he did, his family exiled him; yes, exiled him. It was a long story.

“Take me.” Roan held out his hand. Ava took it. “Troll, you’re coming too.” Roan wasn’t about to trust his life to a complete stranger. After all, Denin said to be cautious of her. Troll might be useless, but he was big and he could shield Roan from any bullets that came his way.

He had seen Denin disappear and reappear quite a few times, but Roan never wondered what it actually would be like. It was like falling asleep quickly and then waking up from a bad dream.

Roan found himself in a cavern wired with light bulbs along the cement walls. Electricity and dank petrol filled the air. The cavern was fashioned out of an old subway station. They hollowed out the wall away from the platform to form an empty arena. Roan’s hooves squelched in damp earth. Water cascaded throughout the area, and the place smelled of vermin. Troll didn’t seem at all fazed by his surroundings. Roan prayed he wouldn’t get laminitis in his hooves. A trip to the vet was the last thing he needed. The doctors always gawked and gaped at him.

“This way,” Ava gestured. Roan tested the ground for stray nails and debris. Ava led them to the subway platform, where someone had modified it with a set of stairs. The light was brighter here, lit with candles that emitted no smoke. The atmosphere was cleaner, as if walking into a bubble of morning air. It smelt like damp earth and cinnamon.

On the platform stood a throne forged from copper and rusted metal. The seat featured copper carvings and silk cushions. The candlelight made the copper glitter electrically. No one was around. Roan sensed a trap. The woman who must have been Rashali stepped out from behind a curtain in the back wall.

"Ah, lovely to meet you, Roan." Her voice was warm and welcoming, as if inviting an old friend into her home. Roan disliked it. She wore a ruby sari that draped around her lithe body and trailed behind her bare feet. She held out her hand. Roan took it with reluctance.

"And you?" she asked, turning to Troll.

"Troll," he replied. "Where's the bathroom? I need to take a leak."

"Charming. Ava, take the gentlemen to the bathroom. Roan, follow me." Roan and Troll shared a look. Why couldn't the damn troll have kept his mouth shut? Roan didn't want to be alone with this stranger. What if she killed him and sold his hooves to a glue factory? Troll made a face, which Roan suspected was an apology as Ava led him away. Rashali held up the red curtain to let Roan pass through.

"I apologise if it's cramped for you," Rashali said smoothly as Roan ducked under the low ceiling. "My home wasn't designed for centaurs. For years we have taken over small segments of subway, some of which were abandoned, and others we made by digging rock away. This is where my soldiers live; they come here to train, to learn. Others seek refuge here. They build their homes, they have made their own societies, and raised their children. Do not think you need to guard yourself against me, Roan. I am here for you; someone needs to defend the Mythica."

"Yes, that's what I'm concerned about," Roan replied. Rashali led Roan into one of the wider rooms. Purple silk draped this room, and matching cushions furnished it. Rashali sat down, and Roan knelt opposite her. His joints cracked from ill-use. He was not a young horse, and a lack of exercise had made him stiff.

"When was the last time you saw grass, Roan? Fresh rolling paddocks of it?"

"It's been a while," Roan admitted. He hadn't raced across a field since he had left England.

"Not since your exile, I'm sure." Rashali's words sent a chill through the centaur. He had always been a private person, never mentioning his past to anyone. The only creatures that knew of his exile were himself and his tribe. Rashali held up a hand to stem Roan's boiling anger. This was a violation. "I know this, Roan, because I was there." Roan bit his tongue. Impossible. "I am a genie, Roan, but of a different sort. I know what you did was shameful to you, and I understand why you do not speak of it. Roan, it may have been shameful to you, but let me tell you a story, your story."

Roan sat there, tongue bitten, as Rashali's words took form in his mind. Even after years of suppression, each face and each moment was as clear as the day he had made the memory.

"There once was a tribe of centaurs that lived on the moors of Cambridge. They were a small tribe, but a tribe of dignity and respect. There in that tribe was a colt, a boy, who raced up and down those hills as if he had been born to do so. He had a wonderful future and a strong sense of nobility to his tribe.

"Then one day, there was a human, only fourteen, who travelled on those moors. She was a seer, and she watched you for days, and these days turned to weeks, then months. This centaur boy did not know she was there, and so he continued to train. He raced against the running waters of the stream; he shot arrows into the sky; he aimed them at trees. He had a good eye, perfect you might say. And during all this time, Roan, that girl never spoke a word of your existence. Then one day this boy's shot was misguided. He had aimed at a bird in a tree, the same tree where the girl was hiding. He shot her."

Roan flinched at the harshness with which Rashali spoke those simple words.

"He shot her right here," Rashali pressed her hand to her shoulder. "The wound was not fatal. The centaur did not run away. Despite his laws and dignity, he approached the girl; he took that arrow out and soothed her. The girl did not feel scared. Roan, she dreamt about you; she dreamt of the day when you would know she existed.

"You took her back to her village. You did not enter; no, you were wiser than that. What was it like, Roan, to carry your enemy home? You remember that? What did you speak of?"

Roan remembered it; he remembered it well. He was naïve back then. Back then, the greed and mercilessness of humans were a distant myth. He recalled the walk back to the village, cradling the girl in his arms. She had wavy brown hair, almost the same colour as his flanks. Her face was pale and thin, and she wore dusty clothes. But her sallow eyes had radiated kindness and curiosity. She had asked Roan for his name, and in return, he gave her hers. Catherine, it had been. A modest, common name.

She had thanked him for carrying her, for not running away. She had told him how beautiful he was, and that for weeks she did not believe such a magnificent creature could possibly have existed. The human's kindness flattered Roan. But children outgrow kindness to become adults.

Roan abandoned the girl where the forest ended, not daring to get any closer to the humans. This left the girl to stagger back to her village. Roan returned to his tribe.

"Everything changed, didn't it, Roan?" Roan itched uncomfortably. Betrayal seethed within him.

"She told them." Human kindness was like fool's gold.

"What you don't know, Roan, is that they questioned her night and day. They didn't let her sleep. They knew something was not right; they sensed it in her; they knew she knew something they didn't, sneaking off to the moors like that. At first, they believed it to be a lover, but then the arrow wound? She tried Roan, she did."

"Well, she should have tried harder!" Roan snapped. His rage fumed like waves of steam. Rashali sank back into her cushions, satisfied with the result.

"Yes, Roan, she should have. The humans came after you; they came after your tribe. They brought the girl with them so that she could point you out. They didn't need to, though; your own reaction gave you away. You had dishonoured them. Roan?"

"Yes?"

"Your tribe. What did they do?"

"They exiled me?"

"No, before that."

"They fought."

"Yes, Roan, they fought and defended themselves, and they kept their honour, they kept their tribe and their tradition. They did not surrender, Roan. For all we know, your tribe is still out there, hiding, but still very much alive, still pure in its traditions. Because they fought. What they did does not differ from what I am trying to do now."

"They're not…" Roan spoke, his eyes off in a distant gaze.

"Excuse me."

"I said, they're not … They're not alive. My tribe is dead. My family crest — that cuff."

"You mean this one?" Rashali pulled the dull gold from the folds in her robes. She held it out to Roan, who took it slowly and with regret. It weighed heavily in his hands.

"Yes, if the humans have it, it can only mean … They're dead, all of them." He had known this from the moment he had seen the cuff in the museum, but now it was only beginning to sink in and Rashali, sitting there, that cuff in his hand, this exiled centaur, Roan had never felt so alone in his life.

"This cuff — what does it do?"

"Protects the wearer from fatal wounds." Roan's voice was distant, empty as if Rashali had taken all his will away from him. Rashali pitied the lost man; his solemn face, his lost black eyes.

"Come, Roan, there's something else I need to show you."

THE MARES

What existed before Roan was darkness, a deep, impenetrable darkness. The sort of darkness that if you fell into, not only would you fall forever, but you would lose all belief that you ever existed at all. Rashali and Roan stood on the cliff that descended into that darkness, waiting for something to appear.

"This is where I keep them," she said.

"What exactly?"

"The Mares."

"Mares?"

"Roan, are you familiar with Greek mythology?"

"Mares? Rashali, if they are what I think they are, then we are all in serious —" a whinnying snarl cut Roan off, and the clop of a lead-heavy hoof silenced him. Roan swallowed, needing to get out of here as fast as he could. Rashali's eyes stuck to the darkness, her feet so solid they became part of the rock she stood on.

"Would you like to see them?"

"Greek centaurs have feared these creatures since they existed," Roan tried to hide the quaver in his voice. "To us they were simply legend, but their terror still strikes us. Our kind had wars against these brutes, slaughtering as many as we could. Their bodies would poison the ground for years so nothing could grow, and anything that did grow carried their venom and was too deadly to eat. ... Rashali?" Rashali stood there as if she could not hear him. Roan stomped a hoof impatiently.

"Would you like to see them?" She formed a glow of light in her hand and then tossed it into the darkness. It hovered in the air before stretching individual tentacles of light in all directions.

Four disgruntled mares came into view. They were the size of rhinoceroses, their bodies flanked with muscles that bulged from their dull black coats. They stomped and bucked at the sudden light, their muzzles exuding venomous foam. Their hooves were the size of Roan's head and made him look like a meagre show pony. They stared up at Roan with blood-shot eyes that seemed to glow. They stared as if he knew what he was. Their nostrils flared to the size of fists.

"There are only four." Roan counted again and again, praying there was not a cavalry's worth somewhere in the subway channels.

"Yes, Roan."

"You can't take over the world with only four horses. They may be dangerous, but the numbers just aren't enough."

"I know," she spoke as if there was a solution to the problem, an obvious one that Roan just hadn't seen yet. "I'll have to breed them."

Roan's heart dropped like a stone. His limbs froze, and gut clenched. The solution was obvious to him now, and the mere suggestion made him want to kick Rashali over the edge and into the mares' mercy. He could not, and never would, breed with such vile things. His kind had spent their lives trying to destroy these flesh-eaters. What Rashali suggested violated the universe. Roan backed away, determined to leave and travel far, far away. He stepped back. Then Rashali spoke.

"Your tribe, Roan, I know where they are."

"I was exiled. It won't change a thing whether they are dead or alive."

"What if I told you they need your help?" Roan should have kept walking, kept walking and ignored every word Rashali had said. He should have done the dignified thing. But his insides contorted. Loyalty to his tribe was still strong even after all this time. The longing to be reunited, accepted, and forgiven again had an effect on him. He imagined himself with his brother, embracing and smiling. His family cuff back where it belonged. Running on the moors of England, bow and arrow in hand. To feel the icy morning air flow through his mane, the muddy dew-wet grass graze his hooves.

The longing seized him, the longing he had suppressed for so long as a future that was now impossible. But it was possible; it was because Rashali had power, a magic so strong it could do anything. It exuded from her like perfume. Roan knew what she was capable of and knew she was not lying.

"If you're so powerful, why do you need me?"

"I may be powerful, Roan, but not even I can defy the laws of basic biology. I have procured a mortal who has dabbled in creating Mythica. You may know him, Roan."

"What do you mean?"

Rashali replied with a mysterious raised eyebrow and continued, "You will be safe, I assure you. You will wear the cuff."

"I can't." Roan turned to leave. Roan made his way back, guided by the dull torchlight along the tracks. Rashali called out to him. "When you change your mind, I'll find you."

#

Zack knocked on Denin's door like a human woodpecker. It was Iloa who answered.

"Zack!" There were dark rings around the girl's eyes, but she still greeted Zack with avid enthusiasm. She looked as if she hadn't slept in days. "Come in. I'm so glad to see you. How did your date go?" Zack was too shocked to tell her. Denin's apartment was askew with everything anyone could want. Empty candy wrappers cluttered one corner, PlayStation games filled another, and books formed towering stacks. On the ceiling, close to the window, was a teardrop-shaped hammock overlooking the city. Iloa dragged him into the kitchen.

"I made cupcakes." She offered him one. Zack made a face. Iloa frowned, remembering.

"Oh, right. Sorry." Feeling guilty, Zack took one anyway. They were decorated with pink icing and sprinkles and were still warm from the oven.

"It's okay, I can still taste." They would give him stomach cramps, but if he had a little, it wouldn't be too bad. He took a bite and grinned. "These are good, Iloa." The feather-haired girl beamed. Her smile faded quickly, as if it took too much effort to hold.

"Iloa, you look terrible. What had Denin been doing to you?"

"Oh, Denin's great. He's teaching me how to read."

"Have you been sleeping?"

"There's too much to do; I never knew there was so much to learn. Did you know that there's a frog in the tropical rainforests that … Zack, where are you going?" Zack marched through the kitchen to the back rooms to find Denin. He had stormed in angry, and he was going to vent that anger where it belonged.

"Denin!" Zack pounded on the bedroom door. Denin opened it halfway, with a towel around his waist. Zack sensed Iloa behind him with wide, curious eyes. He didn't like it, not one bit. Denin had just come out of the shower, his hair still wet. He was two heads taller than Zack. Zack, who stood in front of him, found anger wilting into speechlessness. What was he supposed to say to Denin? Don't steal Iloa away from me? How stupid was that going to sound?

"Yes?" Denin waited.

"I-I've come to take Iloa home."

"Have you now?"

"Do I have to go? I like it here," Iloa said. Zack's insides twisted, and it wasn't because of the cupcake.

"You heard the girl. She wants to say, and she is more than welcome to. Now, if you will excuse me." Denin closed the door, and Zack stared at the white paint, the words that had left him moments ago bubbling up in an incoherent mutter.

"Zack, are you alright?"

"Why are you choosing him over me?" Zack cried before he could come to his senses. Iloa furrowed her brow in confusion. Was she choosing anyone? She was happy here. Denin was nice to her — not that Zack wasn't nice; it's just that Denin's apartment didn't have fleas or smell like garbage island.

"Mav escaped. Roan sent me here to be safe."

"Oh, right," Zack muttered, a little ashamed of himself. Iloa yawned and rubbed her eyes. Zack followed her back into the living room.

"You really should get some sleep, Iloa."

"I try." She yawned again. Her feathers were looking sparse, and Zack saw why. On the kitchen counter was a vase full of long white feathers. They were Iloa's feathers. The girl saw Zack examining them and explained.

"Payment," Iloa said. "Denin takes the magic out of them for me. That's how he got all of this. He's stopped now, though; I don't want to be plucked bald." She finished with a yawn. Zack noticed now the tiny bags under her golden eyes and how she was a little unsteady on her feet.

"Too right you don't." Zack tried to take the bitter edge out of his voice. He sat down on the couch, and Iloa perched herself on the edge of the coffee table, rifling through DVDs and games.

"So, whacha want to do?"

"Huh?"

"Denin will be out running errands this morning, so we've got the place to ourselves. I'm sure he'll let you stay."

"I'm staying whether he likes it or not," Zack said defiantly. Iloa gave a smile.

"Cool. I've wanted to try out the two-player version of this game for a while now." And instantly she jumped off the table, slipped the disk into the machine and bounced back with two controllers in her hand. When Denin exited his room, dressed in his exquisite black suit, Zack made sure he had his booted feet on the coffee table. Denin sneered as he approached. "I see you are still here." He straightened his sapphire-blue tie with a forced smile.

"Yup." Zack didn't look away from the screen; he thumbed the controller greedily.

"Wonderful. Iloa, I'll be back around five. Maybe you could clean this place up a little."

"I'll try."

Denin smiled and strutted to the door, picking up a cupcake on the way and biting into it.

"Wonderful cupcakes, by the way." Iloa beamed at him. He gave a wink and disappeared. Zack glanced at the door, then once he found out Denin wasn't coming back, he paused the game and leapt to his feet.

"What are you doing?"

"Searching."

"For what?"

"Anything. I know the sort of person Denin is. He wouldn't just offer you a place to stay. He's up to something."

"You don't know that. Hey, that's rude." Zack was flinging open drawers and tossing things everywhere. He raced down to Denin's bedroom with Iloa at his heels.

"Why would he let you stay? Why would he give you everything you want? He hasn't tried to kiss you, has he?" Zack scrutinised Iloa's face. She screwed it up to make a funny expression.

"Kiss? What's that?" Zack gawped a little at Iloa's ignorance.

"You've been watching all those movies, and you don't know what a kiss is?"

Iloa shrugged. "I've only been watching nature documentaries. I haven't gotten around to the others, and Denin has been the perfect host, thank you very much."

Zack rolled his eyes and punched open Denin's bedroom door.

His room was immaculate. The mahogany drawers were dustless. They didn't have handles. You had to push them in, and they sprang open. Iloa followed Zack around the room as he pushed open drawer after drawer to find ordered socks, ties and shirts. The man had an entire department store's worth of clothes in here. When Zack opened the wardrobe, he didn't think he had seen so many shoes in his life. He saw pointed ones, shiny ones, ones with a heel, ones from decades ago, and others that looked unworn. There was not a scratch or scuff among them.

The bed protruded from a chocolate-coloured feature wall. He hadn't tried under the bed, or in the bedside cabinets. Iloa perched and balanced on the low mantle at the foot of the mattress.

"He's going to know you've been in here," she sighed.

"Aha!" Zack pulled out a bulky black rectangle from under the bed. "That thief!" The laptop was his. Iloa blinked in surprise, but said nothing. Surely Denin had a legitimate reason.

"He might have found it," she said. "I'm sure he would have told you; he probably just forgot this morning. He was in a rush."

"Or he stole it. He's been looking through my files."

"Denin wouldn't do that. Why would he care about your emails?"

"I don't know. But the point is, he stole it." Zack jabbed a fuming finger at his laptop and stormed out of the room. "When I get my hands on him … Come on, Iloa, we're leaving."

"Leaving? But we can't leave."

"And why the hell not?"

"Because … because Denin had been so nice to me. It would be rude to disappear. You might not like him, Zack, but I do." This made Zack grip his laptop so tightly that he could feel the metal bend under his fingers.

"He. Stole. My. Laptop," Zack said slowly, his voice a growl. Iloa's slender face tightened with stubbornness.

"Denin is hiding me from Mav. Who cares about your stupid laptop?"

"Fine then, I'll just leave." Zack stormed past her out the door. When he got to the kitchen, he turned around and spat. "You're so naïve, Iloa, so naïve. Can't you see Denin is exactly the same as Mav? He's taking what he wants from you, and there you are, his pet, happy as long as you've got whatever you want. You mean nothing to him. As soon as you stop being useful, as soon as he's drained your magic feathers dry, you'll be out on the curb like the rest of us."

He slammed the front door behind him before Iloa could open her tight, beaky little mouth. Zack had been stupid, so stupid to think that anyone would choose him over someone as enchanting as perfect, prissy Denin. Stupid genie…

#

Roan was furious, and this wasn't the kind of anger where you mutter a few curses and move on the next day; no, Roan was furious enough to stampede down a busy city street filled with cars in broad daylight. This was the sort of pissed where you stopped traffic and if they beeped their little horns, you kicked their headlights in. He was surprised the police hadn't shot him with tranquilliser darts yet. Now he could see why Troll enjoyed pissing off these bastards so much. A man had the look of utmost horror on his face when Roan charged for his car and slapped two hoof prints into its bonnet.

Roan continued down the street at a trot. He should be more careful with his legs. They were the weakest part of a horse, after all. Another reason flesh-eating equines were a terrible idea. Put a few tricky hurdles up around the city and you'll have crippled horses in no time.

Rashali was smart enough to see this, surely. And if she was so powerful, why the hell didn't she just crush humanity with a bit of magic? He felt like going back there and laughing in her face, pointing out everything that was ridiculous about her plan. Even if she could breed the mares, how long would it take to make an army of them?

The more Roan thought about it, the less of an all-powerful genie Rashali seemed, and more of a crazy old bat living in the sewers. But the fact that these mares were alive still frightened him. He was so distracted that he almost walked into Zack. Zack was standing in front of their apartment with his phone to his ear and his missing laptop under his arm.

"I know you're there, so pick up the freaking phone." Zack's face fumed like Roan had never seen. "I know you stole my laptop, and I know you're up to no good. Whatever you're up to, you leave Iloa out of this or I'll, I'll, I'll set Troll on you!" Zack snapped his phone shut with force. Roan raised an eyebrow. He must really hate Denin to consider setting Troll on him. He didn't think he had ever seen Zack become that assertive with anyone … ever!

"I see you've finally grown some balls, Zack."

"Where's Troll? I need him."

"So I heard. Is Iloa not doing well?"

"Oh, she's doing fine, fantastic even." Zack flung his arms up into the air. "Has everything she ever wanted, oh, except common sense. Why the hell would you let her go with him?"

"Because Mav is on the loose, which incidentally, I don't think he is a threat anymore. You've gotten lucky this time, Zack, because someone is holding him captive."

“Really, what? Where is he? Where have you been, and why … why do you smell as bad as Troll?”

“Long story, go get Denin, tell him to meet me here, and for God’s sake don’t start a fight with him; you’ll only embarrass yourself.” However, the look on Zack’s face told Roan that the vampire would do exactly that. He rolled his eyes and followed Zack down the street.

Troll was still down in Refuge. Roan had forgotten him until now. But Troll could take care of himself, and Roan could always find him later. If Zack was so worked up about this, the least Roan could do was be there for him. Besides, hoofing a genie in the face might lighten his spirits a little.

They kept to the side streets. Naturally, people stared at Roan, but he would simply snort and glare, and they would move on quickly. Since he had already made one scene today, what was stopping him from making another? He told Zack where he had been and what Rashali was planning. His past was something he omitted. No one knew about his exile, and he planned to keep it that way. Zack seemed to have missed the big picture of it all.

“So, Ava was using me?” Disappointment made his pitiful voice soft.

“Yeah, well, I don’t think she was your type, anyway.”

“But she was so kind and funny and…”

“Had one heck of a set of knockers on her?” Roan mocked in Troll’s gritty voice.

“I keep telling him he can’t say those sorts of things anymore, but does he listen?”

They arrived at the apartment building. It was a skyscraper, and its brilliant new metal walls gave a bluish sheen. Everything about it radiated *no Mythica.* The doorman took one look at Roan and shook his head.

“Excuse me, sir, but you cannot fit into the elevator.” The man was young with oiled brown hair underneath a flat, blue doorman’s cap.

"I'll take the service elevator then," Roan spat back, readying his legs if the man had the guts to refuse.

The doorman must have sensed this too because the next thing he said was, "Right this way, sir. I am accustomed to Master Denin's more … alternative guests." The doorman showed them the way with an outstretched arm. "This will take you directly to the penthouse."

Roan didn't think he had ever been called sir in his entire life. It was such a human title. He wondered whether he should be insulted, or if this was the closest he would ever get to being treated as an equal. The young man gave a professional smile as pressed the floor number Zack told him to.

"Have a good day, sir," he said.

Roan reluctantly offered a "Thank you." Zack itched the entire way to the apartment. He was looking sullen, too.

"When was the last time you ate?" Roan commented.

"I'm not hungry."

"You look like a corpse."

"Like I haven't heard that one before." The elevator doors opened, and they entered the penthouse through an unlocked door.

"Iloa? Oh my God, Iloa!"

THE HOSTAGE AND THE OLD BAT

Troll may have been ugly, but he wasn't stupid. He had an unconscious Ava slung over his shoulder, and he had travelled with her the entire length of the subway. He had found a pothole that had just managed to fit his wide girth. Ava was stirring. He had faked needing to pee to get Ava on her own. The whole recruiting of Mythica to kill humanity seemed a little overdramatic, and he wanted to get it straight.

If people saw a troll with an incapacitated woman flung over his shoulder, they said nothing. It was getting dark, and Troll took Ava to the only place he knew would be safe. If he took her to the apartment, Roan would meddle, and Zack would be tricked into releasing her. Troll knocked a meaty fist onto the black mahogany door. If there was anyone in this city he could trust, it was Margo.

"What?" The door flung open, and Troll came face to face with a female equivalent of his ugliness. Margo was human, and if Troll had to guess an age, he would have said *well past her use-by date*.

"Oh, Troll." Margo's mouth was permanently in the shape of a bulldog muzzle, and her cheeks had fallen to her neck. Her black eyes were puffy with purple bags, and her sparse grey hair splayed tangled around her face.

"Who have you got there?" She may have been old, but Margo had her sight and a sharp tongue to match.

"Let me in."

"She's in trouble, this one?"

"She will be if she doesn't answer my questions."

"Kidnap is it?" Margo let Troll inside, and the little old woman locked the three bolts on her door. Margo's place smelt of musk. No one had dusted for years, and you could see it swirl in the air with the ash. Margo smoked from those long, thin cigarette holders, and there was one in the ashtray waiting to be finished. The archaic box-shaped television sets with the bulging screens played an old game show. Troll dumped Ava onto one of the floral pattered couches. She was twisting now, the great big red bump on her head looking rather nasty.

"She's gonna hate you," Margo said, seeing Troll's catch. "Go get an ice pack from the fridge." There was no arguing with Margo. Troll did what she said. He needed something to tie Ava up with too and grabbed the pink fluffy string from Margo's dressing gown that lay draped over the green plastic and metal kitchen chair. It wouldn't hold Ava for long, but it was better than nothing. He wondered if Margo had duct tape anywhere.

"Margo?" he called, then he saw Ava sitting upright and furious.

"Hello Troll," Ava spat. She made no motion to stand or escape. She was a smart broad, Troll would give her that. No use fighting when Troll could catch her in two hulking steps. Troll grunted in return. He wasn't one for words and didn't know how to begin the interrogation. Fortunately, Margo was there to mediate.

"Now, what did you bring her here for, young man?" she addressed Troll as if he were just a boy. "I've known you since you were a wee tot, and you have never, ever, not once, ever brought a girl into this house." It was hard to tell, but Troll rolled his eyes.

"She's part of this gang."

"It's not a gang."

“It’s a gang that’s trying to take down humanity.”

“Are they now? Well, they’re going to have a bloody hard time doing that. What’s your name?” she barked at Ava.

“Ava.”

“Ava, would you like some tea?”

“Margo, we do not offer hostages tea!”

“Hostage or not, she’s still a guest in my house and, unlike some people here, I don’t forget my manners.”

“I’m fine, thanks,” Ava spoke up. Margo settled a little.

“She’s not human,” Troll growled.

“Well, she could have fooled me.”

“Tell me what Rashali has planned.”

“If you had followed Roan, you would have found out. We were trying to recruit you after all,” Ava replied sweetly, sitting perched on the edge of the seat.

“So, it’s true then.” Margo turned to stone.

“Yes,” Ava nodded.

“I told you,” Troll muttered. A black cat slunk from behind an old cabinet and wove itself between Troll’s legs. This was Blacky. Troll had named him. He had named himself too. He wasn’t very good with names. Troll picked up the feline. In his hands, Blacky seemed no bigger than a mouse. Blacky rubbed her face up and down Troll’s chest, happy to see him again after so long. That was what Troll liked about animals; they didn’t care what you looked like.

“What are you?” Margo inquired. “You don’t seem like a vampire to me. And surely you would have used magic by now if you could. I can sense things, you know? That’s how I found this one.” She pointed to Troll. Margo had a tendency to leap into the past and tell her life story.

“I am half-human. Rashali raised me. I can use small amounts of magic that are given to me. Never quite in this world, never quite in your world,” Ava said with an old bitterness in her voice. Troll, still holding Blacky, opened the cupboard drawers to find a Sigma nine-millimetre gun. He took it out for the *just in case* scenario. Margo gave him a warning look.

"Ava, why is this Rashali trying to take over the world?" Margo demanded. Ava raised an eyebrow.

"You don't think it's possible, do you?"

"What is she using?" Troll demanded to know, the gun pointed at her face. Ava turned and blinked innocently. "Be very careful, Troll, because I can make sure you never speak to Roan again." It was a threat, and from the sound of her voice, a very real one too. Troll rolled the gun under his palm. Blacky was now perched on Troll's broad shoulders, her wide green eyes unblinking.

"Great work, Troll, the first girl you bring home and she's a bitch."

"Tell me."

"Use your manners."

Troll dived a hand into his pocket and pulled out his cell phone. Roan didn't own a phone, but Zack did. He hoped the centaur was with him. Three rings finished, and then Zack's panicked voice picked up.

"What?"

"Is Roan there?" Shuffling and commotion filled the background. Where the hell were they? Zack sounded like he was about to break down and cry. A scuffle sounded through the phone line as the phone was passed around.

"Not a good time, Troll."

"What's Rashali planning? What's her weapon?"

"Horses. Big ugly horses. Dangerous, very scary. She can't take over the world with them.... You have Ava captive, don't you?"

"I might have."

"Roan, get off the phone. Here, hold her..." Zack's voice carried through the phone line. What the hell was going on over there?

"Listen, I've got to go. Just … don't kill her. I've got enough to deal with." The line went dead. Troll pocketed his phone.

"Horses?" he tried not to laugh. "You're trying to take over the world with horses. Animals that small children ride at petting zoos."

"Not. That. Sort. Of. Horse," Ava replied. "These are flesh-eaters, shadow-dwellers."

"Oh, I'm terrified. Did you hear that, Blacky? A couple of ponies are coming for us."

"Troll!" Margo barked. "Haven't I told you it's not nice to mock people?" No matter how angry Troll became, no matter how irritating someone was, Troll never swore at Margo. She was one of the few people Troll respected. If it weren't for Margo, Troll didn't know what he would have done. Margo was a Seer, and forty-one years ago, had found a stumpy, potato-shaped troll child raiding her chook pen.

"What do you think you're doing, boy!" she had cried, then stopped him from leaving by barring the shed with a shovel. Troll had been so shocked to find a human that could see him that he had dropped the five eggs he had been carrying and let the chook under his arm flutter free.

"You're an ugly little brute. What's your name?" Was the next thing Margo had said to him. The troll wore filthy rags. He had been living on the streets, stealing and scrounging what he could. He never knew his parents and, not even to this day, has ever seen another Troll in person. Now and then he would Google search for them to reassure himself he wasn't the only one alive. For all he knew, his species could be done and dusted.

Margo had taken Troll under her wing and had raised him ever since, and by raised, he meant, the place he came to sleep and eat occasionally. Got taken away by the circus at one point, but always found his way back. That was good enough for Troll, and even if he never said it, he appreciated it very much. Troll wasn't big on sentimental crap.

"What are these horses?" Margo asked, bringing Troll back into the present situation, "And perhaps more importantly, why are you trying to kill my kind?"

"Do you really need an answer to that? Look at you, look at how you treat us."

"That's not fair. You can't just assume every individual hates you. You're half human yourself, I might remind you."

"I've chosen my side," Ava sneered, "and I have my reasons." Ava leaned back, tight-lipped. "The humans had their chance to treat us as equals. That time is over now."

"You know what I think? I think you're being a little over dramatic. Where is this Rashali? I want to speak to her." If there was one thing Margo had, it was balls. Even in her pink nightgown and purple slippers, the ancient woman still mustered enough authority to look like someone who should not be messed with.

"Bring her to me."

Ava raised an eyebrow.

"Your minion kidnaps me, drags me here, insults me, and now you expect me to…." From the look on Margo's face, it was clear she would not take any crap. "Oh, fine then, you know you won't be able to hurt her or change her mind." Margo waited for Ava to pull out her phone and ring. She didn't need to speak. She just let it dial for a few moments and then hung up. The next thing they knew, there was a knock on the door. Margo toddled over to open it. A tall, regal Indian woman stood there, her eyes lined with gold and her hair delicately woven into intricate patterns.

"I believe you have my daughter?"

"Your daughter is she now?" Margo mused and let the genie in. Compared to Rashali, Margo looked like something you find attached to the bottom of your shoe.

"In a manner of speaking, yes," Rashali replied and spotted Ava unharmed on the couch. Margo did not offer anyone tea this time. Instead, she lit a cigarette, plunked herself down, and got right into business.

#

Iloa was barely breathing; her heartbeat was so shallow that even the best of doctors would have had trouble finding it. Her eyes were closed and her limbs were lax. It was as if Iloa was in a deep sleep.

They had found her collapsed on her couch. Zack could not wake her. Roan stood there like a useless thing. What was he to do? He couldn't take Iloa to the hospital. She wasn't human; besides, that would cause more trouble than it solved. The humans would never let her leave.

Zack had given Roan his phone to call Denin, but the man wasn't answering. Zack was cursing enough to give Troll a run for his money. Roan tried the number again. No answer. Perhaps he had caller ID and didn't want to deal with Zack anymore. Roan waited a few minutes, then tried again.

"Denin!" Roan barked before he could hang up. "What have you done to Iloa?"

"…leave a message after, well, you know."

A beep interrupted, "Oh, fuck this…" Roan.

"That's your signal to talk!" Zack reminded.

"I know." Roan may not have been used to human technology, but he wasn't an invalid. "What have you done to Iloa?" he barked into the receiver. "I know you're there; pick up now. She's in trouble. We're in your apartment, and if you don't come soon, I will give Zack permission to destroy everything in your wardrobe." Within a minute, Denin had zapped himself through the doorway of his home.

"Don't you *dare* touch my suits."

"Oh yeah, really great attitude," Zack spat, checking Iloa's breathing. "What did you do to her?"

"Nothing." Denin made no motion to enter his apartment. He rested the length of his body against the doorframe, his arms folded.

"What?"

"I have to leave. I can't be here a moment longer. I've taken too much. She needs time." There was something in Denin's voice that told them he was hiding something, that he knew something. For a moment, Roan could have been fooled into thinking the genie felt regret.

"What, you can't just…"

"Denin!" Roan clopped forward, but before he could grab the man by his stupid, perfectly symmetrical tie, he had disappeared.

"How am I supposed to know? I don't even know what species she is."

"We need to find Mav. Mav will know how to fix her. He created her after all."

Roan snorted. Like that was going to happen.

"How's her heartbeat?"

"A little stronger, I think. Roan, what if she dies, Roan?" Roan looked at the phone in his hand. Perhaps there was a way to get in touch with Mav. It was a long shot. It would involve a lot of begging and bargaining, but what choice did he have?

"Do you have Ava's number in here?"

"Of course."

Roan found it and dialled.

#

Whatever Margo had to say, it could not sway Rashali's decisions. This was the course of the earth; this was how the world was to play out. Rashali knew it and had known it for a long time. This was the purging of humans; this was her duty; and this was the time. Talk of innocents, of children — it didn't sway Rashali. She was not heartless, as people had accused her, and she had a soul. She showed pity and mercy occasionally, but this was not one of those times. What right did she have to handpick humans she felt were deserving enough to survive the upcoming massacre? Exactly, she had no right; the ways of death were out of her hands.

She knew her part to play, and she would play it. Humanity believed itself to be divine, delusion itself to think they were the be-all-and-end-all of the universe, when in fact the universe knew they existed as much as an individual is aware of one bacterial munching away happily on their skin or inside their gut. Humans were just too small, but they could not see that. Rashali doubted they ever would.

"And you, you're sitting there." Margo went on and on, jabbing a finger at Ava. "Are you just going to let her do this?"

"The Earth has been waiting for a long time now," Ava replied coolly. That was one thing Rashali had always admired about Ava — how calm she could be, how cold. She picked that up from her. Rashali had raised her well.

"You can't just kill people out of revenge. Sure, we haven't treated you nicely, but —"

"It's not about that," Rashali growled for the hundredth time.

"Of course it is. What? Do you think if we never found out about your kind, you would still do this?"

"Foolish human, don't you see? You had to find out about us. We were revealed so that this could occur. This is just a stepping stone, and you can't move it. You humans also cannot destroy it, as you love to do with anything that does not go your way. This is your purging; this has been prophesied by so many as your judgment day. It is what has been asked of me. It is what the Earth desires." Rashali's eyes were beautifully dark, and her voice grew deep with knowledge, as it does when she speaks unwavering truth. If anyone heard her, they would never dare to question, never consider asking, for they would know Rashali's wisdom was infallible.

"Bull shit. Poppy cock." Margo smacked her lips together and sucked in her last drag of her cigarette and tossed the end into her overflowing ashtray. Troll smirked, patting the cat on his shoulder. And just to break the doomsday atmosphere even more, Ava's phone buzzed.

"Zack, this is not a good time."

"It's not Zack. … where's Rashali? I need to speak to her." Roan's voice was so loud everyone heard it.

"Oh, is this the centaur, is it?" Ava grinned and leant back further into her chair.

"Yes."

"The one who didn't find our plan worth being a part of."

"Now's not the time, Ava," Roan growled, his voice muffled and cracked.

"Phht, plan," Margo huffed. "I don't think you can call culling an entire species a plan."

"Not the entire human race, just most of it," Rashali hissed, half in mind to magic the old bat's lips together.

"What does the horse want?" Ava handed Rashali the phone.

"I heard that!" Roan snarled out of the speaker.

"Whatever it is you want, you won't get it until I get what I want," Rashali said flatly. There was a pause, an endless pause. A scuffle erupted in the background. The longer the pause, the wider Rashali's grin grew. She would have her way; she knew she would. It was destiny; everything slotted into place because it had to be.

"Fine," Roan growled like thunder.

"Perfect. Now, what do you want?"

"Mav."

"That can be arranged."

#

Judge Roan all you want, but what else could he do? An innocent Mythica was dying, and his best friend's heart was breaking. If Roan had not done what he did, Zack would never have forgiven him. He was a traitor not only to his species but also to himself. A cheap whore, a sellout and the bringer of the end of humanity. But when he had that phone in his hand, and his eyes could just see the top of Zack's black hair from over the low couch, he had no choice. Iloa couldn't waste a minute; he could foil Rashali's plans later. "Help is coming," he called to Zack. He did not explain what it had cost him. This was something no one needed to know.

"You called?" Rashali appeared at the doorway just as Denin had done, only this time she held a dirty vagabond of a man by the scruff of his gritty collar.

"Iloa!" Mav struggled to stand. His knees gave way beneath him. Roan sneered at the man, thinking about how times had changed. Roan had feared the man just a few years ago; the man had whipped him and caged him in his pen like an animal. It took a lot of strength to stop himself from kicking Mav in the face. But as Rashali hauled him in, the man was pitiful. He scrabbled, his black pants ripped and white shirt a dirty grey. He scrambled to his feet and collapsed beside Iloa. Zack sneered, but did not draw back. Mav's face was sallow and hollow as he peered down over his creation.

"What's wrong with her?" Zack begged. Mav was silent for a long time, his frail hands fluttering here and there, checking her pulse and breathing. He opened her wide yellow eyes and shook her head.

"And she was just lying here?" Mav interrogated.

"Yes."

"Who owns this place?"

"Denin. A genie."

Then Mav surveyed the apartment. Feathers littered the kitchen bench; bald patches ringed her ears.

"He's been taking her magic, draining her dry."

"Son of a bitch, I'll kill him."

"Some types of Mythica can't help it. It's like breathing air."

“That’s why he didn’t enter the room when we called.”

“I don’t care, I’ll still kill him.”

“She will be alright … I think.”

“If she’s not, I’ll crush you under my hooves,” Roan warned. “And I’ll enjoy it too.” Roan had not forgotten what Mav had done to them. Rashali edged closer to Roan, her long legs taking graceful strides beneath the flowing red fabric. Roan had to admit she cut a dominating figure. Subtly, she took his hand. Her fingers curled around his, and her nails dug in so that he could not pull away.

“You ready?”

“Now?”

“Can’t let you slip on your end of the deal.”

“My family, my tribe? Where are they? You said they were in trouble.” If Roan was going to sell himself, he at least wanted a good price for it.

“Oh, now you want to bargain, do you?” She whipped up the surrounding air with magic, and Roan’s stomach once again shot up to his throat.

#

Ava cursed Rashali under her breath. Why did she have to leave her here in this grubby old shack of an apartment? Margo had offered her tea again, and grudgingly Ava had to take a cup. Troll’s diligence proved inescapable, and Ava lacked the magic to disappear. Hell! Troll didn’t even allow her to go to the toilet without standing outside the door. Thankfully, Margo had persuaded the man to stay out of the bathroom.

Ava had abandoned her untouched tea to wander around the living room, scanning the old photos that lay clustered upon the mantlepiece and sewing machine. Troll scooted around the room with her. If she moved one step, so did he, stroking that cat like a James Bond villain.

“Who’s this?” Ava asked, picking up a dusty, old black-and-white photograph of two young girls sitting side by side on a pedestal. The background was crackly white. They wore high-knee socks and pinafores.

“What’s what, dear?” Margo toddled over. “Oh, that is my great-grandmother and her sister.”

“And these too?” The same two girls stood side by side in front of a small cottage.

“Yes,” Margo’s lips pursed. “My mother said that she died two weeks after the photo was taken. Put it down, girl, stop looking through my things.”

“Thought you enjoyed telling people your life story.”

“Not to the enemy,” Margo huffed at Troll. Blacky wriggled out of his grip and disappeared.

“I should keep her around then. Save me from listening to you.” Somehow Margo beat the height difference between them and smacked Troll hard across the back of the head. Ava didn’t stop scanning the photographs. There were a few roughly sketched pictures of the countryside. The paper was yellowing with age. They were good, but they were coarse, with trees being too large in places where they should have been small, and a lack of detail where it should have flourished. The lines were rugged and faded with time.

“Who drew this?” Ava asked. It looked like a child had done it, a very skilled child, but a child nonetheless.

“Great-great-aunt,” Margo sighed. “Put it down. Sit here and finish your tea. I don’t care how pretty you are, you’re still a hostage, now sit!” There was no defying Margo’s orders, and Ava slumped back onto the floral couch. It was so worn that she sank deep into it and then hit a hardwood plank.

“My aunt had the sight too,” Margo said, angling the photograph to where it was before. Cathy’s wide grey eyes stared at her. Despite herself, Margo still talked, “She had been so young to die. My great-grandmother had only been sixteen when it happened, and Cathy even younger. They had lived in England then.” Troll knew the stories if he remembered them. Margo had told him so long ago. He was the company she had, besides Blacky, of course. But Troll was also unreliable and a downright arsehole sometimes. He would go away for years at a time without a single word of explanation, then he reappeared one day with the excuse that he had been kidnapped by a circus. There's a little scar on Troll's eyebrow. That is from when she had thrown a toaster at him.

"So, you're part human." Troll attempted to start a conversation.

"Yes."

"Your mother or your father, girl?" Margo helped him out. "Which one was human?" The more she knew about Ava, the more she knew about the enemy. It was strange to think they were sitting there with the people who were trying to destroy their lives. If Margo had any sense, she would have grabbed her steak knives and stabbed away. Of course, she was not that uncivilised; perhaps Troll could do it.

But Troll may have been vile, rude, and the epitome of bad habits, but he was not a killer. He showed tenderness only to animals. Even as a young one, Troll loved animals; he would spend hours in the chook pen completely sober. No, Troll could not kill a human, especially one that was no immediate threat. Besides, she was too pretty; even now Troll wasn't looking at her face. *Humph, men.*

"My father was human."

"What happened to him?" Something must have happened because she was with Rashali now. What could have made Ava change sides? Margo scrutinised Ava, her brown eyes penetrating into her blue ones. Ava's lips were tight.

"Are you going to let me go or not?"

"There's no point in keeping her; Rashali will come back anyway and do her teleport thing," Troll grumbled. All his efforts had been futile. There was nothing he could gain that he couldn't have found out from Roan anyway. And now he's dragged Margo into all of this. Roan was right; he was pretty useless.

"Then I can take that as a *yes*?" Ava rose to her feet. No one stopped her.

Only when she got to the door did Margo call out. In a foreboding voice that would have made Rashali proud, she said, "Just one question, girl?" Ava did not turn around but paused with her hand on the handle. "What would your father think of you right now?"

"If he weren't already dead," Ava replied, "I would have killed him myself."

#

"You and I have more in common than you think, Roan," Rashali said, making conversation. They strolled side by side down the subway rails, met by the eyes of Mythica, peering out from the darkness. There were hundreds down here, more than Roan could have thought possible. Perhaps Rashali was doing the right thing. No one should live like this.

"Yeah, how do you figure?"

"We are both fiercely protective of the ones we love." Rashali gestured around her into the shadows. "These are the ones I love; these are my kind, just as Zack and Iloa are yours."

"My kind exiled me long ago."

"Yet you still wish to find them, to protect them. Even though you reject me, Roan, I am still fighting for you. I hope you will see my vision, see that this is meant to be," Roan snorted in derision. Rashali was a visionary; you had to give her that, but history told him visionaries tended to be wack-jobs.

"You're a genie; you could destroy the world anyway you want to. Why like this, why now, why with me?"

"I am not just a genie, Roan; I am one of the Ancients, the noble creatures that have existed before the earth had cooled. I had been energy then, just a cluster of chemicals and something else, something special.

"I had an awareness of the surrounding universe, and in its dust I saw its future. I lived my life in primordial matter, and I experienced being broken down and remade into the vast number of creatures that went extinct before human descendants even began. And in all that time I knew what humans were to become, knew what they would do."

"Then why didn't you stop them? Why couldn't you have made the earth differently?"

"Why did you save that girl all those decades ago, Roan? You weren't supposed to, but you did it. I must do this."

"That's different."

"No, it's the same. Tell me, if someone was there to tell you to run away and leave Catherine to die, would you have done it?" Roan thought for a moment.

"No," he muttered.

"You may not see it now, Roan, but by doing this, I am saving so many lives. I don't expect you to see. Trust me."

Rashali turned to Roan as she spoke, as if there was that universal love in her heart that she spoke of. Roan had believed in his own gods once, long ago. He would pray to them at night and on full moons, and celebrate in victory dances in their honour. Then they exiled him. He lost his faith, lost that part of him Rashali tried to restore.

For a moment, Roan believed Rashali was right, that all these Mythica would rise to see sunlight, to return to their homes, their families, and carry out their ways. That was an impossible dream, because nothing shattered can be mended the same. There would always be cracks, holes, and history. Sometimes it was better to leave the pieces until someone sweeps them away.

"I could kill you now," Roan whispered in an empty threat.

"No, Roan, you can't." She pressed a hand to his flank. Roan flinched, but felt a strange warmth grow from her fingertips. He felt it pulse through his muscles like electricity. It was a threat.

"Why do you need horses? Why not smite them or whatever?"

Rashali snickered. "Personal preference."

"Interesting preference."

"Here we are." They stood in front of a stone wall. They had barricaded the horses in.

"Take this," Rashali handed him the cuff. Roan placed it on his forearm. "There's magic in there, Roan. You're completely safe."

"My safety … that's not…" Roan hesitated. "You don't understand … these mares…"

Rashali stared at him curiously for a moment, then placed a hand, almost tenderly, on his shoulder. "Sometimes, when we must do things that are unpleasant, it is best that we forget."

"That is a coward's way out."

"It is self-preservation. Tell me, Roan, how much calmer would your soul be if you did not remember Catherine?"

Roan considered this, considered it deeper than he ever thought he would.

"The curse will be harmless unless you try to remember."

"And if I try to remember?"

"It will make you forget even more."

"My tribe, will it make me forget my tribe?"

"How about I make another deal with you, Roan? Let me place this curse on you, and after this is all over, I will ensure your return to your tribe in England. You have my word and my blood."

"My tribe, you said they needed me?"

"They do, and I know that if you, and only you, free them, you will be welcomed back. As is the centaur way."

Roan twisted the cuff around his arm and said, "I will do it for them."

THE CURSED BARGAIN

True to her word, Rashali had returned a revived Iloa, unharmed, two weeks later. Zack had not left her side since. “I ain’t gonna not learn no writin’ words.” Iloa stressed each syllable in an atrocious Southern accent. They were doing it again — the accent game. Zack would start an accent, and Iloa would copy him until she mastered it, which she never could, so the games went on for days and days. The week they copied Roan word for word nearly drove the centaur homicidal.

“Yayis, y’all gonna learn them writin’ words,” Zack retorted in perfect Southern speak. Roan had had enough of it; he was going to the museum. Since it was late, he hoped he wouldn’t be seen, especially since Iloa had taken Roan’s vampire escort. He had been going to the museum quite a lot these days, spending hours and hours there, not sure of what he was doing, not thinking of anything either. He just needed to go to get away. Roan picked up his keys and donned his signature fedora.

“Where ya’ll goin’?” Zack asked.

“I’m going to the museum.”

“I’m going to the museum,” Iloa mimicked in her best English accent. It was terrible.

“Yes.” Roan shut the door before Iloa could respond. He could hear the laughter through the walls. When Zack and Iloa were together, they made a terrible team. They were children, stirring up trouble, Googling everything, hacking official government websites and leaving crude messages. Even Troll was in on it when he was home, teaching Iloa how to swear and what gangster jargon meant. Oh God, the day the three of them spoke gangster speak nonstop — now that had been hell. Well, at least he had gotten them to clean up the apartment a bit. Iloa had a knack for cleaning because she liked things with a little order and hygiene. And with Iloa's influence, Troll had even started using an ashtray instead of the couch.

Roan wandered down his usual path to the museum. The air was icy with the end of winter, and his flanks pricked with ice. Things had been bothering him, and sometimes he felt like he was losing his mind. He would find messages in his pockets. They were in his handwriting, but for the life of him he couldn't remember writing them. It was like a forgotten dream. Roan checked his pockets again. The same three messages. Three scraps of paper. His handwriting, written in centaur script. He had wanted no one to read it.

The first message was a name. NEWTON.

The second was CAPTIVES.

The third was REMEMBER.

The fourth was RUN.

Run? Run from what? Who was Newton? What did this have to do with Roan? Roan scrunched up the papers in his deep pockets and approached the museum steps. There was a fresh note every time he left the museum, which was why he kept on coming to this place. He wanted to know, needed to remember. He needed to put all the clues together. This was a secret he kept from everyone, even Zack. This was meant only for him.

The Minotaur were gone. Roan did not know why. The doors were easy to pick, and security never came running. It was peculiar.

"Hello Roan?" Rashali purred in long, flowing emerald winter robes, draped with shimmering gold. Roan remembered everything. Shame riddled his body and left him weak, like a plague. How could he have done this? How could he have let himself sink so low? Roan's legs itched to leave, to race out of there as fast as he could. And that was when his mind went blank.

#

When Zack was with Iloa, he was Zack, just Zack. Not a seventy-three-year-old vampire, not a runaway, not an outcast. Just Zack. It was like living his life when it stopped fifty-six years ago, only now with video games. Seventeen years old in the twenty-first century, watching downloaded movie after downloaded movie, with Iloa by his side. Take that Denin!

Roan had been gone for hours, and Zack had a sneaking feeling Troll would come home any minute. Spike had disappeared days ago. Zack was a little worried, but Roan considered it a blessing. Iloa had mixed feelings towards the chupacabra. It did not bite her, but it shadowed Iloa like a lost puppy, leaving dead, bloated rats at her feet.

Zack avoided one topic around Iloa. It was one of the few things they had differences about. It was Mav, and of course Iloa had to bring it up when the entire evening was going perfectly.

"I wonder where Mav is?" she sighed, swishing her lollipop around in her jaws. Zack had bought her a big tub full on Wednesday. It was half-empty now.

"I always wonder why he made me. I don't know why he did it. Did he ever do experiments on you?"

"No. He dressed me up in a cape once. I got tangled in it when I was performing and fell into the audience." Iloa laughed a light, wispy laugh that made Zack smile. It was true. Mav never made him wear a cape again. What he didn't tell Iloa, though, was that for the next week Mav deprived him of blood as punishment. He had been so desperate for fluids he had tried to lick the morning condensation off the windowsill. Iloa still thought the world of Mav, and Zack had to break reality to her.

"He just doesn't seem the type, you know. To go from circus master to mad scientist."

"Maybe he thought a career change was in order. I mean, we did stuff up his entire business pretty good. Troll smashed everything in sight, and I set fire to the tent." Zack remembered racing out of there like hell, coughing up smoke and trying to smother the flames in his hair. He wouldn't have been able to outrun the fire if Roan hadn't hauled him onto his back. That was the first time anyone from the circus had ever seen Roan voluntarily allow someone to ride him. From that day onward, Zack regarded Roan as a loyal friend.

Spike's door flap thudded, but nothing came through. Another thud sounded, then a third.

"Stupid mutt," Zack sighed, seeing Spike's stumpy grey claws scratch at the hole in the door. "Eaten too many rats and can't fit through again." Zack thrust open the door. "Spike!" Zack jumped back. Spike teetered in, his mouth stretched wide. Between his jaws was a big, gooey, black jellybean pod the size of the chupacabra himself. They watched as a very pleased Spike trotted to his bed and plunked the thing down and began trying to chew through its tough, slimy exterior.

"What is it?" Iloa gaped. When she tried to get close to it, Spike let out a vicious snarl.

"Well, it certainly isn't a rat. Maybe leave him alone; he will get bored with it eventually." Zack slammed the door and approached Spike. The chupacabra raised the sparse, wiry hairs on its back and gave a hissing, huffing warning, like the sound of a clogged blender. Zack had to step back if he didn't want a chupacabra permanently attached to his face. The pod was shiny with chupacabra spit, but no matter how hard Spike bit, he could not puncture the coating. It was like one enormous piece of squishy rubber.

"Well, at least he's got a chew toy."

"It smells funny." Iloa sniffed the air. "Roan will not like this."

"Yeah, well, Roan's not fond of much these days, is he?"

"So, you've noticed it too, how weird he's been acting these past few months."

"Yes." He wasn't even insulting Troll anymore. He was silent and distant, and Zack didn't like it. Roan was hiding something, more so than usual.

"You reckon it's just construction site waste?"

"Huh? What?" Iloa dragged him back into his thoughts. "Oh, yeah, probably. Some sewer junk."

Neither of them noticed how that sewer junk wriggled.

#

When Roan returned at three o'clock the next morning, he did not even notice the putrid stench that had infiltrated the entire apartment overnight.

"There's something wrong with him," Zack said, sipping the blood from his juice box. He narrowed his eyes at Roan as Roan teetered through to his corner, which was his bed. He didn't have a room; his desk was his room, and sometimes, if he was exhausted, he would just fall asleep there after a night of reading. Iloa perched beside Zack on the back of the couch.

"How does he sleep standing up?" she whispered. At seven in the morning, Spike was too busy with his new toy to ask Zack for breakfast.

"It's the horse in him. Something to do with ligaments in his legs or something. He says there's one in his back too, to stop himself from slumping." They examined Roan in silence for a while. The centaur stood facing a wall, his body leaning against it.

"Must be uncomfortable. He doesn't even have a pillow." Zack chuckled a little at Iloa's comment. Sometimes she would say the most unusual things.

"What's that?" Iloa pointed to Roan's pocket. He had fallen asleep with his cloak and fedora still on. Scratches marked his fetlocks, and grime coated his coat. Roan had been lying. He had not been going to the museum at all. Then what the hell was he doing? Why was he keeping it a secret?

"What's what?" Zack asked. Iloa jumped from the couch towards Roan.

"Be careful; don't wake him."

Iloa rolled her eyes. "Yeah, 'cos waking a cranky old centaur while I'm taking his stuff is exactly what I want to do." Zack replied with a finger to his lips. Roan had fidgeted in his sleep. Iloa crept forward. What she had spotted was a little scrap of paper peeking out of his coat pocket. Iloa took it with ease. Zack watched her ghost-white eyebrows furrow.

"What's this mean?"

"Let me see that." Zack dropped his drink and snatched the paper out of Iloa's hand. It was Roan's handwriting all right; he could recognise that calligraphy scrawl anywhere.

"Should we Google it?" Iloa offered. Zack had taught her well.

"It's in centaur script. Even Google can't transcribe it. Believe me, I've tried."

"But you said Google knew everything."

"That's called an exaggeration, Iloa. As much as I hate to admit it, the internet does not hold all the answers. This is something we're going to have to find out for ourselves. Roan will never tell us, so we can't ask him about it. We need another centaur."

"We don't know any other centaurs."

Roan, for a moment, jolted as if he were about to wake. Instead, his eyes opened and rolled sightlessly around the apartment.

"Roan, hey, Roan," Zack waved a hand. Roan did not respond. Instead, those dreaming eyes locked onto the far corner of the room, somewhere near Spike's den, on that dumb rubber chew toy, and widened.

At that moment, Roan let out a shocking scream. His body fell against the wall, then, in a daze, stumbled back, knocking over his desk.

"Iloa, get back," Zack snatched the bird-girl out of the way before Roan's rump collapsed into his typewriter, the rest of his body following, and before they knew what had happed Roan was unconscious on the floor, his desk in pieces and his memoirs, which were usually securely locked away, were now released from their now shattered draw.

"Roan! Roan!"

"Zack, we need to get help."

"Troll, I will call Troll; he can help us move him."

"Move him where?"

But Zack was already on the phone, "Pick up, you oversized potato!" He screamed when the phone went to voicemail. He tried again and let an equally insulting message before raking his hands through his hair in panic.

Every single thought was for Roan, Roan the centaur who had saved his life, who stood by him, who looked after him even when his overprotectiveness wasn't necessary. Roan, who made snide comments every time Zack dressed up for another let-down date. His dry sense of humour and ridiculous English accent. If anything happened to Roan, Zack didn't know what he would do. Well, he would be stuck with Troll for a start, and that would be anything but pleasant.

"Denin," Iloa said. "Zack, I know you don't like him, but I think we need him right now." Reluctantly, Zack picked up his phone again and dialled the genie's number. At least this time, someone picked up.

"Zack, surprised to hear from you. Has Iloa finally come to her senses and wants to return to living a life of luxury?"

"No."

"Need me to de-flea your apartment again?"

"Shut up. Roan has passed out on the floor, and I'm gathering it's not because of a hard night of drinking."

"He didn't just ... fall down in his sleep?"

"Get here now." Zack snapped his phone shut again.

"I'm sure Roan's alright," Iloa offered, touching Zack's wrist. Zack didn't reply. He bit his lips together, focusing his eyes on Roan's unseeing, open eyes.

A moment later Denin appeared behind them, dressed in an emerald smoking jacket and an open-collared shirt.

"You realise I am not a horse vet," Denin said, "or have any medical training whatsoever."

"You and I both know this isn't something medical," Zack growled, stepping aside to allow Denin to examine the centaur.

"Hi Denin." Iloa pushed her way past Zack.

"Hello, my dear." Denin gave her a polite smile while checking Roan's jugular pulse. "He's still breathing, he's got a papillary response and if I kick him..." Denin shoved a shiny boot into Roan's chest. The centaur huffed as if something had winded him. "He feels it."

"What the hell is going on here?" said Troll, who was suddenly at their door. "There better be a good reason I've left my poker table."

"Look at him!" Zack flung his arms across the room at Roan. Troll's face did not show any expression.

Instead, he gave a muted grunt and said, "I'm guessing the state of this apartment finally got the better of him."

"Very amusing, Troll," said Denin.

"Har, har, very funny. Listen, if you're going to be a pain in the arse, you might as well be doing your job."

"I'm assuming I'm going to get paid for this job?" Denin's eyes flicked to Iloa. Zack let out a growl. Denin raised an eyebrow in amusement. Troll thrust a fist into his pocket and threw the last wad of Iloa's cash at him. A business card also fell to the floor.

“I don’t need money,” he said. “Three feathers, same as before. I’m sure you can spare me that, Iloa.” Iloa nodded eagerly. It was Zack who protested.

“Haven’t you taken enough from her?”

“Zack, stop this!” Troll growled warningly. Surely the vampire could spare his pride to save his friend.

“No, Denin almost killed Iloa.”

“Shut up, sit down, and let the man of his job.” Troll barked in a voice that could have caused an avalanche. Zack was so surprised to hear such a threat in Troll’s words that he shut right up. After all, his friend was in trouble, so surely Zack could put his hatred towards Denin aside for a few hours at least.

“He’s been acting strange these past few weeks,” Iloa offered, rummaging through her feathers to find one she could spare. “He is all dazed and confused. We found this in his pocket.”

“I’m going to try something. I’m going to bring Roan back into consciousness using magic; it’ll be like slowly waking up from a sleep.” Denin knelt beside Roan’s head and clasped his hands over the centaur’s eyes. Denin closed his own and remained still. The entire room was silent. Even Zack didn’t speak. Roan’s breathing became rapid. His flanks flinched and hooves kicked as if trying to toss off a blanket on a hot night.

“Get away!” Roan’s voice was a hoarse whisper, as if he were trying to scream but could into find breath.

“We’re here, Roan,” Denin soothed. “Where are they?”

“Everywhere. There’s more. Everywhere.”

“What do they look like?”

“Darkness,” Roan gasped, and then kicked the leg of his desk. Iloa jumped, and Zack steadied her.

“Roan? Roan?” Roan didn’t answer. His face twisted, and he yelped. Tears streamed from his eyes.

“Roan, who is there?” The centaur fidgeted but did not answer. “Roan, what are you afraid of? What is there in the darkness?” No matter how many times Denin asked,

Roan would not reply. Eventually, Denin sighed, rocked back on his heels, and opened his eyes.

"He leaves himself notes," Iloa offered. She was sitting on Roan's desk, and the scrap of paper had been beside her. She handed it to Denin. "Can you read them?"

"I can't read centaurion," Denin said, not looking up from Roan as he rubbed the stubble on his chin in thought. Behind him, Zack collected the notes Troll had thrown on the floor. Among them, he found a business card.

"I think I may have found a centaur," Zack said under his breath, and he raced out of the apartment before anyone could tell him this was a terrible idea.

#

Zack stood in front of Adam & Co. funeral parlour. The building was single-story, weather-worn, and the lettering on the door had faded to grey. Zack rang the small bell, and the next thing he knew, there was a click and the door opened.

"You do not have an appointment." The receptionist was a slender woman who looked as if she had never seen daylight. She donned a black suit and skirt and square glasses. She wore her hair in a tight bun.

"Er, yeah, sorry about that." Zack approached. The woman did not blink. Before Zack could explain, a man walked through the door. Zack saw that the woman and the man were not only brother and sister but also twins. Then it clicked. These strange, pale people were not people, but Mythica. Only Mythica could look as they did.

"You're a vampire," the man said.

"What do you want?" Their voices had changed; they had become light. It felt unnatural, yet they spoke with ease. "You know what I am; what are you?"

"What an —"

“Impertinent question.” The two siblings shared a tight smile, their identical eyes locking onto one another.

“We are the Vetali twins.” The man replied. His hair was also long, but tied back.

“I thought you guys were just a myth.” Zack stared wide-eyed at the twins, who stood side by side. They even blinked in unison.

“Allow me to elaborate,” the man interrupted. “I am Kayn, and this is my sister, Lath.”

“We are children of ancient times, born at the moment the first man fell and Death came into existence.”

“We take new form but remain unchanged, our offspring born in the womb and our life given to them. Always twins, always us, born with our memories.”

“We can give temporary life to the corpse of a loved one, momentarily sacrificing our own to do so.”

“In return, all we ask is a few years of the life of the one who seeks our … talents.”

“So, I guess the funeral parlour is a cover for you,” Zack gave an awkward and humourless chuckle. “I ah … will it work on a —”

“Vampire?”

“Everyone dies, even the enchanted.”

“On the one hand, he could save his friend; on the other hand, he was giving up years of his already prolonged life. He could certainly spare a few years; who knows how long his life could be, anyway? He could live for centuries, so what’s two or three years off that?

“It will cost you five years.”

“Are you willing?”

“I suppose so.”

“Who is it you need? We need their body.”

“Come, I’ll show you.” Zack had Roan’s memoirs with him, and the scrap of notes he took from Roan’s pockets. Zack turned, and the Vetali twins followed him like two ghosts. They did not speak, and Zack didn’t ask the dozen questions brimming on his tongue. How were they to take his life? How were they to give it to the centaur? Did they know how long *he* would live? How long had *they* lived?

It seemed like hours before they made it to the museum, picking a lock to a maintenance door to enter. The twins followed like cats. They didn't make a sound. Zack's throat was dry. His heart thudded with blood that was not his.

"This way." He edged his way into the main rooms, then into the entrance hall where the dead centaur stood, taxidermy and poisoned, front hooves raised in a gallop. His glass eyes weren't his, and they stared forever into the hallway ahead of him. It was as if he were running to a place he would never get to. Zack stared at the man with sadness. Would the creature know that he was alive? Would he do what Zack asked for? Will he attempt to escape? Would he attack? Suddenly, this didn't seem like a good idea at all. Zack could still back out. He turned around to see the Vetali twins standing impatiently.

Zack swallowed a gulp full of fear and asked, "What do I need to do?"

"Get him out of his case."

Zack examined the casing for a while, then decided the best approach was the break the wood frame and slide the glass out. The twins did not help. They didn't even move. They were like taxidermy figures themselves. Zack struggled with the weight of the windowpane, praying he wouldn't set off any alarms. With the main panel gone, Zack reached out to touch the grey, mottled, dusty flank of the centaur. What would this man's first words be? What were his last words?

"Stand back."

Zack did as he was told.

"Shall you take this one, or shall I?" Lath asked.

"I thought we agreed I would take this one," Kayn reminded with a tight smile.

"How could I forget?" Kayn stepped forward and placed his arms on either side of the centaur's lifeless face.

“This is your last chance,” Lath sang.

“No, no, I’m sure.” Zack was anything but sure. Then Kayn gasped and fell to the floor. Zack edged forward, but Lath held him back with a reflex grip. Zack looked to see her crying, her tears single watery lines down her flawless face. Kayn was on the floor, eyes wide as if dead. Was this the method? One would die to bring another back to life? Was the bond between the siblings so strong that even temporary death would make Lath cry?

Zack waited for something to happen, but all he felt was hollow anxiety in his chest. Perhaps this would not work. Kayn was dead.

Then the centaur gasped, his chest expanding in a horrifying shriek. His eyes and mouth were both wide. The centaur expelled his first breath in a choking fit, and his bones cracked from disuse. His arms flung themselves forward to stabilise himself. His feet were secured to the stand. The centaur tried to move, panicking with fists against the glass in front of him. Zack had to say something, to intervene, because Lath wasn’t going to.

“Stop, stop.” Zack waved his hands to get the centaur’s attention. The man saw Zack but did not calm down, still heaving for breath. “What’s your name?” The man had a rounded face; his grey mane cut short like a mule’s. His features were softer than Roan’s, except for a jutting chin. His pallid skin mirrored the dusty white and grey pockmarked appearance of his coat. A layer of thin, short white hairs ran all the way up to his chest.

“Horak,” the centaur wheezed, then examined his legs. The bolts went around the fetlock. Horak tried to pry them open with his hands.

“Here, let me.” Zack fumbled with the screws as he explained. “I know this is confusing for you, but we don’t have much time.” Hell, Zack hadn’t even asked how much time they had got. Neither twin had moved. “I resurrected you, but only briefly. I need a centaur to translate something for me.”

"Why?"

"Because it will save my friend's life. He's a centaur too." Two legs down. Two more to go. Horak flexed his legs, testing.

Seeing the faint bluish lines around the coronary band of his hooves, he said, "I was poisoned."

"Yes, Roan's told me just about every time we pass you."

"Roan?"

"Yes."

"Your friend?"

"Yes."

"A centaur?"

"Yes."

"From Cambridge?"

"How did you know?"

"I won't help you." Horak's tone was the same tone Roan had when he had come to his decision, and neither hell nor high water would change it.

"Why not?"

"Because this Roan you speak of is a blood traitor to our tribe." Zack left the last leg secured and came to face Horak, the anger raging in him.

"Listen here, I've given up five years of my life to save my friend, and you're the only one who can help. So, you better do what I say, buddy, or … or?"

"Or what?" Horak raised a bemused eyebrow.

"Because he may not be a part of your tribe anymore, but he is a part of mine, and I need him. We all need him." The centaur stared sadly at his discoloured hooves. Zack waved the papers and the scrappy notes under his nose.

"Alright, let me loose and start reading." Horak was true to his word and as the centaur wandered the museum with Zack at his heels.

"He keeps reminiscing about his tribe. There's so much regret in his words."

"Roan never speaks about his tribe."

"And for a good reason, too. He brought shame upon his family name."

"Why? What did he do?"

"It is not for me to say. In these notes he speaks of the Valsha curse. I do not know what this is, but this is what plagues him. It is rotting his mind. He is trying to remember, he wants to remember. Rashali tells him not to, but he cannot help it." They had circled the museum and then returned to the room that had given him back his life. All the while, Horak stopped, paused at each exhibit, and gave a sigh as if mourning every item. The sparkling cauldron was gone; closed for maintenance, said a white plaque in elegant script.

"How long do you think I have left?" He sighed, seeing the twins; Kayn still dead on the floor while Lath, an unmovable statue.

"I don't know. I never asked."

"I can sense it won't be much longer." The sadness in Horak's voice penetrated Zack. How hard it must be to know you've not much longer to live? To know you've died, and your loved ones long gone. "What has become of my tribe?" Horak asked. "Roan spoke of trying to find us. He speaks of trouble, but does not know what it is."

"Do you remember how you died, perhaps that…"

"I don't remember. It was so long ago. I remember a golden chalice and deep red liquid. That is all. I remembered feeling cold, too. The most distant memories are the clearest to me," Horak took in a deep breath. "I have read of Roan's memories; I understand what the humans have done to us. You do this to save your friend, but tell me, if Roan's life were not in danger, would you still wish to stop Rashali?"

The clop of horse hooves paused, the last of them echoing down the corridor as Zack did not move.

"Of course," he said, a little too fast. "I mean, it's not right for innocent people to die. I was human once, too."

"Indeed. But at what point does someone stop becoming human and become a monster? Perhaps when they poison your goblet, chain your hooves, or grind down your fangs?"

"You read that part, did you?"

"Roan was forced to perform circus tricks while suffering from laminitis. Do you know how painful hoof rot is? Like wooden stakes under your nails," then he gave a thoughtful look at Zack up and down at the mention of wooden stakes and muttered, "apologies for the analogy."

"Don't apologise. I get it. Life is shit for us. But killing everyone? That's not the way."

"Do you believe there is another?"

"There has to be, you know?"

"I do not. It is not our way. Perhaps that is why your friend has done what he has done. In our world, freedoms were won through battles and treaties. This is not the human way. Their world is too big for treaties, and they do not respect this power."

"You don't think we should stop Rashali?"

"I think you should protect your tribe, Zack. You have already given five years of life to save your friend. That is noble of you."

"Yeah, well, Roan's a good man."

"Yes, he was," Horak paused, his eyes glazed, reminiscing. "It was his kindness that led to his exile. He would have been a tribe leader and I, his kinsman. When I am gone, please ask Roan for my forgiveness, for I hold him no ill will. My only regret is that I could not have wished him farewell. Give him my best of luck and that my soul will be with him." Horak then returned to his cell, placing his hooves into position. Zack forced himself to meet the centaur's eyes, and the centaur returned the look with a comforting smile.

"Both you and Roan have my blessing. If he finds our tribe, we will welcome him back with open arms."

"I will."

Horak took one last breath. He did not exhale.

#

Zack was in no position to linger and give idle chit-chat with the Vetali twins; if anything, they really freaked him out. So, once Horak had returned to his dead state, he raced back to the apartment, not bothering to see if Kayn had returned to life or not.

"It's a curse." Zack gasped as he flung the door wide. Roan remained prone on the floor, only now someone had placed a lounge cushion under his head. Denin was still here, much to his disgust, but he had now acquired another two feathers from Iloa. Greedy bastard.

"The Valsha curse," said Zack again. The only movement in the room was Spike, still chewing on some rubber toy no one could get near.

"How do you know this? Where did you go? You were gone for hours."

"Never mind," Zack said to Iloa, diving to kneel between her and Denin. The papers Zack had been carrying scattered. Iloa picked up a few scraps curiously. What had Zack been doing?

"If it's a curse, how do we break it?" Zack looked to Denin, who gave a shrug.

"I have no idea."

"What do you mean you have no idea? You're a genie."

"Exactly, genie, not a witch, you buffoon."

"Buffoon? Of all the insults you could call me, you call me a buffoon? What are you, from the eighteenth century or something?"

"At least I don't dress like a teenage boy band."

"Oh, and cravats are so much better."

"Hey!" Denin pointed a finger at Zack. "Cravats are cool."

"Boys!" Iloa barked. They looked at her, surprised that such a voice could fit inside such a tiny frame. "What about Roan?"

“I might … know someone who dabbled in curses long ago.” Denin offered with great reluctance in his voice.

“Great, let’s go.”

“It’s not that simple.” Denin explained. “He and I are not on the best terms. However,” he eyed Iloa curiously, “I’m sure a creature like yourself would convince him.”

“What the hell is that supposed to mean?” Zack just about launched over Roan’s body to get to Denin.

“I mean,” Denin said calmly, “is that magic makes people more … cooperative.”

“So you want to bleed her dry again? I will not allow it.”

“I feel fine, Zack,” Iloa assured, “I’m totally recovered.”

“Iloa knows her limits now; we understand how she works.” Denin assured, “I trust her.”

“I don’t. And least of all I trust you.”

“You don’t trust me!” Iloa puffed out her already triangular chest in rage.

“Looks like somebody is in trouble.” Troll cackled.

“Shut up, Troll,” Zack spat, flustered as three sets of eyes were on him.

“What is that supposed to mean?”

“It just means … that’s not what I…”

“You don’t think I can take care of myself.”

“I think you don’t comprehend when people take advantage of you. You think Mav is a saint still.”

“He saved my life, didn’t he?”

“He locked you in a basement. And this dick-wad here just about killed you with greed.”

“I can’t control it.” Denin pointed out with a lift of his finger. “And I have apologised since.”

“I’m coming with you, Denin,” Iloa said before turning to Zack, “You can stay here and tend to Roan.” Iloa huffed, rising from her backward-protruding knees.

“Have fun with the horse.” Denin chuckled as they left. Zack remained on the floor with no one but Spike to keep him company. That was until the thing Spike was chewing cracked.

#

Their destination was a small maintenance cavern under one of the city's main bridges. Above them was the scream of peak-time traffic, and below them was the lapping sludge of the foul waterways. Iloa wished she had shoes as she picked an empty fast-food wrapper from her heel. If her expression was bad, it was nothing compared to Denin's, who had resorted to creating two impenetrable magic bubbles around his ankles. When he saw the state of her feet, he made bubble shoes for her too. Troll didn't look fazed. He had been in worse.

"Who lives in a place like this?" Iloa asked as a few homeless people shuffled in the shadows.

"I must warn you, Iloa, he's a bit, well, strange," Denin said.

"I think we are all a bit strange," Iloa said, unfazed. Troll and Iloa shared a look as if to say Denin was the only normal one amongst them. Denin wrapped a tentative hand on a rotting wooden door, and before he had a moment to step back, it flung open.

An exasperated, sallow face stared at them through ice-white eyes. He was bald but his skin was decorated head to toe in markings. These were not tattoos; these were different, and if Iloa stared long and hard enough, she swore she could see them move. Veins rimmed the deep blue, almost black ink markings, making it appear as though his body had become one with the symbols.

He wore only a scrappy old sweatshirt and black boxer shorts, and when Iloa saw his gritty fingernails, they were blue. The man stared at her, his eyes wide. When he spoke, his lips hardly moved. He was haunting, and with every muscle movement, he twitched as if fighting against a body that was not in his control.

"What do you want?"

"Talon. So nice to see you again," Denin spoke carefully, as if one wrong word would send the man into a spiral. "May we come in?" Talon stepped aside and allowed them to enter his home. Iloa couldn't stop staring at the man; his bare skin rippled. Talon caught Iloa's wandering eye, and he made a face, which she supposed was an attempt at a smile.

"What is this interesting creature?" he cooed as if she were a parrot or a swan.

"We will get to that later, Talon," Denin said as if he were bored already. "Sit down."

"You don't give the orders around here."

"Neither do you anymore, either." Denin said back. Talon gave a chortled laugh as if it was just a joke between them.

"Are you after the … you know? Did you decide that a life of freedom is not for you? Has the pretty bird caught your heart?" Talon turned to Troll, cocking his head, "Or do you find yourself possessed by this … thing?"

"Not a thing." Troll growled with warning.

"No, no, of course not. Denin would never give up his freedom. No, no tricked me, tricked me he did."

"You did this to yourself." Denin sighed, his eyes catching on the copper bangle hanging from the man's bony wrists. To change the topic, Denin looked around and said; "I see you did not take my advice and redecorate," he mused. Talon attempted another smile. His body hunched, his limbs appeared too long, and his arms draped on either side of him like a gibbon's. Iloa could see the faint shadow of markings underneath that shirt.

"Home decor is not my forte, Denin," Talon replied.

Colder than the outside, the cement floor leeched all warmth from Iloa. The place was lit with light bulbs in holders that looked like they had been gathered from roadside junk. The room was large but, for the most part, empty except for lingering rancid incense. There was a single bed in the corner and a black metal locker in the other. Old-style inkpots and quills rested on an old writing desk. Denin examined the place with a look of boredom.

"Who are they?" he fastened his eyes on Troll and Iloa. Again, Talon lingered on Iloa a little longer than the others.

"Friends," Denin replied.

"This one has magic." He pointed an accusatory finger in Iloa's direction. "Both you and I could use her Denin. We could be great again, powerful. She could break my curses."

"She cannot break your curses. You know this."

"No, no, you want to keep me cursed, don't you?"

"I can't say it's not a deserving demise."

"Then why are you here? I'm busy, very busy."

"Today, I need you to teach me about the Valsha curse."

Talon drew in a hissed breath. "I will not perform it for you," he snapped. Denin let out a crooked smile.

"You misunderstand me, Talon. I need to know what it is. We believe someone used it on our friend."

Talon let out a crackling laugh, the sort of laugh you would hear in your nightmares, like nails on a chalkboard. Iloa could not help but put her hands to her almost non-existent ears.

"Please," Iloa begged, "he is really sick."

"You see, the curse will rot your brain. The more you try to remember, the faster you rot. The more you rot, the more you change. It can make the kindest man a murderer and the most virtuous capable of the vilest acts." Talon cackled again. "Or it can cure the mad and make them sane. It is impossible to know what will happen once the memory is gone."

"It erases your memory?" Denin confirmed. Talon nodded.

"Yes, yes, if your friend stopped trying to remember, he would be just fine, just fine. But he is thinking," Talon hit the side of his temple with his open palm. "If he thinks, he goes mad."

"He is leaving himself notes." Iloa said.

"The curse must be taken willingly," Talon added with another cackle. "Whatever your friend is trying to forget, he has chosen to forget."

"But now he is trying to remember."

"We always want to remember what we have forgotten, even if it is … painful. I tried once … not enough magic, not enough magic." Then his icy eyes flickered to Iloa, "but you, with you…"

"Not a chance in hell, Talon," Denin warned.

"Then I won't help, no, no. Won't tell you how to break it."

Iloa gave a sigh and plucked a stubby feather from her neck and dangled it in front of the creature. "Tell us, and I'll give you this." She pulled it out of his reach before Talon could snatch it back.

"So proud," Denin clutched his heart, "They grow up so quickly, don't they, Troll?"

"No counter-curse." Talon said. Iloa dropped a feather to the ground, and Talon caught it before the grimy dirt could mar those pristine white barbs.

"You must … kill the caster or die yourself."

"Well, it's simple then, isn't it, Talon?" Denin said, dusting off his suit as if being here too long meant the dust would cling to it. "You will find the person who cast this curse and kill them. I would start in the sewers if I were you. I suspect that you will find them there."

"Why would I do that?"

"You owe me."

"I owe you nothing!" Talon lunged and then withdrew as if regaining control of himself.

"Please," Iloa begged, searching her hair for more feathers. She could only imagine what Zack would feel if he lost his friend. She had to do anything she could to save him. Roan, with all his secrets and dry humour —

she couldn't let him change into the monster Talon so predicted.

"Curses like this are not easily traced; I'll need more magic." Iloa threw a fistful of feathers at the creature, who sniffed them with hunger. "And I will need something of your friends."

"Like this?" Iloa pulled the tiniest scrap of Roan's handwriting from her pocket. Talon sniffed this too.

"It will have to do."

"Break the curse," Troll said, stepping forward, "I'll pluck the chicken bald." He tossed his head towards Iloa, "You don't break the curse … I'll take those pretty little tattoos off of you one slice at a time." Troll pulled out a hunting knife and raised it to Talon's maddening face. He did not look scared; no, the word Iloa would use was eager.

"Well said, Troll," Denin agreed. "Now let's get out of here before the cretin loses his mind for good."

"Cretin, you dare call me a cretin!" But as Talon was hollering, Denin ushered the three of them out the door and into the sewer-stained air.

The streetlights glowered as they returned to the main street. This was the time of night Mythica emerged from their burrows and back alleys. Troll appeared right at home; Denin, on the other hand, walked briskly.

"Denin, Denin, who was that?"

"An old captor."

"And you … did that to him?"

"No, don't be foolish. He did that to himself."

"But why?"

"Not intentionally, of course. His obsession turned to curses and defence against Mythica enchantments. He was fooled, you see, long ago, into loving a Mythica elf. He ordered me to… Never mind … long story short, he riddles his body with so much obscure magic that my bonds no longer recognised him as my master and I was released."

"And what about him?"

“He has become a cretin, not quite human, not quite beast. He fights to remain in control of his own body. The regret of his own actions consumes him.”

“How … painful.”

“If you knew what he had ordered me to do, you would not be so sympathetic.” Denin said no more and, with an air of irrepressible regret, he disappeared.

THE WOUNDED TREE

When Troll and Iloa had returned to the apartment, they found Zack standing on the kitchenette bench with a frying pan in his hand, swinging it like a bat. Roan remained passed out on the floor, a blanket now covering his body.

"Watch out, get away!" Zack screamed, dancing as if he were burning on a hot plate. Troll pushed Iloa back and entered the room himself. Roan was still on the floor, twitching in his sleep. Spike was growling on his bed, but not the menacing sort of growl, but a nip-at-your-heels playful growl.

"Relax, Zack, he just wants to play," Troll sighed, walking over to Roan where Spike was and scooping him up in his arms. "You good, Spike? Yes, we go for a walk? What have you got?" Spike was sticky with a black-green goo.

"Troll, behind you!" Zack screamed. Iloa also yelped. Troll turned. Standing on stilted, shaking legs was a black foal. Its eyes were huge and glassy, its mouth open with sharp white teeth visible underneath flared nostrils. Its hair was still shiny with placental slime.

"Kill it, kill it now!" Zack screamed.

"No, Troll, run!"

"Don't touch it!"

But Troll did not do any of those things; instead, his beady black eyes widened, and he clasped a massive hand to his chest and said with what could be mistaken as softness in his voice. "Relax, it's only a baby." Troll moved towards the little foal, its tiny body shaky on skinny legs.

"Hello fella. Has Spike been chewing on you all week, has he?"

"Troll, it will kill you."

"Venom ain't working yet. Just born. Spike would have been dead by now if it weren't."

"That does not mean you can keep it as a pet," Zack reminded securely on the kitchenette bench, despite the foal not taking any interest in him whatsoever.

The foal stepped forward as Troll approached, teetering on unsteady hooves. Troll was there, right by its side, helping it to balance like a proud parent.

"Where else is it gonna go?"

"Oh, I don't know, maybe *back where it came from*!"

"Nah, then it'll grow up all evil and then I gotta kill it."

"Oh, I'm sorry. I think I misheard you. You're saying we only need to kill it if it grows up? Troll, that's what baby animals do; they grow up!"

"Get a vet to take out its poison glands."

"Why don't we grind down its fangs while we're at it? And besides, no vet in their right mind would go near a thing like that."

"Train it not to bite?"

"That has to be the stupidest thing I've ever heard you say. They're carnivores, Troll! And besides, you don't have the best track record with training animals; Spike still thinks Roan's desk drawer is a litter tray."

In reply, Troll gave a cunning smile, telling Zack Spike's misbehaviour was completely intentional.

"It is just a baby, Zack," Iloa said, creeping into the apartment cautiously.

"Iloa, stay back."

"Don't tell me what to do." But Iloa didn't dare get too close to the foal, who was now nuzzling Troll's hand.

"You hungry? Zack get me a juice box."

Zack threw a juice box filled with blood across the apartment. Troll stabbed it with his hunting knife, and the foal suckled madly.

"It's not staying here." Zack said.

"Why? I let you keep a centaur. I'm not killing it."

"Maybe we can find somewhere else for it to live?" Iloa suggested.

"Yeah, like who is going to keep a savage brute like this?"

Troll gave a cunning smirk. "I know someone."

#

"Well, I'll say, it's downright better than the last thing you brought home." Margo said, referring to Ava as she stared at the foal stumbling around behind the chain-link fence of the front yard. Margo's house was not big, certainly not big enough to house a horse, but it was better than an apartment.

"The trio watched from the front porch steps, the behemoth of a Troll gently scraping away the creature's placental juice.

"You said Spike brought the thing in."

"Thought it was some construction site rubber." Zack said with a shrug. "We had bigger problems on our hands than to worry about what the cat dragged in."

"I'm assuming this is Rashali's doing?" Margo said. "That Ava girl said something about horses. Although this thing looks pretty harmless." They watched the foal follow Troll around in circles. They would have to move the creature into the backyard before the sun rose and people started their morning walks.

"It doesn't look dangerous. Maybe Troll can train it."

"If anyone can train a vicious creature, it's a vicious creature himself." Margo said, "Or perhaps the person who trained him in the first place."

"Troll won't let you get near it. They are venomous, you know."

"Only if they bite," Margo shuffled back into her house and returned with a Styrofoam tray of mince. "Not sure if it will eat it." She flung the tray of meat across the lawn, where the foal leapt backwards and snarled.

"Margo, you can't throw food at it."

"It's what I did for you." No one could argue with that, and Troll scraped up the meat and offered it to the foal in small handfuls, which the foal took with hesitation, sniffing it before nibbling.

"Likes blood better."

"Probably like milk for it."

"Great, my blood supply source is thin enough as it is. You realise what I have to do to get my blood right? I line up at the blood bank like a freaking junkie once a week. I am not sharing."

"Relax, we can just get some from the butchers." Margo said, "Never said it had to be human." This settled Zack down a little.

"I don't understand how Rashali plans to destroy the world with some baby horses."

"They grow up, Iloa."

"They're kind of cute."

"You've been spending too much time around Troll."

"Troll, bring that thing around the back before anyone sees it. Come in, I'll make us all a tea."

"I think I'll call him Bitey," Troll said as the creature tried to nip Troll as he hoisted him over his shoulder to the back door. Where the venom dripped, it left an acidic hiss over Troll's thick hide, which would have burned through anyone else's flesh. If that is what a newborn was capable of, these things were going to get dangerous, and quickly.

"Great, he's named it," Zack flung his arms up in defeat.

"He'll be sending me werewolves next," Margo muttered under her breath before pouring them a coffee. Zack accepted for the smell, because human food wasn't his thing anymore.

"Coffee is gross." Iloa stuck out her tongue and made a face.

"It is when you drink it black. Give it here, girl." Margo retrieved the cup and added milk and half the sugar pot; she had learned early that Iloa would only eat exceptionally sweet items.

"Try it now."

"I suppose it will grow on me." Iloa made a face but swallowed.

"I thought Rashali said she had Mares of Diomedes." Margo said, with her coffee cup paused halfway to her lips.

"Yeah, something like that, so?"

"Well … they are mares."

"Yeah, horses."

"Female horses."

"So?"

"So how did they get a foal?"

Zack and Iloa looked at one another. Iloa looked confused, but Zack was anything but.

"Roan."

Zack spilled his untouched cup of coffee as he sprang to his feet.

"Zack, I don't understand." Iloa called after him.

"Rashali is using Roan to breed horses and wiping his memory. That bitch. That awful, awful bitch." Zack raked his hands in the air before reaching into his pocket to call Denin. That was until Troll's scream thundered through the window.

#

"Well, it's definitely dead." Denin nudged it with his boot. Troll had not said a word. He was digging a hole behind the chicken coop, flinging dirt across the small yard.

“He says it just dropped dead,” Margo explained, understanding Troll better than anyone, she was the only one who could decipher his grunts and growls.

“Did it do anything beforehand?”

“I don’t know. When we came out, it was seizuring on the floor and then it just … stopped.”

“I wouldn’t ask him; he’s very upset,” Iloa said, wringing her hands together, flustered and unsure what to do.

“Hm,” Denin mused. “Would not have picked him for a sensitive type.”

“Only for animals,” Margo explained, watching Spike bounce around Troll’s boots, oblivious to his owner’s emotional turmoil. Troll dumped his shovel and trudged towards the foal. It flopped in his arms, looking no bigger than a Kelpie dog by comparison to his hulking chest. He unceremoniously dumped it into the pit, dusted his hands, and when he thought no one was looking, wiped a tear from his eye.

“Shouldn’t we do an autopsy or something?” Zack asked, watching Troll kick dirt over the shallow grave.

“Just be glad it’s dead.” Denin muttered. “So, what do you want me to do about this?”

“We think Rashali is using Roan to breed these horses.”

“That’s…”

“A bit messed up, yeah, we know,” Margo said. “So, go tell your girlfriend to stop meddling with the horse. We’ll be keeping a close eye on him now.”

“Really? Who is with him now, then?”

#

Rashali stared miserably down at the dead foal before her. In the darkness, the mares whinnied a mournful cry. In her own misery and rage, she let down her defences, allowing the horses to gather too close. Mav trembled as he knelt to examine his failed experiment.

"You know what this means, don't you, Mav?" Rashali said cooly.

"I don't understand. I don't understand. I was sure the seed pods would work. But, they do not live past a day."

"Do not be foolish enough to try to deceive me."

"I would never, never, I swear," Rashali knew Mav was being truthful. He was too much of a coward to lie.

Rashali turned away from the dead foal. Mav scooped it up into his arms and carried it out of the cavern. The floor was sticky with empty eggshell casings, soft and rubbery, like the egg pods of a shark.

"You have created creatures before, have you not? Or have you deceived me?"

"I have, I have."

"And they have lived beyond a day?"

"She was different; she was…"

The tunnel lights greeted them, and Mav was grateful to be away from the wretched darkness of the Mares. They were confined to a pit, a cavern below a cement cliff face.

"What made her different, Mav?"

"I don't want to say."

"You are honest. But you know I will torture you until I get my answer. So, let's skip that part," Rashali allowed Mav to walk beside her. There was nothing that the mortal could do to harm her.

They returned to Mav's prison quarters, a makeshift laboratory, you could call it. Instead of test-tubes, spell books lay open, and cauldrons bubbled with black tar. Mav laid the dead foal on a cement slab, and Rashali waited for answers. The genie was patient; she could have waited centuries, and Mav knew she would have too. Perhaps it was best to answer.

"Iloa was an experiment." Mav sharpened a set of knives and sliced the foal through its centre. Black ooze seeped across the table and onto his bare feet. It was as if the entire inside of the creature had been decomposing for days, when it could not have been more than a few hours.

"Have you heard of the Icarus feathers?"

"A mortal name." Rashali's curiosity piqued when she considered the ancient trail of feathers that mortals would follow. "They believed it to be the trail of feathers Icarus left after flying too close to the sun."

"They are mistaken."

"Naturally."

"Icarus feathers lead to a phoenix. Have you ever seen a phoenix, Rashali? Gigantic birds, untameable, follow the Icarus trail, and it will lead to your death."

"And yet, here you are."

"I was fortunate to find it as a chick, freshly hatched, not a single feather on it. When it started to get too big and wild, I would kill it. I began a circus, collected many creatures, but the phoenix was always the showstopper." Rashali observed Mav's work as he dismembered the deceased foal, setting aside limbs as though he intended to repurpose them.

"Phoenixes are naturally violent," Mav explained. "Few people know this; they get big too, huge, think ostrich with an attitude problem."

"How did you contain it?"

"Killed it before it could get too big. It would be reborn. Its corpse became its eggshell."

"You are turning this into an eggshell now, aren't you?"

"Nothing gets wasted. When my circus burnt down, I lost everything. My creatures either ran away or burnt, except for the phoenix, of course. Phoenix don't burn. It was the only thing I had left, still contained within its eggshell days off hatching once again.

"So, I began experimenting with it. Figured I could create some sort of immortality, make a fair bit more money than any circus could give me. I experimented. Iloa was my greatest success story. Every time that phoenix died, I changed it just a little, just a tweak here and there, until I decided not to kill her anymore. I decided I would let her grow. You need phoenix magic to make these things live, Rashali."

"Will it kill her?"

"Would it matter to you either way?"

"I am no monster, Mav," Rashali warned.

"Not if we do this carefully." Mav rubbed his sallow cheeks, wondering how he might achieve that.

But before he could think further, a war cry sounded from down the corridor, towards Rashali's private rooms.

Mav and Rashali raced from Mav's quarters, following the continuing screams. Metal pipes clashed, and static electricity crackled. Rashali and Mav knew that sound. It was the sound of magic.

"Avalin!"

In Rashali's private quarters, fabric silks rippled, suspended in the air. Ava stood before them, arms outstretched, silver magic streaming through the cavern. That magic was suspending a monstrous creature just off the ground. Ava and the monster were both splattered with blood. Ava's magic was waning; the monster was reaching forward. Its body was thin and warped; his head was bald and every inch of him was covered in tattoos that rippled like a sickness under his skin.

"Rashali, I'm out of magic," Ava cried before collapsing. The monster raced forward, but not towards Ava; the beast flung himself towards Rashali.

Rashali held no sign of fear on her face. She waved a sharp hand towards her fallen silks, and with a rapid madness, the silks wrapped and bound the monster with a strength silk should not have. In a moment, the monster was cocooned as securely as a newborn baby, with only its head visible.

"If you had given me more magic, I could have killed it," Ava panted, collapsing against the closest pillar.

"This is exactly why I won't give you any more." Rashali stepped closer towards the creature who, swaddled in silks, looked a little more human than before. She saw that a knife blade had been dropped on the floor.

"You were trying to kill my daughter?" Rashali asked. The monster's eyes were human, ice-white and full of fear.

"No," it rasped as the silks choked threatening around its neck. "You."

"Me?" Rashali prowled around the suspended creature. "Why me?"

"The Valsha curse. Only way to break it."

"So the horse sent you?" Ava recomposed herself. "I knew we should have kept him captive."

"No. Horse is sick."

"What is your name?"

"Talon." He turned back to Ava and said, "You look … you look." A guttural snark of pain rippled through the creature, becoming less and less human as if remembering something changed him, making it impossible to recall what he was about to say.

Rashali looked the monster up and down with a mix of pity and curiosity.

"You have created quite a monster of yourself, haven't you, dear Talon? I would say you know a fair deal about curses. Tell me, did Roan ask you to kill me? After all, it is the only way to break the curse, which, if you remember, is a curse that can only be willingly received."

"I came here to break it, you are correct. But it was not Roan who sent me." Rashali loosened the silks and allowed Talon to stand steady on his own two feet. Ava swiped the dropped knife from the ground, an action which did not go unnoticed by Rashali.

"Who, then, sent you?"

"Why would I tell you that?"

"You are also seeking something. I can tell … by your curses. Let's see … memory charms mostly…" Rashali ran her eyes up and down over almost indecipherable tattoos. "I see there you even searched for … lost blood… interesting. Who are you searching for?"

"None of your business."

Rashali squinted at the set of coiled lines on Talon's wrist. Old lines, bleeding under his skin as if searching for something. Her eyes flickered to Ava, who was too busy flicking the knife around to notice.

"Give me your hand," Rashali demanded, using magic to pull Talon's wrist forward. Upon that wrist was a loose-fitting bangle. Rashali did not notice the bangle; it was the tattoo that she took far more interest in. Ava, now intrigued, approached, only she did not care for half-hidden tattoos; no, what she saw was the copper bangle and only the copper bangle.

"You want to forget more than anything else, right?"

"Yes," Talon breathed as if he were finally going to get his wish.

"Who sent you to kill me?"

"The genie." Ava's eyes lit up; that bangle finally making sense. Rashali sensed it too.

"You were once his master?"

"Until my curses … I became unrecognisable."

"This is what happens when mortals take too much power, Ava." Rashali warned, slipping the cuff off of Talon's wrist, but not placing it upon her own, she held it out, just away from her, as if it could trap her too.

"As they become greedy, they change themselves. They lose themselves. They meddle in magic they do not understand. Keep this safe, Ava." She handed the cuff to Ava. "Do not let Mav near it." She added before turning back to Talon. Talon's eyes followed Ava, as if to say something, craning his mutated neck as if to catch one last look at her.

"I could kill you, my poor creature, or I could give you your heart's desire. For a price, of course. There is a Mythica made of phoenix and flesh. A bird child. She may have been with the genie or the horse."

"Yes, yes," Talon cried.

"Bring her to me; make sure no one follows. And then I will perform the Valsha course on you and you will never have to remember whatever it is that you are trying to forget."

#

"Where is the horse?" Troll grunted at the empty space in the apartment. Spike was sniffing an old stain, then rolled in it. He was no sniffer dog, and he followed his own stumpy tail before giving up and rolling around in a wet patch that smelt like horse urine.

"Who do we call? Denin? Animal control?" Zack paced manically. Iloa watched as Spike bounded up to the egg casing remains of the foal, opened his mouth wide and swallowed it whole.

"Relax," Troll slumped himself down on the couch and turned on their busted television. The pixels were dead in the top left corner after Troll had thrown a shoe at it last football season.

"Television, now! At a time like this?"

"Relax," Troll flicked through the channels and turned on the news, "If there is a mentally ill centaur rampaging around the streets of New York, it will make the news."

"And what if he is not on the streets? Did you think maybe he was kidnapped?"

Troll shrugged and flipped the channel again.

"Come on, Iloa, let's go." Zack thew a beanie and a cloak in her direction to cover her feathers. They left Troll on the couch. He would be useless anyway and probably end up on the news himself.

"Can't believe we left him alone … stupid… I'm so stupid."

"Cheer up, Zack. We will find him. He's probably just gone for a walk or something."

"In the middle of the day? With humans around? I don't think so."

"You think Rashali has taken him?"

"It's the only logical explanation."

"You could call Ava?"

"I don't think she is going to be helpful."

"I could trade more feathers."

"Iloa, you can't keep giving your feathers away. You need them."

"No, I don't."

"Yes, you do. You can't let people take advantage of you."

"I'm not; I'm trying to help my friends. If you had gone missing, I wouldn't hesitate to pluck myself bald to find you … even if you think I'm naïve."

Zack halted mid-step. "Thankyou." He muttered despite himself. "I would do the same."

"So then it's settled. Call Ava."

"I really do not think will help us," but Zack pulled out his phone anyway. It rung out.

"Call again."

Zack did.

Nothing.

There were still enough people around to be a threat. Iloa wasn't exactly normal-looking, but just normal enough that she could pass for a sickly human. Humans were so self-conscious that way, always diverting their eyes when someone looked the slightest bit unusual. This worked in her favour, at least, and Zack was glad that Iloa could walk somewhat freely down the street.

"If I were a centaur, where would I go?" Iloa said when Zack abandoned the effort to call Ava.

"He likes the museum; well, actually he hates the museum; he likes to go there to complain, mostly. He would really like Central Park, but even he isn't stupid enough to go there this time of day."

Then screams resonated two streets away. People began running, others paused, confused, then snuck into nearby stores. Iloa and Zack shared a look. That must have been Roan. Against the flow of people, the two of them raced towards the screams, around the corner, through halted traffic, expecting to find Roan's miserable face, maybe a few police cars. But that was not what they witnessed.

Before them was a monster, a creature forming before their eyes. An inky creature rose, unfurled, its long arms elongating further, neck extending, jowls growing.

"Is that a … werewolf?" Zack grabbed Iloa's hand. Iloa stared into the creature's eyes. She recognised ice-white pupils.

"It's Talon." She gasped before resisting Zack's tug.

"It's a werewolf!"

"He's technically a cretin." Iloa called back, still rationalising that she could reason with the man she had spoken to not hours before.

"Talon! Talon!"

The cretin did not recognise Iloa; his eyes glazed over her in favour of a street lamp which he wretched out of the cement as if it were a flower in a pot.

"Iloa, we need to get out of here." Zack pulled Iloa back. This time, Iloa didn't argue, only, with that swift movement, her hood fell down off her head. Her feathers were revealed.

Talon sniffed the air.

Those manic eyes locked onto Iloa's, and he lunged like a hound who had scented blood. In his hands was a feather, Iloa's feather, the one she had given him under the bridge. He rolled it around his snout before sniffing the air in Iloa's direction.

"Run," Zack begged. "Iloa, run!"

Talon leapt over cars and buses and taxis as if they were nothing more than cracks in the pavement. The cretin seemed to engorge in size, his arms elongating and stretching out close, too close. Claws whipped across Iloa's feathers.

Pedestrians were all running in the same direction. Zack pulled them left, right, down a street, then another. But they could not shake Talon. The cretin had caught her scent, and he followed them as if attached by an invisible lead.

Zack felt Iloa's wrist slip through his fingers. Iloa screamed. Zack turned to find Iloa being flung into the air. Talon had tossed her lithe body up as if she were a paper plane, and caught her between his open jaws.

For a moment, Zack was sure the cretin would bite her in two. He flinched instinctively at the anticipation of blood. But there was no blood. The cretin did not crunch. Instead, the cretin bared his teeth one more time before opening his jaws and letting Iloa's limp body fall into his arms. The cretin seemed to shrink, his jaws becoming more human-like.

"I'm sorry," he said, before racing away with unnatural speed, Iloa limp over his shoulders.

#

"Ava, surprised to see you here." Denin closed his apartment door slowly. With her arm on the mantel, Ava stood by the fireplace wearing her usual inappropriate attire, which this time was a black leather outfit from a specialty store. Ava liked to dress up just as much as Denin did; only Denin could walk the streets in his clothing and not get arrested.

"Special occasion, is it?"

Ava had been visiting a lot, usually for nefarious purposes, but also to get whatever information he could out of him, not that Denin gave anything away. There wasn't any information to give. Rashali already had the upper hand: a justified cause, faithful minions, a centaur…

"You could say that," Ava did not move from her position. Denin had to come to her. He looked her up and down, the leather tight around her waist and legs, donned in fishnet tights. She looked like a whorish cat-woman, and Denin had to admit it was a bit try-hard, even for her.

"I know Rashali put the Valsha curse on Roan. I knew she was using him to breed the mares." A cunning curl of a grin adorned Ava's face like the devil's. It transformed her into something evil. Denin narrowed his eyes.

"Now, Denin, didn't we agree not to discuss business like this?" she purred innocently.

"Our deal was not to discuss business while we're naked, and unless I am mistaken, we are both, more or less, clothed."

"I can fix that."

"No, you won't," Denin pinched her chin and forced her to look him in the eye. "As unorthodox as it sounds, I actually don't mind the horse. I would almost even consider him a friend; no, that's going too far, an acquaintance. What Rashali is doing is no better than what the humans have done to him in the past, worse even."

"Except that Roan chose this," Ava replied calmly. "You forget the Valsha curse can only be cast willingly." She ran her hand up and down Denin's suited arm. He tried to pull away, but she held him firm, not wanting him to move from the spot. "She wipes his memory clean so he will not suffer regret and guilt. It was Roan's choice. He did it so he could find his tribe."

"Find his tribe? Hell, I could have found his tribe for him. Dumb-arse horse. Why didn't he say?"

"There's something else," Ava said.

"What?" he snapped.

"I need to show you." She beckoned with her hand to come closer before reaching a hand to pull something out of her snug pockets.

"I've already seen everything underneath that ridiculous outfit," Denin replied, but came closer anyway.

"I don't think you have."

As Ava spoke, her arm shot out to his. Denin's heart froze as something clicked around his bare wrist. It felt like needles digging into his flesh and hot metal flooding poison into his blood. He had not felt like this in centuries, and he prayed he never would again. He could not move.

Denin stood aghast, feeling his mind shrinking as freedom left him, replaced by servitude. The bangle, steeped in her blood, sank into his flesh. That blood rippled through him. Magic twisted beneath his skin. He always knew he could not trust Ava, but never suspected this. How could she have found that bangle? Foolish! Foolish!

He tried to move his limbs, lift an arm to strangle her, push her out the window. But his body was stone; it was not his own anymore; it belonged to Ava to do with as she so desired. Gasping for air, he stared at his new master.

"You're mine." Her red lips kissed his cheek. "If I can't have magic all to myself, I will take the next best thing; my own personal genie."

"No magic for yourself, huh?" Denin sneered. "Doesn't Rashali trust —"

"Hush now."

Denin's jaw clenched shut and his voice left his throat. A red nail raked down his lips.

"My first command is simple."

Denin rolled his eyes. It would not be simple. It earned him a playful slap on his cheek. "I see we are going to have fun. I'm so glad we could take our relationship to the next level. Now, tomorrow I want you to do something for me. I want you to kill Roan."

#

Roan was breathing in the fresh grass, the petrichor air and the raw musk of his own primal sweat. Part of him knew he was dreaming; part of him knew he was living in a memory. He knew this because his knees were bulbous in a way only a foal's could be. His mane, too, was short and wiry as if it had not grown out yet, and his bow and arrow still felt awkward in his hands.

"Roan, you're too slow." His brother laughed in his native tongue. Drystan was six years younger than he was, but moved with the speed of a bolting filly. As he was prone to tripping over rocks or divots, Roan could always catch up. Their father warned Drystan to slow down. A stubbed hoof was one thing; a broken leg was another.

Roan cantered towards his brother, remembering this day well. It was the day he was to teach Drystan to use an arrow for the first time. Siblings honoured each other by passing on knowledge. Of course, their father was not far away, ready to step in if Roan struggled or if Drystan got out of hand, but this was a moment between siblings. This would cement the next generation of the tribe.

And the tribe needed bonding, their territory cut in half by the village. Rumours described colossal cities, forests of brick and steel, taking shape. Of course, this was not new to Roan; he had heard of the humans before, building, encroaching, ripping trees out and planting crops. It was best to stay out of their way.

"Roan!" Drystan called again. Roan found him by a little stream, splashing his hooves and bucking.

"A little further up the stream, we will practice there," Roan ordered, wondering how he was ever going to hold his little brother's attention for more than a few moments.

"Here, hold these." He slung a set of arrows from his back and onto Drystan's. "Maybe if you carry something, it will slow you down."

"Nothing will slow me down."

"Indeed, you have the spirit of a pine marten." Roan agreed.

Drystan obeyed, slinging the woven satchel across his back.

Roan's eyes flashed dark; Drystan whinnied, his face elongated and turned black. His eyes glowed a feral red.

But before Roan could react, Drystan returned to normal, and the fear was gone.

As they followed the stream, soaking Roan's aching fetlocks. The river festered, a sea of rotting slime soaking into his senses.

Then. Gone.

"Can I hold your bow?"

"Of course. But hold it like this." Roan showed how he rested it on his forearm, but where his arm was, there was no bow, but a snarling mouth of a mare suspended in the air. Roan recoiled, but it vanished.

"I think you should stop trying to remember," Drystan said. "It's just hurting you."

"But when I try to remember," Roan said, "my mind takes me back to here. I like it here."

"How long have you been here?"

"Just a little while."

"Are you sure?"

"We're here. I'll show you how to hold the bow, then I will give you an arrow to string."

They had made it to a clearing where there was a single tree punctured with generations of arrow holes, some healing, some afresh. Between the trees were the eyes of the mares, waiting. Roan's nostalgia was so strong that he couldn't feel fear. These horses could not harm him. The horses were the memory; it was him and his brother that were real.

Drystan pulled back his first arrow, which, when he released, fell to the floor. Roan strung another one for him. He tried again. They spent the entire morning together, and as the sun reached its peak, Drystan was not far off from the wounded tree.

Of all the memories to retreat to, Roan always came back to this one. And when the memory faded, when the mares turned their hindquarters and retreated from the forest edge, the acrid stench of his worst nightmares returned. Rashali always pulled him away before he could see where he truly was, and he wandered the streets as he awoke from his trance.

He returned before dawn each night. But he found himself living deeper in his memories even after Rashali took the mares away. Sometimes she would tell him things. He would write them down in his own language for later because he knew he would never remember them.

"Roan? Roan, did I do well?" Drystan pointed to an arrow wobbling in the bark of the wounded tree.

"See how well you can do when you stop, breathe, and concentrate?" He ruffled his younger brother's mane.

This memory was wonderful. Yes. He could stay in here forever.

#

"Are you sure you want me to do this?" Denin asked, staring at the pathetic centaur wobbling in the middle of Central Park. "He is sleepwalking. Like shooting fish in a barrel."

Roan was sleepwalking; he had been sleepwalking for the past hour. They watched the centaur with morbid curiosity from the tree line. Rashali had released him for the night, and now it was Denin's duty to fulfill Ava's command. Ava, unfortunately, had come along to ensure Denin didn't find any loop-holes. Genies could be sneaky that way.

"Why do you need me to kill him, anyway? Surely you could get a gun. He's a horse, for God's sake. You could just break a leg, and that would be the end of him."

"I don't like getting my hands dirty." Ava replied, dressed in black.

"You worry Rashali will punish you if she finds out you were behind this."

"I don't have to answer that."

"Why have you decided to double-cross her, anyway? What changed?"

"Just shoot the damn horse."

"In good time, my dear. I want to find out more about you first, you know, since we are bound forever until all eternity." Denin slid a mocking scowl towards Ava, who flared her petite nostrils with a scowl.

"Let's just say I would rather be a Mythica in a mortal world than a mortal in a Mythica world."

"Ah, I see," Denin chuckled, watching Roan sway and draw an imaginary arrow into his bow. "You feel that if the Mythica come to power, they will treat you like a mortal."

"Rashali already treats me like a mortal. But I command you to never tell her I said that."

Denin mimed zipping his mouth shut.

"Perhaps this marriage between us won't be so bad at all. After all, I quite enjoy the way my life is at the moment. I mean, maybe we could do something other than shoot the centaur? Perhaps we could just hide him?"

"Nah, that's boring." Ava shrugged, feigning boredom. "I command you to shoot him now."

Roan released his imaginary arrow.

Denin released a very real bullet.

#

They had returned to the underground. Ava bounced with a smugness in her step.

"Don't you think you've had enough?" Denin sighed, dangling upside down from one of the many chambers of Refuge. Denin had been upside down for hours, and Ava had forbidden him to use magic to return the blood to his feet. It gathered in his brain. Whenever Ava felt like it, she would push him so he swung back and forth a little. Well, at least he was wearing clothes.

Ava sat on her cushioned daybed, book in hand. She wore jeans and an oversized t-shirt.

"No, I quite like you there," Ava replied. "Sort of abstract art, don't you think?"

"I'm thinking you can call it a lot of things, but abstract art is not one of them," Denin grumbled. "You know, they have a name for girls like you."

"Oh, I know," Ava sang, her eyes never leaving her book. She began twirling a finger through a lock of her hair.

"Would you like me to name a few?"

"I don't think that will be necessary."

Denin did so anyway, "Sadist, Dominatrix…"

"Enough, Denin."

"I can't say this has been the most exceptional evening we've spent together."

"Quite on the contrary, I'm finding this book fascinating."

"Shows how much I satisfied you," Denin muttered under his breath.

"Hush now, Denin, abstract art doesn't talk." Denin dangled in silence, then took up the annoying task of whistling. Ava ignored this for a while until he began to sing too, just a little tune under his breath. That was when Ava slapped her book down. Before she could say anything, Rashali stood at the door.

"You know, if he keeps that singing up, hang him by his thumbs."

"You need something?" Ava inquired.

"Yes, I need to know why you did not tell me your plans to capture a genie."

Ava just shrugged, "You seemed busy, didn't want to disturb you."

"I am no fool, Avalin; I know you are mad at me."

"If I really did not want you to know about Denin, I wouldn't have brought him down here." Rashali then turned to Denin, who was still swinging a little. Rashali wore the expression of a disappointed mother, but it was deeper; her golden eyes twitched with betrayal. She composed herself. This was an ancient being; no matter how angered Rashali was, Denin doubted he would ever see the woman so much as raise her voice.

"From one genie to another, Denin," she said, "I'm disappointed in my daughter."

"I know where she got the cuff from," Denin said.

"Sending a cretin to end my life, how … amateur," Rashali replied.

"What did you do to him?"

"I gave him what he wanted."

"He doesn't deserve that."

They spoke as if Ava were not in the room, and she was growing tired of it.

"If it's any consolation, I made him relive every moment before he forgot it for good," Rashali paused, as if wanted to tell Denin something without Ava knowing. "Interesting," she began, staring at Ava, who was still pretending to read her book. "How mortal blood has a way of returning to haunt us."

Denin, still dangling upside down, turned to scrutinise Ava. His jaw clenched, his stomach seized. From his silence, Rashali knew he understood.

"What do you want? Or is the only reason you are here to scold me?" Ava asked, growing bored with this interruption.

"I came here to invite you to dinner. We have a special guest. Make sure the genie wears something nice."

Rashali turned her back with an elaborate sweep of her robes. It was time for her to patrol Refuge, to ensure her Mythica received her best care. She walked barefoot across the exposed rock and iron, proud of the tents and stalls the Mythica had created. Sure, some retained mortal habits and brought money and clothes, but it was unavoidable. Once the mortals were gone, the Mythica would return to their natural ways. They would recover their languages, their stolen artefacts. They will emerge and disperse, and return to their true lives.

Elves bowed as she passed. In return, she let a little of her magic drift from her fingers to the saddened collection of bonsai trees that struggled to grow in the lamplight. After replanting, they would grow impossibly fast, reaching a size large enough to house an entire tribe.

Gnomes were rock-breaking new trenches, and pixies chased each other above her head. Refuge was dark, grimy, and crowded. But it was free, and soon it would rise.

"Ra-ra!" a booming voice bellowed, followed by a thunder of footsteps. Rashali recognised who it was before turning.

"What is it, Kit?"

"Horse man, come." Kit gripped Rashali's wrist with her own oversized and sickly pea-soup green mitten. Kit was a troll. She was the size of a large wrestler and had the face of one too. Makeup plastered her skin, and she wore a horrid pink dress and a fluffy scarf. She covered her sparse tufts of hair with an ugly, woollen koala beanie. The two white pom-pom ears had turned grey with dirt.

"Ra-ra must see. Bad, bad horse-man." Kit almost stepped on a scurrying gremlin as she took Rashali onto one of the subway platforms.

Rashali assumed Roan had done something stupid, like get himself caught by the rangers, or try to wander deeper into the tunnel system.

"I told him to always wait by the will-o'-the-wisp," Rashali said. "What has he done this time?"

But Kit did not need to reply. She saw the body. Dried blood stained Roan's chest. A single bullet hole painted his chest.

"Found on elf patrol. Kit, bring here."

Rashali bent low over Roan's body, placing a hand on his shoulder.

"I do not think it is an accident."

"Kit, ask the elves what they saw."

Kit turned to leave, but Rashali said, "Actually, no, Kit, let's move him first." Kit, with ease, scooped up the centaur in both hands, his human torso left to dangle down by her hip. Rashali reverently clicked her fingers to levitate the man's head up to Kit's shoulder so he would not have to suffer the indignity of having his head bump against the ground.

"Where to?"

"My quarters. If this was murder, it is best no one knew about this."

"Not even horse's friends?"

"It may have been his friends who pulled the trigger."

"Bad friends."

"Agreed, Kit. Agreed," Rashali led them to a silk-draped room, only these silks held the strength of marble. The emerald fabric parted only for Rashali, and with the grinding of stone, fused together once more. Rashali's quarters glittered with gold and wood; the walls were not cemented, but pulsed with veins of crystallised magic. The floor became a carpet of brown clay and dirt. Kit laid Roan down upon it, then stood for further orders.

"Want me to dig a hole?"

"No Kit. I want you to bring me Mav and the bird-girl he is with."

THE RESURRECTION

Iloa had not said a word to Rashali since her capture. *Understandable*, Rashali thought. So, she figured it best to be truthful with the girl. Iloa was not like Mav, who could be controlled with fear; no, Rashali knew Iloa was cut from a different cloth. Iloa had a heart as pure as a phoenix and deserved to be treated as such.

For Roan's honour and Iloa's sensitivities, Rashali placed a forest green silk upon the centaur before calling the two in. Mav stumbled forward; having been held captive for so long, he no longer tried to escape. Iloa, on the other hand, was wrestling Kit with two balled fists and kicking legs.

"Punch is like being poked with a stick," Kit muttered before dropping the girl to the ground. "I leave now; take out splinters." That was troll humour. The satin curtains returned to stone as she left.

"Let me go!" Iloa screamed, huddled in the dirt.

"I'm not draining her dry," Mav growled.

"Relax. I will not harm her. Although I can't help but express how impressed I am that you have grown some shred of morality, Mav."

"Then what do you want from me?" Iloa cried.

"I need your help, Iloa," Rashali crouched down before the girl and held out a hand. Iloa did not take it.

"You could have asked for it. You didn't need to kidnap me."

"Would that vampire have trusted me?" Iloa flinched, knowing the answer. "I figured if I brought you here, you could make up your own mind free of … influence."

"And what about Mav? You've kidnapped him too."

"I have rescued him from mortal prison. You've been to jail, Iloa. Remember how unpleasant that was? Mav must stay down here so he won't be caught." Rashali glowered at Mav, daring him to contradict her. Smartly, the man kept his mouth shut. Iloa unfurled herself a little but still dug her clenched toes into the damp earth. It didn't feel dirty, or sullen; this earth felt … pure.

"It's different, isn't it?" Rashali ran her palm through the earth too, then picked up a handful to let it trickle through her fingers.

"Can I tell you a story, Iloa?"

"I want to go back home."

"Of course you do. But I have a friend of yours that needs you, needs you and Mav to work together."

"I don't care about your story."

"Of course not. Perhaps I will tell it to you later. It's important that you understand."

"Is that Roan?" Mav gasped, his eyes cast behind Rashali to the body of the centaur. Iloa shrieked, her golden eyes widened with horror. She lunged at Rashali with her talon-like nails outstretched.

Rashali caught her, but not before the girl swiped a deep cut across her cheek. She healed it with magic.

"It was not me, Iloa." Instead of pushing her away, Rashali cradled her. Iloa tried pulling away, then sobbed. Of course Rashali would not kill Roan; she needed him. Instead of fighting back, Iloa let the ancient genie rock her while Mav watched with cynical eyes.

"What happened?" Mav asked.

"Murder," Rashali replied. "Sabotage."

"By his friends?"

"No, Zack would never, never." Iloa muttered.

"There may be a way to bring him back to life, Iloa."

"Don't give the girl false hope, Rashali."

“Did Mav ever tell you who you are?”

Still cradled to Rashali’s bosom, Iloa shook her head.

“You are cruel,” Mav scoffed, understanding where this was going.

“I made a promise to Roan,” Rashali ignored Mav’s comment. “I promised to return him to his tribe if he helped me breed the Mares of Diomedes.”

“You cursed him.”

“He chose the curse. Now, someone, I do not know who, has killed him, likely because of his choice to help me. You might just have the power to bring him back from the dead, Iloa, but I need something more from you.”

“You’re going to drain me dry, kill me.”

“I promise you will be safe.”

“He was wearing the cuff; why didn’t it … why didn’t it keep him safe?”

“That is a good question, Iloa, a wonderful question. Perhaps if you help us. We can find out. Will you help?”

“Why did you kidnap me? Why didn’t you just ask?”

“Whoever killed Roan might be after you next. I am so sorry Talon frightened you.”

“No, I’m done being a captive.”

“You are not captive, Iloa.”

“Sure feels like it.”

“A fair observation. It is your choice, Iloa. Stay here and save your friend’s life, or return to your friends and bear them the news of Roan’s death.”

To Iloa, it was not a true choice.

#

Troll had never seen Zack so pale; this was corpse-like pale. This was the sort of pale that would get him arrested for being not-human.

“Found him?” Troll asked, still clicking channels for any news on rogue horses. He had been doing a terrible job and had been watching some trashy reality show called *Love, Lust and Losers* for the past half hour.

"Kidnapped," Zack gasped, panting against the kitchen counter. "The monster, the big bad monster. Got Iloa. She seemed to know it. Said its name was Talon. Ripped up a streetlight. On the news. Bad. Got Iloa."

"Ah, Talon," Troll grunted, rising from the comfort of his couch. "I know where he is. Knew he was a creep." Troll hoisted Zack up by the scruff of the neck.

"Drink some blood. We'll go there tonight."

"No, we have to go now!"

"No, we don't. Much as I enjoy terrorising humans, if Talon has made a scene, best someone as ugly as me lies low." Troll wandered over to the fridge and threw three juice boxes at Zack. "Now sit, Carmen just found out Justine is cheating on her with Sam."

#

"That was the longest three hours of my eternal life," Zack groaned, now caught up on the ins-and-outs of *Love, Lust and Losers*. They had bypassed Talon's crime scene that spanned five blocks and returned to the maintenance shack under the bridge.

"Make a bridge joke and I'll throw you in the river," Troll warned.

"After watching Sam throw a full pizza at Justine, you have stiff competition for the definition of troll."

"Hah."

This was one time Zack was glad that Troll was as large, menacing, and hideous as he was.

"Talon! Open up!" But Troll didn't give the cretin a chance. With a solid boot, Troll knocked down the door. They expected to see the beast that had stolen Iloa. Instead, they found a shocked man dressed in ripped jeans, a stained t-shirt, and a plastic bag filled with random objects.

"Where is she?" Troll demanded, marching to close the gap between them. Talon, still covered in tattoos, just made it past Troll's belly. He was no longer twitching as if his skin caused him physical pain.

"I'm sorry?" Talon said, dazed, not at all the response you would expect from a man confronted by an angry troll.

"Where did you take her?"

"Take who?" Talon looked confused, his eyes still oddly glazed.

"Err, Troll, something is off about him."

"Yes, he doesn't remember."

"Remember what?"

"You literally cleared out three streets by becoming a monster and stealing Iloa, you know, bird girl, this tall, hair full of feathers."

No recollection crossed his expression.

"Who forgets something like that?" Troll looked to Zack.

"Excuse me, I need to go. I, ah, have some family who have agreed to take me in."

"You're not going anywhere," Troll flung the cretin over his shoulder. Zack expected Talon to say something, to fight, to at least throw a punch.

But he docilely obliged and said, "I don't really want to stay here anyway. Where are we going?"

"Troll, I don't think this is a good idea. He's clearly got a screw loose, and what if he changes back into that weird wolf thing?"

"Nah, he won't do that."

"How do you know?"

Troll just shrugged, which was not good enough for Zack. They bickered the entire walk to … where was Troll taking them?

"You thought you would bring him here!" Margo held a wooden pasta spoon, still dripping with sauce. "Look at him, he looks like a criminal."

"And I look like a troll, so what?"

"Fair point. Sit down. Don't touch anything. I would rate him second on the list. The world-ending horse still has first place. Ava last. Don't touch that." Talon recoiled a curious finger from the photo frame. Spike stared at him from the spare cushion beside the man. His tongue lolled out the side of his mouth, between his sharp fangs.

"Are you my great aunt?" Talon asked Margo.

"Yeah, sure," she muttered before waving the sauce spoon at Troll. "His brain has been addled. Drugs, I recon."

"Nah, he wasn't like this the first time I met him. He seems … normal now."

"That's concerning." Margo said nothing more but returned to the kitchen to serve her dinner. Zack continued to pace, wringing his hands. There was a beat of silence as Troll and Zack stared cluelessly at the cretin who was attempting to pat Spike without losing his fingers.

"So you don't remember what you did?"

"I've spent most of my life trying to forget," Talon said plainly. Something told Troll and Zack that they were not talking about the same event.

"And now you have forgotten?" Zack asked before turning to Troll. "I think he has been Valsha cursed too."

"Denin said he would never do that to him."

"Maybe he changed his mind."

"Could it be Rashali?"

"What would she want with Iloa?"

"Well, her horse idea may not be going to plan and everyone wants to use Iloa for her magic."

"If you ask me," Margo called from the kitchen, "horses are a stupid idea. I mean, how many flesh-eating horses do we need to take over the entire planet? Illogical, futile. She will be breeding them for centuries. And how is she going to transport them across the world?"

"She is a genie, Margo," Zack reminded.

"Well, then, if she's all that powerful, why does she need a bunch of horses to end the world?"

"Is the pasta ready yet?" Talon asked.

"Okay, so if we run with the theory that Rashali has kidnapped Iloa and wiped Talon's memory, where does that leave us?"

"Guess we've gotta go save her."

#

Months of work, months, caverns of placental eggs and deeper into the shadows, the four mares whinnying, disgruntled at the intrusion in their lair. Rashali stood beside Mav and in front of Roan's corpse, which Kit had moved down to the depths of the subway tunnels. Iloa, despite herself, was clutching onto Rashali's robes, and Rashali pressed a comforting arm around the girl. They stood before two ageless figures, one dressed in a suit and the other in a pencil skirt.

"You have quite a home here," Lath said politely, but in her light tone it came across as mockery.

"Shame about the … infestation." Kayn's eyes, instead of narrowing at the eggs, narrowed on Mav.

"I've invited you here to seek your counsel," Rashali explained.

"Yes, this *end of the world* plight," Lath added.

"We don't understand, why now?" Kayn asked.

"After so many years."

"And with horses."

"When you could just wait."

"And let them destroy themselves."

"Far more entertaining."

"Far less effort."

"But I sense you do not have the patience for that."

"Or is there another reason for this haste?" The twins tilted their heads in unison, eyes wide, unblinking and curious.

Rashali did not flinch under their scrutiny. Instead, she asked, "I have invited you here for your expertise in the matters of life and death."

"You want to resurrect the foals without starting again." Lath turned a head towards the placental eggs, some kicking, rocking in their foetal state.

"They are alive now."

"They don't live beyond a day once they hatch," Mav explained. "I have Iloa with me; she had phoenix blood in her. But the magic to combine it all, it's beyond me."

The twins, as if on purpose, avoided making eye contact with Iloa.

"And there is the matter of the centaur," Kayn added. "I assume you want him alive?"

"For the rest of his natural life, yes," Rashali said.

"Centaurs live for centuries. The maximum service we provide is forty-eight hours."

"I am sure you understand how our powers work?" Lath clutched her brother's hand as she spoke, as if fearing to be apart from him for even a moment. "We are just here for your counsel." Lath and Kayn let their eyes wander towards each other, as if having their own private conversation.

"Our advice will cost you the same number of years and foals you wish to raise."

Rashali paused for a moment, then raised a finger before dropping her knees to the gritty earth. She pressed a palm to the ground, and her henna glowed up her forearm. Iloa watched curiously, those pigments pulsing as if in conversation. The Vetali twins, too, were curious, then shared a silent conversation. The only one who did not notice was Mav, who was wringing his hands with apprehension as if a foal could hatch at any moment and devour him while everyone was distracted.

Rashali rose to her feet with a sweet smile. "I have over two thousand foals in this station alone, which I intend to take across the world."

"Two thousand years of life for our advice."

"It had better be good advice."

"It will be." Lath's eyes lingered on Iloa for a moment too long. She could not resist Iloa. Kayn's eyes found her too, and did not blink.

"And this … centaur?" Kayn asked.

"You take pity on him," Lath mused in her angelic voice. "He has served me well."

"Curious," said Kayn. "That the cuff did not save him."

"Yes, I was curious about that, too."

Rashali bent down to touch the cuff on Roan's stiffened arm. It was glowing hot, dying almost. There had not been enough magic in it to save him from a direct wound. All that magic had gone into sparing him from the mares. Soon it would be nothing more than a ring of decorative gold.

"We suggest you look at what killed him," Kayn said. "That advice we will give for free."

"As to who killed him, well, if you require that information, you are not as intelligent as we gave you credit for."

Rashali bent lower over Roan's lifeless form, her palms splayed over his corpse. Iloa gave a muted whimper as the body twitched. Roan's bloodied chest spasmed as Rashali pulled on an invisible string. A bullet wretched from the corpse. The bullet had tiny markings etched on it.

"I wonder," Lath sang, "who would know such curses."

Rashali said nothing but clenched the bullet in her fist. Expecting Roan to jump to life now that Rashali had removed the bullet, Iloa tugged at his mane and rolled his shoulders. Roan's body remained lifeless.

"You think phoenix feathers will let you escape death," Lath said, her eyes glazing curiously over Iloa's form.

"That's what the mortal told you anyway, wasn't it?"

"An all-powerful genie such as yourself, asking for help from a mortal."

"He created her. He is useful to me."

"No, he stole her," Kayn said simply, stepping towards Iloa. "She has changed, but her eyes are the same."

"In all our years of searching, searching. We never expected her to be like this."

"Rashali, what are they talking about?" Iloa asked.

"You scare the girl."

"She should not be afraid. Do you not see the resemblance? Pale skin, one of the same flesh?" Lath crouched down to where Iloa was trying to make herself as small as possible. "A phoenix, to die and then be reborn. She is one of us."

"No, no, I'm not. I'm Iloa." Iloa tossed a stray pebble between the two siblings, who dodged it smoothly.

"She does not remember us, Kayn," Lath spoke with great sadness in her ancient voice.

"The mortal has violated her memories."

"Mutated the laws of Life and Death."

"I wonder if she can be reborn again?"

Iloa was not prepared to find out and ditched another stone, this time at Kayn, hitting him on the bridge of his nose. Both Vetali twins flinched.

"But we sense Iloa had a kinship with this centaur."

"I do." Iloa peeped. "Please save him."

Lath and Kayn stared at one another, then turned to Iloa. With a whisper they said, "We have been searching for you. If you can remember us, we travelled here, to this place, to find you."

"I don't understand."

"Lath, she does not remember."

"I want my friend back. Here, take these," Iloa pulled out a fistful of feathers. The twins gasped as if Iloa had done something horrible. Behind her, Mav crouched with greedy instinct.

"You belong with us, Iloa."

"No, I belong with my friends."

"And when you die, you will be reborn, and perhaps then you will remember who you are."

"We will find you."

Iloa flinched. These two ghost-like Mythica in front of her offered her nothing but ice. Their expressions were cold; they may have been alive, but it felt as if their hearts were long dead. To find out she belonged with them felt worse than being imprisoned by Rashali, worse than being drained of magic with Denin, even worse than a sunless room underground with Mav.

"We are scaring her."

The twins retreated sadly.

"In a gesture of familial faith, we shall bring Iloa's friend to life, a full, centaur life."

"Unless he is foolish enough to be shot again."

"Take him far away from here," Iloa begged, stroking Roan's mane.

"I will honour my vow to him." Rashali soothed, stroking the girl's back. "But you must do something for me."

"What more could you want from me?" Iloa sobbed, wiping a rebellious tear from her golden eyes.

"Learn from the Vetali twins who you really are. And Iloa, don't tell Denin or Ava about this."

That evening Iloa, the Vetali twins, and Rashali all sat down in Rashali's quarters for dinner. They sat cross-legged on a low mahogany table, the curtains around them turning to sharp stone once they were inside.

"An interesting abode," Lath said smoothly. "Your lamp?"

"Most do not notice," Rashali agreed.

"You mean this is your lamp?" Iloa asked, touching the earth as if she rubbed it hard enough she would find copper or gold underneath.

"Mortals, yet again, have a way of poisoning our past," Rashali spoke as she waved a hand across the table, spreading it with unusual sweets, coconut-crusted squares and bowls of syrup.

In front of herself she conjured steaming copper pots of curry, and in front of the twins, a clear broth. Iloa did not ask what was in it.

"When the earth began, we did not have bodies as we do now. I was bound to the earth. My brothers and sisters were bound to wind, water and even Death." Rashali turned to the Vetali twins and scooped her curry into a fold of roti. Iloa stuck her tongue into a bowl of maple syrup. The twins did not move, but stared into their clear bowls wordlessly.

"As mortals advanced, they became aware of us; they altered us."

"Is that what they did to you too?" Iloa asked the twins.

"We come from death; it was only a matter of time before the mortals tried to harness us, tried to stop us by binding us to human form."

"But death still occurs."

"Indeed."

"Why?"

"Death comes in many forms."

"And in threes."

"And what am I?" Iloa asked, not feeling like she was anything more than herself. She did not feel like an ageless force of nature; she did not feel like life or death. She just felt like Iloa.

"You are a bird of magic, of Life and Death. You have been in our care ever since."

"That's it, I'm just a bird?"

"Our understanding is that when the mortals who tried to trap death, they also trapped something else … loss."

"Grief."

"Sadness."

"I don't feel sad; I don't feel any of those things."

"Of course you don't."

"Grief is not yours to feel."

"I don't want to feel it … I don't… I don't." Iloa shook her head in distress.

"Iloa, remember, a phoenix is not about grief, or loss, or death. Don't forget, they are reborn." Rashali soothed. "Perhaps what the twins describe may have been you many lifetimes ago, but what you are now, well, that is something entirely different, don't you agree?"

"I've … never even seen a phoenix. I don't know what I am supposed to look like." Iloa wiped a tear away from her eye, a distant memory emerging — the memory of her picture book, of the bird with the bright yellow beak.

"Like this." Kayn tipped his bowl of clear broth across the table and intricately waved his hands across the shimmering surface. Iloa realised now that it was not water, no, but mercury, and it moved magnetically across the wooden table until Kayn had drawn the outline of a magnificent bird with a long neck, an even longer tail, two solid legs with large talons.

"You would have grown taller than us," Lath explained, "and fed on the dead."

"Ew, no, no, that's not me." Iloa swiped the mercury away from in front of her in disgust. She could stomach nothing more than sweets; to even think about eating dead flesh was repulsive. Rashali soothed her once again.

"No one will make you eat anything you don't want to. You are not a phoenix anymore. Say, I wonder, have you ever seen a bird before?"

"Of course, there are pigeons everywhere."

"No, no, like a big regal, majestic bird, a bird of prey, the sort that might make you appreciate who you used to be." Iloa stared down at her mercury-stained fingers, seeing a flash of gold as it caught her eye. That bird in her book came to her mind. That bird did not scare her.

"How about I ask Denin to take you to the zoo tomorrow?"

"What if Ava says no?"

"I'm sure she can spare her toy boy for a few hours."

"We will come too," Lath said.

Iloa gave the twins a disconcerting look. Denin may accidentally and inadvertently drain her magic dry to the point of death, but compared to the twins, she would take her chances.

#

The eagle opened its vibrant sunrise-yellow beak. They reflected in Iloa's wide eyes. Both were the same colour as each other. Seeing an eagle alive and moving was a dream come true. The keeper held out a dead rat, and she watched as the eagle lowered its head and flared its wings. Then it sprang from powerful legs into the air as the keeper flung the rat into the sky. The bird caught it mid-flight and just about devoured it before it landed. The keeper said something, and everyone clapped.

The dead rat reminded her of what the twins had told her she truly was. She buried the thoughts that clung to her happiness like a nightmare. She was seeing an eagle for the first time! She could not think of it now. No, she did not know how to begin to process this information, and so, she decided, it was best not to try.

Denin sat by her side, looking ridiculous in a fluorescent green tie Ava had made him wear. It was a ghastly combination with his bright orange clown suit. Ava insisted he expand his horizons in the suit department. Iloa was dreading the day he would have to wear his birthday suit. Denin said that it would be by far the most attractive suit Ava could make him wear.

The Vetali twins sat one row behind them, failing to blend in. They dressed entirely in black with wide-brimmed hats as if one shard of sunlight would burn them to charcoal. They looked utterly vampiric, and there was a conspicuous distance between them and the nearest tourists.

The twins had insisted that Rashali not keep Iloa locked away underground, and Rashali had insisted that she did not return to her friends. She was still mulling the bullet over in her fingers as she had spoken. Iloa did not want to be left alone with the twins, and so they had compromised and brought Denin along as a babysitter. Ava was compliant in letting her genie go for an afternoon, unaware of the events of yesterday. Rashali had explained that the twins had now joined their cause, tired of exploiting mortals for their years of life. Ava had not cared to listen to the rest of the lie Rashali had spun.

"He took away her wings." Iloa heard Kayn mutter to his sister.

"Perhaps they will return in her next life."

"I can hear you, you know," Iloa hissed over her shoulder. She wore a thick shawl over her head and a pair of sunglasses to cover her eyes.

"So rude," Denin scolded with mockery. He was enjoying not being the complete bad-guy for once. Or maybe he was just enjoying an evening away from Ava.

Things were not going well between Ava and Rashali. Iloa heard them fight through the corridors. The words were hissed, but whispers sometimes travel further than shouts. They fought about the horses and about magic. Rashali still had not forgiven Ava for capturing a genie. It went against everything Rashali fought for: freedom.

The bird show had ended, and Denin was the first to rise from his seat. Everyone's eyes were on him, and he glowered back angrily, gripping the bangle on his wrist. It had fused with his skin, forming smooth metallic scar tissue. The Sanskrit glittered in the light.

"So, Iloa," Denin asked, "what do you think of zoos?" The Vetali twins were not much for conversation, so Denin had to pick up the slack.

"I like them."

"Would you like to be in one? Gawked at day to day, wings clipped, so to speak. Look." Denin pointed to a sign, a large plastic banner coloured with powdered colours of blue and red and purple. In bright white writing were the words.

MYTHICA!
COMMING THIS AUGUST.

They were building a Mythica exhibit. They would be housing Mythica here. Iloa twisted her lips a little.

"It depends on the Mythica, I suppose. I mean a chupacabra…"

"Humans don't make that distinction," Denin snapped a little roughly. Then, with a sigh, added, "Sometimes a think Rashali is right."

"No, don't say that."

"Humanity has a serious superiority complex."

"Denin."

"Hmm?"

"You hate humans, right?"

"I find their presence a burden upon my existence, yes." He fidgeted with the immovable bangled burned into his flesh.

"I'm impressed you have not tried to escape."

"Not until I know Roan is safe."

"Not to mention the horses; don't want to get caught when they rampage through the streets."

"I need to warn Zack and Troll."

"Don't ask me. I've just been ordered to take you to the zoo, no detours allowed."

"What about these two," Iloa motioned a head behind her.

"The creepy twins? They can do what they want. What are you to them, by the way? Are you their pet? Their third wheel?"

"I don't know." Iloa had not figured it out yet. "If you ask me, they don't seem like the best company to have for all eternity."

"We can hear you," Lath warned.

"And to answer your question, we are custodians."

"Can you send a message to Zack? I want him to know that I am okay." Lath and Kayn looked at one another as if their child had just asked for a pony for Christmas.

"Fine," Kayn said.

"But after the lion show."

"I wonder…"

"If they still feed them Christians."

The zookeeper's lion show disappointed the Vetali twins; the keeper only threw meat and lectured on conservation. After the show, the Vetali twins slipped away to the address Denin had given them, which was useful because Iloa had no idea where Zack lived.

"He gave it to me the first time I had to save his ass," Denin explained, still getting side glances from tourists from his ridiculous attire. They wandered around the zoo for a while, seeing tigers and elephants. Eventually, Iloa had enough courage to ask.

"Has anyone ever asked you to kill someone?"

After a long silence, Denin replied, "Yes." Iloa nodded, uncertain how to continue. Instead of asking further questions, Iloa put a comforting hand in his, her long fingers wrapping around his clenched fist.

"My last captor, not so long ago." He didn't know why he was telling her this. But Iloa was kind and did not judge. She would listen and see the best in him, as she always did.

"An antique store owner found the bracelet and the urn. I thought they had been buried deep within the Egyptian tomb of my last pharaoh, but somehow it surfaced.

"I had to tell the store owner about the Mythica. He wished for mundane things — treasure, a big house, wealth, you know? I made him very rich. Antique store owner to billionaire." Denin felt vulnerable, as if all his power was a curse. "He fell in love with a Mythica — no, not love. The woman had placed powerful enchantments on him. She was an elf. Elves belong to the entertainment Mythica category, so job opportunities were limited to children's birthday parties or … something else. The moment I saw her, I knew who she was, but she pleaded with me to keep quiet. I obliged. I felt a little sorry for her. And it was nice to have another Mythica around for company.

"Because of those enchantments, he gave her everything she wanted. Then, he grew suspicious. I had no choice but to tell him what she was, and that I had known all along. In revenge, he ordered me to kill her. I staged it like a mugging; no one would question it. She was pregnant. I spared the child because I had not directly ordered to kill it. Taking the child with me was not possible. I left it bundled beside her dead mother. Perhaps I should not have.

"My master became obsessed with curses and forced me to arm him against each one. Consequently, he became a cretin, and the magic that bound me to him broke. It no longer recognised him as human, and I was free."

Denin remembered the feeling of the bangle breaking from his skin. It was like losing a weight from his wrist. Denin relapsed into a moody silence. The fact that everyone was staring at his suit did not help.

"Do you know what happened? To the baby, I mean."

"It survived," Denin said, remembering the look Rashali had given him and the words she had said; *mortal blood has a way of returning to haunt us.*

How had he not seen it before? How had he not recognised…

"That's good," Iloa hummed, "that it survived. Can I get an ice cream now?"

THE LOST HORSE AND THE FOUND TRIBE

"We could not find him," Lath reported as Iloa sat on a large, cold chunk of cement. She did not like being down here, did not like it at all. Mav had collected more feathers than she had cared to give him and had crushed them into a fine dust.

"I don't believe you."

"There will be plenty of time to find them later." Rashali was eyeing every single movement Mav made. But he was doing nothing but stirring a mercury-like liquid into a crucible of Iloa's ground feathers. He was creating an iridescent opal liquid. He also had a large syringe and an even larger needle beside him.

"No, I want to see him now. Where else could they be?"

"We checked the apartment," Kayn assured. "There was no sign of them. They may be somewhere else, somewhere safer."

"Or less … pungent." Lath crinkled her nose at the memory.

"Are you ready?" Mav asked before Iloa could demand anything further. He had drawn the liquid into a syringe and carefully, under the torchlight Rashali provided with the flick of her fingers, approached the first globule cluster of eggs. He injected each with a drop or two of the serum, which flushed and pulsed under the shell. The black-green eggs now radiated a sickly opalescent sheen.

"Give it time. They will hatch and remain alive," Mav assured. And as if fate had heard his words, there was a crack and hatch of an egg echoing down the dark tunnels. A hungry whinny echoed. Mav shuddered with an odd mix of fear and relief.

"Try Roan now. And remember, if he dies, so do you." With that warning, Mav crouched down and pressed a hand to Roan's chest. The bullet wound was puckering around the edges now, too large for any needle, so Mav took the needle off and wedged the syringe hub to Roan's flesh. Roan did not flush with an opalescent sheen like those eggs. In fact, he did not move at all.

Iloa slipped down from her cement ledge. Mav had been her only hope. It was either that or implore the Vetali twins to yield forty-eight hours so Roan could bid farewell, but she would not do that without Zack and Troll. They deserved to say farewell too.

Roan did not move.

"Shame," Rashali said after a minute went by. "I truly believed that you feared me enough to do a good job."

"No, no, it will work, it will work."

"Roan." Iloa knelt forward, her heart retching. The hope of seeing the centaur again dissolved. The liquid from the syringe was seeping out. With desperate fingers she tried to scoop it all back in. Roan's eyes were lifeless and turning milky with death.

"The living cannot be brought to life without death." A shivering voice whispered in her ear. It was Lath.

"Very different from something that was never dead to begin with." Kayn hissed into her other ear.

"If only we had an insignificant mortal life we could use to gift Roan."

"And then perhaps your phoenix blood will carry him through beyond…" Iloa looked at Mav who was on his knees, begging Rashali, pointing madly at the cluster of opal-green eggs.

"I made them, didn't I? Show mercy, please. Please!"

"She is going to kill him anyway."

"Probably make him suffer."

"Would be kind to take his years before she does."

"Better than letting them go to waste."

"I can't. He is Mav. He … he…" She remembered what Zack told her. Mav had made her unnatural, but she could not hate him for that. But she could hate him for holding her captive, for hiding her from the world. Mav had kept Zack, Roan, and Troll captive and done horrible things to them. A horrible feeling twisted in her gut; a feeling that maybe Zack was right. Roan was part of her family now, and he deserved for Iloa to at least try….

"Fine," Iloa gulped. "Do it."

And as Lath collapsed beside her, dead in an instant, Roan screamed an ungodly scream and kicked his hooves in a dangerous seizure of panic.

Mav collapsed, and Iloa saw something remarkable, something impossible.

"She see's it, Lath," Kayne said, clutching his dead twin's stiff hands. A trickle of opalescent shimmer trickled from Mav to Roan, and just as the liquid had flushed and pulsed through the egg, it pulsed through Roan's beating heart too.

Rashali realised what was happening and turned to Iloa with curious eyes. Then, a calm smile spread across her golden face.

Lath gasped, alive beside Iloa, and Kayn clutched her wordlessly. Roan, still gasping, wide-eyed and panting, remained alive.

"He can't stay here," Rashali said, and with a click of Rashali's fingers, the ground underneath Roan gave way, and he was swallowed into the earth.

#

Pandora's cauldron looked empty; that was exactly how it was meant to look, but wise eyes knew differently. The cauldron was small, no larger than a school backpack, and appeared rusted through. This was not rust, but blood, layers and layers of it. The cauldron was made from the sacrifices it was offered. Rusty blood flaked into intricate but seemingly accidental patterns. Mav's blood, which dripped slowly into the rim, was unseen.

The hands that held his wrist constricted, running sharp fingers down his arms to squeeze enough blood for the purpose. Mav's body hung wide-eyed and limp, suspended in the air above. Shadows formed around his eyes and lips. His would be the first blood to be spilt, the first blood in centuries. Blood that will lead to more blood, so much more.

The humans should be more careful about what they leave lying around in museums.

Two half-breed eyes watched Rashali from the shadows. Of course, Ava had not been privy to Rashali's entire plans. Why would she? She was, of course, half human, and full trust could never be placed in her. Ava touched the empty spot on her neck. When she had ordered Denin to kill Roan, she thought she had put an end to Rashali's plans. But no, her mother, if you could even call her that, had pushed her further and further away. Rashali longer permitted Ava to enter certain parts of the caverns, saying they were *not safe*. She was no longer trickling magic towards Ava either because, in Rashali's words, *she had a genie now*.

Rashali was oddly pleasant to Denin, which pissed Ava off even more. She offered him his own room, suggested he spend time around Refuge and even offered some of her own enchantments, so he didn't drain Iloa dry.

With a twist of her hands, Rashali spoke in a tongue too ancient for any living creature to understand. The henna along her arms pulsed, and she raised them above her head. The cauldron, which appeared nothing more than a rusting artefact smoked. With another hand, something rose from the darkness.

“My sister,” Rashali spoke into the cauldron. Ava remembered that word from her childhood. Rashali had tried to teach her once. “Drink.” She remembered that word, too. Ava did not understand the rest, though it seemed Rashali instructed the cauldron to do something. Suspended above the cauldron, Mav’s flesh peeled away from his bones. Blood, clotted and coagulated, dripped and plunked into the cauldron in chunks, sucking Mav dry. Rashali watched, almost affectionately.

The grey mist plumed up, then the bottomless cauldron greedily sucked it back in. Then shot up into the air in tendrils as if finally being released, then as quickly as the swirls of mist rose, it plummeted down into the earth.

The end has begun.

#

Roan,

You are in Cambridge. Your tribe is being housed at the Newton Stables. You were shot. Go into hiding. Find cover, hide, and do not go into the mist.

There was no signature at the bottom, but Roan could remember now that the curse had been broken. Rashali had come through on her agreement. His tribe was a long way from home. What was happening to them? Roan looked up from the letter to the street where he had appeared, covered in dirt as if he had emerged from a grave. A residential area — well, at least it was quiet. The early morning air bit with cold. Roan flared his nostrils at the scent of fresh grass. There was a park nearby; he could smell it. Fog obscured the sky, and the sun’s orange haze dominated the clouds. He needed a map, or at least to know where he was. He wandered forward in search of a street sign or landmark, or anything. Roan twisted his lips. Where the hell was that?

He pressed on, wondering what the attitude towards Mythica was in England. Not the best considering his tribe was stuck in the stables, but would he be able to ask for directions without being tranquilised? Well, he was soon going to find out, wasn't he, when everyone woke up?

Perhaps he should head to the park, just in case. He could hide in brambles or bushes. He followed the street, hoping the clop of his hooves wouldn't wake any early risers. Roan's arms goose-bumped, but it was not because of the morning wind. He felt vulnerable.

He came to a main road, and a few cars passed by. Some slowed a little as they approached him, but no one stopped or leaned out of the window to throw abuse. One businessman pulled out his cell phone, but that could have been for any reason at all. Roan was growing paranoid. He really did not want to be shot in the arse by anything. He needed to contact Troll and Zack too, to let them know he was alive. Did they even know he had died? Had he just gone missing? Roan pulled out Rashali's letter. It mentioned nothing about that. He screwed up the letter again.

A fence secured the park, so he followed the painted iron until he found a gate. It was a large botanical garden, and Roan hoped he would find a place to hide before joggers came on their morning run. Roan cursed the weather again. Why couldn't it rain? It was England, after all. He just *had* to arrive on the one sunny day of the year.

Roan found a secluded portion away from the path. There were a few trees and some rather thorny bushes. He made his way into them as far as he could. There was a little empty circle in the middle that was far too small to fit his entire body, but at least his front was thorn-free. Roan waited, wondering if he would see any centaurs passing by. If only he could talk to someone.

The first runners came through. Roan edged back into the shrubs. A few more students walked past. Roan held his breath. They were close. He caught snippets of their conversation.

"I just don't understand why we are studying it. It's an Australian text," a male spoke.

"It exemplifies racism in all cultures…" a woman's voice trailed off.

"Amber?"

"Huh? Thought I saw something." She had seen Roan, looked him right in the eyes, half hidden in the bushes.

"Yeah, getting back to helping me pass this essay."

"Where's my fifty pounds?"

"Oh fine. I swear you're ripping me off…." The voices trailed. Roan still could not find breath to breathe. Amber must have seen him; he had blinked right into her blue eyes. Had she kept her mouth shut? Was she going to alert the authorities? Roan couldn't move; more and more students were passing, but fortunately they were far more interested in themselves than their surroundings. Roan couldn't shake the image of the tall brunette. Those eyes were sure to have connected with his. He was certain.

Hours passed. Students were lounging in the sparse sunlight. Some were wearing Cambridge University hoodies. So that was where Roan was — the Cambridge Botanical Gardens. This was bad, terrible, too many people, snoopy, nosey people. That was when he heard someone talking to the ranger.

"Just there, officer. Standing there for a while." Roan froze. He didn't know where the ranger was, but he knew he was close by and talking about Roan. The next thing he knew, rifle-wielding officers were approaching. Roan did not move a muscle. These were men prepared to shoot and just waiting for an excuse. It made Mythica's treatment in America seem like high school. At least there he could walk down the street.

"No collar," called one.

"No branding either. This one's a stray."

“Better shoot him then.” Great, how ironic, to be brought back to life only to be shot again. Roan opened his mouth to shout, but it was not his voice that came from his lips.

“I said wait!” Roan’s eyes flickered to a girl racing towards them, chestnut hair trailing over her shoulders. Her face was flushed pink. It reminded Roan for a moment of Catherine.

Instead of stopping to talk to the police officers, she leapt right into the bushes beside Roan. Roan was so shocked he didn’t know what to do.

“Hold these.” She shoved a small book from her hoodie pocket into Roan’s hand.

“Ma’am?” the ranger called.

“Follow me,” Amber hissed.

“I’m leading him out now. He won’t hurt anyone, no need to shoot. My mother just paid a fortune for him.” Paid a what? For whom? Roan bottled his outrage and his questions. As long as he wasn’t feeling bullets in his backside, the girl could say whatever she wanted.

“You own this horse, Miss?” the oldest, most pot-bellied police officer inquired. He had lowered his gun and was reaching for his notebook. Was he going to give Amber a ticket? Roan almost wanted to laugh. Amber must have seen the smirk on Roan’s lips, and she dug her nails into the back of his hand as a warning.

“No, my mother does. Bought him yesterday. Cost a fortune because he doesn’t speak a word and does everything you say. If you had shot him, my mother would have had you off the ranks in an instant.”

“Where is his collar? Branding?”

“Obviously, I haven’t had time to do that yet. Mum’s busy with the baby. He wouldn’t have been out here like this if it weren’t an emergency. I’ve got an exam in an hour, and I need my book.”

“And where is this book?” Roan, on command, lifted his hand to read *No Sugar* by Jack Davis. The policeman made a sour face, as if he was looking forward to shooting the centaur. It took all of Roan's willpower not to raise his eyebrows in a mocking smile. Instead, he played his part and kept his head low, not making eye contact.

"Why was he hiding in the bushes then?"

"He was waiting for me. Safer than just bustling into the lecture theatre."

"I'm still going to fine you because he's not wearing identification."

"Do you have a collar in the car I could use? I don't want him shot on the way home."

"The university has stables."

"I need to be registered to use them."

"I'm sure if one of us escorts you, they'll make an exception."

"They better," Amber muttered and let Roan's hand go. Roan wasn't stupid enough to run away. Not only would he get shot, but it would cause a lot of trouble for Amber as well, and even if he didn't like humans, the girl had just saved his ass. Two policemen urged Roan forward from behind. Amber led the way. The officer with the ticket book, followed.

"Your name?"

"Might I ask how much the fine is?"

"If you can afford the horse, you can afford the fine."

"Fine … Jona Wayland. Forty-three Brandridge Road." The policeman scribbled a bit more on his ticket, then ripped it off and handed it to Amber. Amber tossed it over her shoulder to Roan, who crushed it in his fist. They were silent all the way to the stables. Amber and Roan lingered back while the police convinced the stable hand to let Roan stay there for a day.

"I told you I can't let him in until I see his vaccination records. Branding and collar too; kids bring in strays sometimes, and they cause all sorts of havoc."

Roan's stomach clenched at that. So, there were others like him, fighting for their tribes.

The police turned over their shoulders at Roan and Amber. Were they suspicious now? Roan's hooves itched to run. The policeman nodded to one another and approached at a quickening pace. They were drawing their guns again. Amber stiffened beside him. That was when they saw it, out of the corner of their eyes.

The dark shape, with red eyes glowing from the shade of the trees. The heat from its breath rose in steam clouds, and the drool from its foaming mouth singed the grass at its feet. Roan gripped Amber's arm. The police had their guns raised.

The stable hand muttered, "What the … that's not one of mine!" That seemed to be the signal for the flesh-eater to attack. It galloped forward, launching itself right at them.

The mare trampled the nearest policeman, crunching its razor teeth around his torso, crushing an entire body's worth of ribs. The dead man gargled blood as his partner shot a barrage of bullets to little avail. Black, opalescent blood seeped from small holes in its flank. It seemed to do nothing more than if the man had fired a Nerf gun.

Roan backed away, Amber already sprinting for cover. The bullets were shooting in his direction now as the Mare of Diomedes lost interest in its first victim and flared its nostrils at Roan. These monsters loved centaur blood. Out of all the different meats in this world, the flesh-eater would always, always hunt and tear a centaur first.

The sun had disappeared, and the air turned to ice. Roan wasn't sure why this was happening. In fact, he just thought his mind was playing tricks. He was in shock after all, and just about to die for a second time. His hooves lifted, and he spun around and flew into the air, kicking the beast in the neck. The horse howled. It was an unnatural sound; it was the sound that belonged to a bear or a wolf. Roan knew he couldn't outrun it, and so he leapt from side to side, hoping to dodge its blood-dripping jaws. The mare took a moment to recover from the kick, and in that time Roan ran for the gardens.

The horse was huge, twice as wide as Roan, and he hoped the beast would get stuck in the trees. Something snagged his tail, ripping hairs from his behind. The mare's hooves pounded like hammers. It picked up speed, moving up alongside him. Roan dodged as he heard teeth snap shut where his rear had been moments before. Something stung his skin. Had it bitten him? It was acid. Venom. He should have dropped dead by now if he had; the poison was instant. It hurt like hell; he could feel burning, like needles in his veins. He almost hit a tree.

The entire botanical gardens were empty now. Then he spotted a face — a face in a tree. It was Amber. She clung to the highest branch. She cried out to him.

"There's more!"

Roan was a dead man.

THE MIST

Three more. They came from behind and the sides. Roan was surrounded. Had Rashali planned this all along? This was it. He was going to die. The horses closed in, their heads low and dripping with white froth. The horses flared their nostrils. They were hungry. The one on his left snapped at the other. Perhaps, perhaps he could pit them against one another and then get away.

"Yoho, over here!" Amber called, scrambling from the tree. She clapped her hands together, trying to snatch their attention. "Over here, you ugly brutes." One of them altered their gaze but made no motion to move.

"It won't work!" Roan barked. The girl should get back up into that tree. Should he tell her about his tribe? Would she carry out a dying centaur's wish? Would she laugh at him for even suggesting it?

He knew he had moments left. He knew they were about to strike; he could see it in the way they bent a little lower, flexed their muscles, tightened their flanks and drew breath. They were not horses. The Greeks had it all wrong. They were indeed monstrosities.

Then something caught Roan in the throat. He could not breathe. Behind him, he heard Amber scream. He felt as though he were being strangled. His vision turned grey. He was not passing out; no, this grey was in the air, like a dense smoke but different. This grey was dense, so dense it was like they were potholes in the fabric of space and time. If you fell into it, you would disappear forever.

Roan felt disoriented within it. He could not see his feet or anything above his head. Was he dead?

Around him, the squeals of horses tore at him. Bone crunched and blood splattered into the air. Whatever inhabited this mist was consuming these creatures. Whatever could do that, he didn't want to be in its way. The sound of cracking bone and ripping flesh made Roan wretch. The beasts cried and wailed like newborns. Was this hell?

Then it reached for him, reaching out like coldness in his chest. Roan gasped in shock, then everything around him contracted. In the next moment, the mist was gone, retracted back into the trees, into the earth. Surrounding him were the dilapidated corpses of four horses, their bodies ripped like shrapnel. Roan looked at his arm. It blazed white-hot. His family cuff. So that's what had saved him.

Amber was no longer in the tree. Roan's heart fell. That meant.... His eyes spotted the corpse of the girl who had saved his life. Why did every kind human have to die at his hands? Roan clenched his fists as he knelt to examine her. The creature drained Amber's body, yet her flesh stayed moist, resembling a tomato left in the sun. Her face was pale; her entire body was white. Her eyes were open and mouth wide as if the mist had sucked the life from all orifices. Roan's hands lingered over her face. Should he touch her? Shut her eyes? Or run?

Roan rose to his hooves and examined the scene. The horses were not at the forefront of Rashali's plans. No, no, it all made sense now. The horses were bait if the dead beasts in front of him were anything to go by. Whatever this mist was, it wanted to devour the Mares of Diomedes. Her actual weapon was soon to come, and bullets could not kill it. Roan had been in that mist and had survived. He could still feel its touch all around him. This was no ordinary force of nature. It felt alive, alive like he was; he could sense its pulse and its greed. This was how Rashali was going to wipe out humanity. Well, he had to admit; it was a bit more foolproof than a couple of horses.

Roan abandoned Amber's corpse, yet he lingered. What would he do with her? Carrying around a dead girl's body would be incriminating. The less he had to deal with humans, the better.

"Amber?" A young woman screamed from the footpath and raced forward. She had jet-black hair, a heavy fringe and a bullring in her nose. Roan had to stop now, at least long enough to explain. Tears streamed down the woman's cheeks, streaking her mascara. She was a slight woman; her black leggings ripped in a way Roan supposed was fashionable. Roan stood frozen, uncertain what to do. Uncertainty seemed to follow him around a lot these days. Surprisingly, the woman addressed him without looking up from her friend.

"How did this happen?"

"The horses came. Then a mist. When it was gone, the horses were dead, and so was she." Roan approached slowly. The woman did not seem scared, nor did she shy away from the scene. Amber's body remained intact, unlike the horses'. Her shoulder was at a funny angle, but that was because of how she had landed.

"What's your name?" Roan inquired.

"Shannon." Shannon wiped her eyes daintily with the back of her wrist and rose to her feet. She looked Roan up and down. "No collar."

"I'm a stray," Roan replied warily. Shannon looked back at her friend.

"What do I do with her?" Her voice was meek. Roan almost reached for her shoulder in comfort.

"The police will come soon. They will take care of her. Stay. Tell them what I told you. People need to know what's going on. The horse attacks will only get worse, and with them, there will be a mist. The horses are being used to lure the mist, I suspect."

"I don't care about the damn horses!" Shannon snapped. Then snuffled. Roan lapsed into silence.

“I’m sorry,” Roan spoke after a pause. “Was she your friend?”

“Help me take her back.”

“No,” Roan flinched at his own words. Catherine had been alive when he had taken her back to her village. There had been a life at stake. Catherine had been screaming, then when he approached, she had simmered to a whimper. She had asked, begged. This time, Amber was dead. Shannon could find someone else. This time, Roan would not make the same mistake. This time, he would choose his tribe.

If he was going to save his tribe, now would be the moment, now that the mist had frightened the mortals away, at least for a little while.

He turned a shaking hoof and returned to the stables.

The stables were silent. There were at least thirty stalls, each one housing a centaur. Reaching chest height, the steel stable door was rimmed with sharp steel spikes. The icy place had already chilled Roan’s legs. The woman centaur in the first stall was still staring, her straw-coloured hair unkempt and her skin too pale for a centaur. She was almost white, as if she had not seen sunlight in years. Creatures like him bore tanned olive skin, even the English ones.

“Stad,” the woman replied in their mother tongue. He had not heard his own language in many years. It felt foreign yet familiar, like someone else’s memory. She looked to the cameras; Roan understood now. They were being monitored.

“Who are you?” Roan asked, his dialect a little rusty from years of neglect.

“Eila,” she replied, the coldness not retreating from her eyes. “Who are you?”

“A stray.”

“And the gunshots?”

“Wild animal.”

“The humans?”

“Dead.”

"Are you going to make me keep asking, or are you going to explain?" Eila jutted her jaw defiantly. This was not what Roan had been expecting. Although he could not remember what he had been expecting. Centaurs attached to carts? Paraded around like freak shows? Morose, defeated?

Before Roan could say another word,

"It's about time you came to your senses and stopped sympathising with those bipedal abominations," a face half hidden by a stall post followed a familiar voice. Roan recognised that voice.

"Drystan?" Roan followed that voice to the far stall. His brother just looked at him, studied him like one would study a painting they would never see again, or a memory long since passed. Roan's brother had aged. Silver streaked his hair, and grime covered his face. Time had changed Drystan's face from that carefree colt, but his eyes were the same. Roan would recognise his brother anywhere.

"What took you so long?" Since Drystan was only a child when Roan was exiled, perhaps he never grasped Roan's betrayal. If he had, he would not be welcoming his brother like this. Then Drystan gave a laugh. "Roan, it's been decades!" Drystan looked much younger when he laughed; those furrowed creases became healthy laugh lines. And those eyes lit up like a child's. Roan didn't know how to respond.

"Our father ordered my exile, Drystan."

"Father's dead," Drystan replied, his expression sobering. "So are our brothers. They fought, they resisted, and they were killed." Drystan crossed his thumb over each cheek. Roan did so too. It was a sign of remembrance. He noted everyone else in the stables did the same thing, too.

"We thought you would come back after the Revealing."

"They shipped me to America," Roan explained, recounting his capture and miserable time under Mav's control in the circus, then … as he felt it welling up in his throat, he told them about the mares.

"That's what the gunshots were. There are mares out there. I created the stuff of nightmares, all so I could get back to you, brother."

Roan kept his head down to his hooves; there was silence, utter silence, and it seemed like hours before any of them spoke.

"Roan?" Eila asked gently. Roan lifted his head in response. He saw Eila look to Drystan, and Drystan nodded. "Thank you." Roan gulped down his shock. Thank you? Roan did not need to ask for an explanation; his confused expression must have been sufficient.

"Roan, you do not know what it's like to live like this. You were lucky; you got out of here. If you knew how they treated us, that we have to live with day by day, then you would not judge yourself so harshly. I am sure that all of us here, if we had been in your place, would have given our bodies freely to Rashali's cause.

"You see, Roan, our enemy now is not the mares, not even the mist and not Rashali, but the humans, and if we have to use the horses to kill them, then this is our weapon and we will use it."

"You don't think Rashali is wrong? She will kill innocent people too!"

"Humans have made their choice here," Drystan explained. "They have had years to protest, to make change, but they continue to act like cattle, following one another in submission. If they choose to behave this way, then we will treat them this way." Drystan had a lot of time to think through this, and who was Roan to contradict him? After all, he was technically the tribe elder; he was the leader. Roan was a stranger, an outsider.

Roan stood there, uncertain what to do now; what would happen to him. Did his tribe want him?

"We're not all from the same tribe," Eila spoke kindly. "But we are all centaurs, and we need to put aside our differences in times like this. What Rashali is doing, we cannot stop, and so perhaps we should just let fate take its course. Maybe after a few days here, Roan, you will not judge your brother so harshly." The brothers met eyes, and Roan saw vestiges of fellowship with his tribe.

"Now, brother, have you just come to visit, or will you help us escape?"

"What about the mist?" Eila asked.

"I'll take my chances with the mist and the mares over humans any day." Drystan answered already, rearing his hooves at the stable door.

"Hold your horses," Roan sighed, which earned him a sneer of offence from the palomino centaur beside him. "I'll get the keys." Roan returned to the front of the stables where the stable hand lay dead. There was a mist still lingering around the pathway. No one had come to the stables yet, despite the previous gunshots. Shannon would bring someone soon, and they were best to escape now. Whether it was safe to pass through the mist remained unknown, but Drystan was right; he would have better chances in the mist than against a gun.

Roan opened every single stall, freeing his new tribe. The last to leave was Drystan, who clasped his brother in a long overdue embrace.

"Where do we go?" Drystan asked Roan.

"That is for you to decide, brother. You are the leader now."

Drystan surveyed his clan who, Roan now saw, were from different places. Some had the roughish, stocky features of the north, and others the slender features of the south, and others Roan could not place, but all were staring, waiting for Drystan's orders.

"We hold no weapons; it would be foolish to retaliate unarmed. We will perform a tactical retreat, and if my brother is correct, the mares and the mist will weaken our enemy. Then we will attack."

"But the mares will hunt us down."

"The mares lure the mist, right, Roan?" Eila asked.

"I think so. But the mist will kill us too. I only escaped because of this." Roan touched his cuff.

"Then we must march into the town. The mares want centaur blood; there is nothing more that they want. Then the mist will follow and destroy all our enemies. Then we will outrun the mist." Eila's plan earned a hearty cheer and a thump to the chest from the centaurs.

"No, no, that is foolish and dangerous," Roan panicked. He had just found his brother, his tribe; he could not lose them again, not like this. But he was not the tribe leader. He had no say, and Eila was right; Roan had no idea what they had been through. Who was he to tell them to run?

Eila turned to Drystan, who nodded.

"We will be safest together." Drystan picked up a gun from a fallen police officer and asked, "How do you work this?"

"Give it here." Roan snatched the gun from his brother. "I don't like this plan, but I'm not leaving your side."

"Wouldn't expect anything less from my elder brother." Drystan gave a sideways smile as the centaur herd ventured back into the town defenceless and praying they did not meet a mare.

But as they approached the town, through the botanical gardens towards the university, they did not meet any humans. It was eerily quiet until sirens echoed streets away. Then, as the sirens emerged, so did the people, some racing across the footpath's phones in hand. Nobody seemed to notice a herd of rogue centaurs.

"We should stay back," Roan suggested, but the herd was already marching forward. They were willing to sacrifice themselves to avenge their tribe; they were sure to either get shot or ravaged by a mare. They were placing too much trust in this mist, a mist that Roan wasn't even sure was going to return and save them. He couldn't lose his tribe again.

A tremor ran through the ground. The fountain in the centre of the botanical gardens spluttered and stopped. Then, with an impossible force, the earth split, and from it emerged five horses. Each one erupted from the ground as if they had been born from the earth itself.

"Are you sure this genie is on our side?" Eila asked as the horses took a moment to hoist their twisting, awkward, skeletal forms onto solid earth. Their bodies were narrow, their limbs too long, and their heads too big. They were abominations, nothing like the four original mares from Roan's nightmares, but they were deadly nonetheless. Roan couldn't help himself; with a shaking hand, he raised the gun. He shot before he realised what he was doing.

"Roan," Drystan stepped back, gripping his frozen brother. "Roan, this is where we run," but Roan could not; he could not move. Fear flooded deep inside him. With the Valsha curse broken, he could remember everything: every acidic bite and every brush of sweaty flank. He remembered Rashali's golden eyes watching him, Mav talking to him about eggs, about magic, about things he could not understand.

Drystan gripped Roan and pulled him away as the horses found their footing and sniffed the air.

"Through the town centre!" Eila called. He could hear the horses now chasing them, whinnying madly.

Roan followed, galloping, his heart pounding. They galloped through the streets, ignoring students as they dropped their books.

"This is not a good idea," Roan screamed, seeing more and more people exiting their stone-spired homes and shops. But once the humans saw the five horses chasing the hoard of the centaurs, they didn't seem to care about the centaurs too much.

"Where is the mist?" Drystan called back.

"I don't know. I told you, it was just a theory." The centaurs had galloped towards King's College Chapel. More horses spilled from all corners of the town. Blood dripped from their snarling muzzles. Gunshots were following them, but bullets did nothing. Humans and horses now surrounded the centaurs.

"I'm sorry, brother," Roan gulped, seeing the crowd cluster now. "I got it wrong." There was no mist to be seen; the sky clear as an English sky could be. "We need to get out of here now. I can't lose you again." Roan ripped the cuff from his arm and shoved it onto Drystan's.

"Brother?"

"Wear it, please," Roan spoke with such desperation that Drystan did not retaliate. Instead, he pressed a hand over Roan's and nodded.

"Drystan, you need to get out of here now."

"No, I'll stay with my tribe," Drystan said with such conviction that Roan knew there was no way his brother was going to leave his tribe, no, of course not, it was not the centaur way, it was not his family's way. Still, Roan did not remove his hand from Drystan, lest the centaur try to remove the cuff from his arm.

Roan, with his other hand raised his stolen gun and fired at the rampaging horses, who were snarling and darting around the grass, attacking whatever human dared to approach. The only thing that was prowling closer were now ten horses the size of cars.

"I thought you would have raised your offspring better than this," Drystan joked.

"Yes, well, I thought a family reunion was in order." Roan aimed his gun at the closest horse, not that he figured it would do very much. If the humans couldn't stop them, a few extra bullets wouldn't do any significant damage.

"Look!" Eila pointed to the ground. The mist was seeping up, seeping through the grass. Roan jolted his hooves up, expecting pain, expecting death to feel like something. The mist was rising now and swiftly.

"Run!" he commanded, but there was nowhere to run, nowhere to go. His entire tribe would be sucked dry; their insides would evaporate, all except for Drystan who was still wearing the cuff.

"Go!" Roan tried once again to push his brother, to urge him to escape, but it was futile. The horses from all corners charged forward. The mist plumed from the earth like a dust storm, covering their sight. Rumps and hooves clattered and clanged. Roan held his breath, trying to hold in what life he had left.

The pain did not consume him. Rancid blood splattered hot over his face and rained down. The horses' whinnies were silenced. The mist surged forward around them, rippling out like a shock wave. The mist formed rippling tendrils, snaking across the grass, up into the cathedral and beyond. Roan could see now, through the mist, that the human screams were not from his tribe; no, those screams were human, real mortal humans.

Surrounding him as the mist thinned enough for them all to see, they witnessed Rashali's plans. Mortals were screaming, writhing, their insides sucked dry, just as Amber's had been. There were so many of them, dropping to the ground, others running away but not getting very far at all. The mist was like an acid, like salt water pickling them dry. The mist indiscriminate killing, screams echoing from streets away. Entire families were massacred. Roan felt more fear that he ever had before, no, not fear, but guilt. For the first time he saw what Rashali was doing, the consequences of his choice. Was this worth finding his tribe? All this death? He watched as the mist continued, rising in the air and spreading out across the entirety of Cambridge, spreading, consuming. Mortals became wilted leaves on the ground.

"What have I done?" Roan breathed with an emptiness in his chest. Beside him, Eila breathed in whatever life was leaving Roan.

"It's over," Eila laughed, then screamed louder, bucking her hind legs, gripping Roan's arm with one hand and Drystan's with another, her straw hair now shining in the natural light. "It's finally over."

THE VAMPIRE AND THE RESCUE

Zack's army was pathetic. It was the worst army he had ever seen, like a gang of shitty superheroes lacking both the super and the hero. But they had suffered weeks of waiting and in that time Zack had been planning.

Margo had offered her place as a base since no one dared return to the apartment after Roan disappeared and Iloa was kidnapped. There was Troll, of course, who was just looking for an excuse to kick ass.

Then there was Talon, who really was not much help beyond making Margo tea. And of course, Spike, who had devoured almost everything in Margo's pantry like a hungry Labrador. For a creature that was meant to only feast on blood, he ate a lot of garbage.

"The entrance to Refuge is through the potholes in the ground. It's via a will-o'-the-wisp. Talon tells me there are guards that allow the will-o'-the-wisp to eat you or let you go, so how are we going to get around that?" Zack commanded the meeting.

"Say we want to join?"

"Won't work; they know who we are."

"We will split up to increase our chances of finding her."

"I have curses," Talon said in the silence. "I have them all here. Curses that can protect you and some that will hinder the enemy." But a moment later Talon returned to his lucid state and asked Margo if she wanted more biscuits.

"Fat chance of getting any curses from him now."

"Don't think I want any, anyway." Margo looked the cretin up and down, who was concentrating hard on the biscuit between his fingers. "I've been thinking," Margo said. "If Rashali is a genie, then she must have had a lamp and someone could trap her."

"We need to trick her inside the lamp, then we smash it. That's how you kill a genie." Troll said, slamming hist fist on the table. Zack wasn't sure how true this was.

"What about me?" Margo butted in.

"You stay here." Troll said.

"Like hell! I'm a seer; they may accept me. You could bring me along, say you want my safety."

"That will not fool her."

"If we agree to her plans, she will."

"She's already won. Didn't you see the horses on the news? And this weird mist. We would be going there to surrender."

"I reckon I could take on a horse." Troll said with gruff defiance.

"I'm sure you could," Zack assured.

"Margo, this could be dangerous."

"I'm sixty-nine years old, I smoke like a chimney, my blood pressure is through the roof, and I've got enough padding around me to survive a two-story fall, in case you hadn't noticed, walking up the stairs is dangerous for me. I'm already living on the edge."

"Well then, I suppose … I mean, there is a fair chance you will die," Zack said as if he were reminding someone of a credit card transaction fee.

Zack eyed Spike, wondering how he could incorporate the creature into his plans.

"Don't worry about him," Troll said, noticing where Zack's eyes had trailed. "I've seen him do some crazy shit." Zack was more than willing to take Troll's word for it.

“We ready?” Margo loaded the cartridge into her gun and polished it up for the third time tonight. She had donned a grey velveteen tracksuit and white orthopaedic running sneaker. At least it was an upgrade from a musty floral nightgown.

There was no way in hell Zack would ever be ready. The butterflies felt more like boiling acid in his stomach. There was a fair chance he was going to get himself killed, and frankly, if that was the case, he would have liked to have sat down and watched his favourite movie one last time. But now with Iloa gone, watching movies seemed a little empty. There was no one to laugh with him, no one to make stupid comments.

Zack’s heart ached for the girl and he blinked back bloody tears that threatened to clog his vision. He was doing this for Iloa; he didn’t know why he was doing this for her, or if it would make her proud or upset, but he needed a reason to do what he was doing, any reason at all, and Iloa was the best reason he had.

#

They split up and took two separate entrances, hoping to find Iloa faster. Zack and Margo went together and so did Troll, Talon and Spike. Zack swallowed, but it did nothing to ease the lump in his throat. It was one of those moments when you just wanted to hold someone’s hand, to know you weren’t alone, but let’s face it, he wasn’t exactly about to face certain death hand in hand with Margo.

They came to the camouflaged pothole — well rather, the will-o’-the-wisps gaping mouth.

“Are you sure this is the entrance?” Margo inquired as they felt something cold wrap around their ankles.

“It’s what Talon told us in his lucid moments.”

“Are you ready then?”

“Not a chance in hell.”

"Good, perfect time for it then." And just as Margo had finished her words, they felt themselves being pulled feet first down the pothole, their backs dragging along cold cement, their heads banging against the ground. Then, their bodies jerked down, and they landed in something squishy. It covered them as if they were inside a great big intestinal tract. There was slime everywhere, and Zack scrunched his eyes shut and prayed he did not run out of breath. He did not know where Margo was, but before he could scramble around to find her, he felt himself falling through icy air. Again, he landed in something soft, but this time it wasn't so slimy or suffocating. Zack tried to lift himself up, but he found he had lost his entire right arm in the flesh-coloured folds. Was this the will-o'-the-wisp? It was a butt-ugly beast.

"Margo!" Zack called, then spotted her a little while away; her entire bottom half had disappeared. Zack wrenched his arm free; it felt like he was ripping his skin from his bones. The will-o'-the-wisp had suckers with barbs in there. Zack looked at his hand. There were at least two juice boxes of blood seeping down his elbow. Well, it could have been worse. He could be Margo.

Zack scrambled towards her, the will-o'-the-wisp moving and bulging, trying to suck him in. Margo was only a few meters away, but by the time he got there, the will-o'-the-wisp was juicy with Margo's blood. He could feel the contractile pulses beneath him. His feet were slipping, being pulled down.

"Margo!" Zack reached out a slippery hand to the old woman. She was being sucked up to her shoulders now. She was unconscious, her face pale and lifeless. Zack tried to pull; he saw between the folds of will-o'-the-wisp the yellow of fat splattered with blood. It had known, must have known Margo was mortal and devoured her even faster. A peak of Margo's leg sprouted out of one of the distant folds, and the will-o'-the-wisp coughed out one of Margo's orthopaedic sneakers.

Zack pulled his hand back, understanding it was too late. His own skin prickled from the digestive enzymes. Zack was about to run, to escape, when he saw the glimmer of a gun simmering in fat and blood. Zack wretched his hand down into the folds and snatched it, just before the contractions could take him as well. It ate her so fast, too fast for Zack to even process what he was seeing. Margo was gone. Gone. Swallowed like a pill. He couldn't think about what he had just seen, or what it meant. *No, don't think. Just look. Pay attention.* He was still inside the will-o'-the-wisp.

The will-o'-the-wisp had to end somewhere. But Zack was being pushed back into its flesh; the lips of the creature were rising like a tidal wave. Zack scrambled forward, leaving Margo behind. Troll was going to kill him.

There was no guard at this entrance, which Zack supposed was because they figured the will-o'-the-wisp would finish anyone off.

But what was his excuse now? His cover was blown. When he walks up to Rashali's, what is he going to say? He didn't have Margo anymore to ask for refuge. All he had was himself and a gun. He would get killed in a second. Zack stashed the gun, making it as inconspicuous as possible. The pink, snot-like goo-thing that covered the entire room, which now that he was out of it looked like an electrical supply room or something. He wondered what happened when it got too big. Would it take over the entire station?

The stations had been blown apart to create a cavernous hall bustling with tents and stalls. So, this is what Refuge looked like. All manner of creatures lived here — elves, trolls, gremlins, vampires, even some Zack had never seen before.

"Buy a charm, love?" A woman with a face concealed by a nest of grey hair asked. She held up a knotted bulb, which Zack had the sneaking suspicion was her own pubic hair. He tried not to cringe as he shook his head as politely as he could and continued down the stalls.

There was a cage of chupacabras with the sign: *you pick 'em, we roast 'em*. Troll wouldn't have been happy to see that. Zack felt a sudden swell of pride towards the chupacabra for evading capture all these years. The air was dense with smoke, and in the corner of his eye he saw a table and a man bleeding into a bowl. His arm was tied off with a tourniquet, and a small tube was tapped into the vein in the crook of his arm.

"Fresh blood, want a bowl?" The man grinned, looking a little pale. Vampires queued in a line. One vampire was taking their money. She gave Zack a wink, and the bleeding man beamed. Zack was curious, so he approached.

"Excuse me, sir..."

"Twelve dollars a bowl, big bowl, filled right to the brim," the man smiled cheerily.

"Are you captive here?"

"Haha, no, no." A vampire hid a smirk as he took his full bowl of blood away. Zack tried his best to quench his thirst, but he had not drunk fresh blood in years.

"Shouldn't let your fluids drop so low, son," the man warned. "Go on, get in line." The line was short, with only two people. Zack checked his wallet. At least he had enough cash. Zack wondered why they needed cash.

"You're new to Refuge," the woman vampire said as a matter of fact, handing him a large black bowl.

"He's not a captive here?"

"He volunteered after word got out about the mares; humans have been begging me to take them. It's better to bleed here than to be ripped to shreds up there." Her voice was smooth, like toffee before it hardens, but with a roughness underneath it that told Zack she was a far older vampire than he was. "Bleed him a few times a week. Give him rest so that he doesn't die. He likes it, don't you, John?"

"I sure do, my queen." The vampire gave a patronising smile, but John did not seem to notice.

"Besides, we need a human to go up there and grab supplies sometimes when Rashali gives the *all clear*. I hire him out to do the groceries. It's starting, you know, the horses, the mist?"

"Yeah, I heard something on the news about that, over in England."

"It will happen here next."

"That's what I'm afraid of."

"Oh, no don't be afraid, it's a good thing, it will be a good thing for my mistress and her kind." John interrupted in earnest.

It was Zack's turn to place the bowl under a freely dripping tap of blood. How long had it been since he had drunk fresh blood? It smelt so good, not that coagulated stuff in juice boxes that always had that glug at the bottom.

As Zack drank, he let his eyes wander over the scene. This place was so alive, with so many creatures. Did they deserve to be down here, sending human slaves up for their shopping? What if someone got sick? Did they die down here? Did they have a healer? What if they needed a hospital? Well, he supposed it wouldn't differ greatly from the situation now. Doctors often refused to treat Mythica. They rarely had insurance, and the doctors' training was limited.

Zack drank his bowl, wanting seconds; hell, he wanted thirds. But he felt a little guilty. He slid a glance at John, who had finished his plastic bottle of water and biscuit. Of course, he needed to keep his fluids up. Zack thanked both John and his vampire mistress and continued down the subway tunnel.

He wondered what would serve as currency if the humans died. Would they return to trading? Did each store have a different way of purchasing? It made sense that way; he supposed. Not everyone needed money to survive; some grew their own food, or caught it, like the chupacabras. Some had magic, and some did not even need to eat or drink at all.

Zack approached an elderly creature whose limbs were tree roots and asked, “Excuse me, do you know where I can find Rashali?” The man looked at him with emeralds for eyes. He opened his mouth, but the sound came from behind him.

“Zack!” He felt a blast of arms embrace him from behind, skinny, bird-like arms. Iloa spun him around herself.

“Zack?” Zack backed away faster now, his mind beginning to spin. This must have been one of Rashali’s tricks.

It was a trap; it had to be. Zack blundered through the crowd of Mythica just to get away. Iloa would not be free to roam. She would be locked away, trapped. Someone snagged his arm. An iron grip kept him there, even though his feet were still moving.

“You know, you never were the brightest crayon in the box, were you?” Zack turned to find a man in a lady’s bright pink jumpsuit. Floral print decorated the low neckline and flamboyant sleeves. There was a yellow plastic belt around his waist. It was something out of the sixties. Great, he was being restrained by a man in drag — no, not drag, just the worst dress-up costume of all time. And he even had bright blue pastel eyeshadow and a ridiculous amount of blush to match.

“Denin?”

“Well, at least you got that one right.”

“Let me go.”

“Not until you shut up. What are you doing here?”

“Zack?” Zack froze again. Iloa was right behind him. Did he dare turn around? “Zack, I’m sorry I didn’t tell you I was alive, but … I tried. The Vetali twins, I sent them to the apartment.”

“We moved to Margo’s.”

“Of course you did,” Denin said, rolling his false eyelashes.

All Zack could do was hug Iloa in a sloppy, mushy hug. He was crying now, only a little, not enough for anyone to notice, at least he hoped not. Relief and happiness flooded through him as he squeezed his friend, and when he let go, he was so happy; he kissed her. He couldn't help it, right on those bird-beaked lips. It was a brief kiss, more like a peck, but it was enough for Zack. Zack waited face to face with the bird girl, wondering what she would make of this rash action. His hands still clasped her face, his fingertips in her crisp white feathers. She blinked a little. Was she waiting for another kiss? What was Zack supposed to do now? A wave of awkwardness hit him, and he wanted to apologise then retreat into a hole.

"Oh, yay, sappy love scene. Everybody go *nawww*," Denin interrupted sarcastically. This broke the tension. The boy had never been so happy to have Denin open his cynical mouth. "By the way, you call that a kiss?" he sniped to Zack, and that was when the vampire had returned to normal and resumed his unrelenting desire to punch Denin in the nose.

"Didn't want to overdo it, you know, in case you burst out crying and your mascara runs," Zack replied with deadly stealth. "We're getting out of here."

"I'm afraid I can't do that." Denin stepped in their path. "I had specific orders to take her here for a tour and bring her back for dinner."

"What are you? Her nanny?"

"I prefer the term caretaker," Denin replied. "On Ava's orders." He reluctantly flashed his bangle. Iloa whispered across the Zack, loud enough for Denin to hear.

"He's my babysitter." Denin gave the girl a warning scowl, which made Zack grin even more. God, it was good to have Iloa back. He gave her hand a squeeze, and she tightened her grip in reply. Fine, if Iloa was going to be a hostage, so was he. After all, you don't argue with a genie, even one in drag, especially one in drag.

#

"Oi! You two!" said a voice that sounded like sandpaper in a blender. "Three of you, huh?" the voice corrected as Spike plopped out from the squishy pink lips of the will-o'-the-wisp. The will-o'-the-wisp was moving underneath them, grumbling like a hungry stomach. It's folds lingered on Talon, then spat him back out like a bad taste.

Troll was more terrified of the other big, pink blob rampaging toward them. That was no ordinary rampaging pink blob; that was a rampaging pink *troll* blob. Troll had not seen another troll since he was the size of a potato sack, and even then he couldn't remember them very well.

Leaping off the edge of the will-o'-the-wisp, Troll gawked at the most beautiful thing he had ever seen. She wore a knitted koala beanie with two big grey pompoms for ears, a pink fluffy coat, and slacks that were more holes than fabric.

"What are you looking at?" Troll took a moment to close his mouth and blink at the oval face scowling at him. Her skin was a little greener than his and, instead of being rigid with calluses, was soft and pockmarked, as if someone had smashed a bed of needles into it and left it to heal in little dents. Her nose was broad and flat, and her eyes were a shiny blue.

Before Troll knew what was happening, a fist landed a crunching blow to his nose, and he fell backwards into the will-o'-the-wisp that gurgled greedily.

"Get your ugly mugs out of here!" The troll barked in a grating bellow. Troll, despite his looks, was capable of quick thinking.

"Was told there was a troll down here, thought I would take a look."

"You got a look, now leave."

"Don't wanna."

"Oh, yeah? You fall on Pinky, Pinky don't like that. Think you are food. Pinky told not to eat Mythica, you tease." Pinky must have been the will-o'-the-wisp. Coming at him again, the troll side-stepped. Troll reached out to grasp her arm almost tenderly, and in that moment of awe of being so close to another of his kind, Troll gave the lady a powerful right hook that knocked her sideways. "Run!"

Troll took a moment to stare at the only other of his species, bent down and stole her koala beanie.

"What?" Troll barked at Spike, who was waiting for him. "I like it."

Spike was in the lead, hopping along the dark walls. Talon toddled behind. Troll wondered why the hell they bothered to bring him.

"Anyone know where we're going?" asked Talon.

"This way," Troll guessed. He was good with darkness, not so good with directions. He supposed it came with being a troll, but not knowing any other trolls, except the one he had just punched in the face, he supposed he would never find out if it was a troll thing or a *Troll* thing.

He wondered what was happening to Zack and Margo. He was getting a bad feeling; he shouldn't have brought Margo along, especially after what that troll had said. If it was this dangerous for them, then God knows what would happen. The tunnel echoed with the sound of the grating of metal and the fall of dust as they passed under a functioning substation. The city ran deep in these parts.

"Oi! You stole my hat!" Great, the troll had recovered.

"Run faster!" Troll snatched Talon up by the neck. The ground thundered dangerously as the troll chased them. Spike hissed angrily into the darkness.

When they saw the drop, it was too late. Troll tumbled forward, unable to scream a warning. The next thing he knew, Talon was falling too, followed by a yowling Spike.

There was no way of telling how far they were going to fall, and that made the feeling of falling ten times worse. Their stomachs were in their throats. They landed on something soft, something slimy, and they bounced twice before sliding off small, oval ovular shaped objects. Then the stench of rotting fish assaulted them. Troll knew that smell.

Talon scrambled to his feet beside Troll.

"What a pretty horse," Talon hummed, lifting a limp head towards a shining obsidian hoof.

"We're dead men," Troll replied.

#

"Where are you taking us?" Iloa inquired.

"Back to your room, both of you. You're going to stay there and not get yourselves killed. If anyone asks, Zack's here because he wants to join Refuge and just happened to see Iloa, and now he *definitely* wants to join."

"Why are you helping us?" Zack asked. "I always thought you hated my guts."

"Because, believe it or not, jumpsuits aren't really my thing." They passed through Refuge at a remarkable pace. Denin had been quiet the entire way, checking his phone, assuming some genie magic meant he could get reception down here. He seemed preoccupied, not even bothering to torment Zack, not even a little.

Dainty white script painted Iloa's bedroom door on the gritty metal. Zack noticed that now a few of her feathers were missing. Did someone take them from her? What was Rashali using them for?

Denin opened the door and shoved them both inside. The door shut, and Zack faced a vast, cavernous room. Lavender paint covered its low ceiling and jagged walls, and a glowing ball of sunlight circled the ceiling, resembling a lost moth. Iloa's bed was a teardrop hammock, like the one she had in Denin's house, and the rest of her room was an absolute scramble of objects.

Iloa somehow always got what she wanted. Zack suddenly felt furious about this. With Iloa so content, did she even try to escape? Did she try to reach him?

"Zack?" Iloa sensed something was wrong.

"You didn't let me know," he said, sounding like a child, but he couldn't help it.

"Zack, I tried, but —"

"Tried? You probably just asked politely, and they said *no*." Iloa recoiled. Zack diverted his anger into exploring the room. Another door opened into a small bathroom complete with a magical waterfall bathtub. God, Iloa had everything she could ever want in here, except for freedom, but he supposed she didn't want that.

"Zack, what are you doing?"

"Finding a way to get out."

"But Denin said to stay here."

"I know what he said. But unlike you, Iloa, I don't want to be babysat for the rest of my life." Zack punched a wall, causing a crack to form in the cement. The blood he had drunk lent him strength. He forgot how strong he could be with a decent breakfast in him.

"Zack," Iloa said, puffing out her chest. "Don't you dare think I'm here because I want to be babysat."

"Then why are you here?"

"I had to, to save Roan. I made a deal. You would have done the same thing. So don't you dare think I'm here because I want to be babysat."

Zack looked sheepishly down at his shoes.

"Roan? You know where Roan is?"

"He's safe. Rashali brought him back to life."

"He died!"

"You see why I had to make my choice?" Iloa said firmly.

Zack nodded and muttered a quiet and regretful, "Thankyou."

"And I tried to find you, I really did try, but you weren't at the apartment and the horses are alive and

Rashali is setting them loose around the world, so I thought it best to stay here. That and Denin is well…"

"Yeah, Denin. Is he still at the door?" Iloa did what she was told and looked out the little peephole.

"Yes."

"Now ask him for something."

"What?"

"Something he can't just conjure up."

"Zack — he's a genie," Iloa replied flatly. "Conjuring things is their life's work." Nevertheless, Iloa opened the door a squiz and asked in a meek little voice. "Denin, could you go fetch Rashali for me?"

"I think she's gone out," Denin replied. There was something strange in his voice. "Distributing hatched horses."

"What about Ava?"

"Why would you want her?"

"Girl talk?"

"Pathetic lie."

"Do you really care?"

"Not really."

Denin knew this was a trick; he just had to figure out what it was. But if he knew, he played along with it. After all, the genie was on their side, wasn't he?

"Don't go anywhere or Ava will have my head." Iloa shut the door to the sound of high heels clomping down stone.

"Stay here," Zack demanded, reaching the door Iloa had just closed.

"What?"

"You heard me."

"I'm coming with you."

"This could be dangerous. I do not want you to get hurt."

"You were just complaining about me being babysat and not sticking up for myself. Well, this is me sticking up for myself." She puffed out her sharp pectoral chest.

"Better babysat than dead," Zack countered, but Iloa was finally, much to Zack's irritation, not backing down.

"I know this place better than you do. You're going to get lost."

Iloa had a fair point there, and Zack contemplated this, watching her, hands on her hips in impatience.

"Do you even know what you're doing?" she asked.

"I've got to find Rashali's lamp. You know how Ava trapped Denin with that bangle thing of his? Well, Rashali is a genie, I think, so she must have a bangle or something to trap her too."

"And you think she's stupid enough to leave it lying around?"

"No, but I know where her lamp is, but it's not what you expect." Iloa replied as if it were the most obvious answer in the world. In response, Zack flung open the door and marched out of there. Iloa was at his heels. Zack knew there was nothing going to stop her, and besides, he kind of didn't want Iloa to leave. Selfish, yes, but a couple of hours ago he thought she was dead. He wasn't about to lock her in a room and leave her there.

"You're heading the wrong way," she said.

"I knew that," Zack replied defiantly, then realised how stupid he sounded. That was when they both burst into laughter. For a moment it was as if they had never left the couch of their old apartment, watching movies and eating bags of marshmallows.

"Rashali's throne is this way. It's usually guarded, though. Who else is here?"

"Troll, Talon, and Spike." He did not mention Margo. He did not want to think about Margo.

It didn't take long for Iloa to lead him to Rashali's cavern. A busted archway of construction steel support frames, which twisted like veins up into the cavern, framing it.

The cavern was immense, with rock and metal snaking along the walls with emerald draped silks like some wretched modern art exhibit. But the throne — no, there was nothing new about it. It radiated ancient magic, sending a copper glow across the vast, dome-shaped room.

“Have you been in here many times?” Zack whispered, wondering if the others were nearby. He could see the copper fragments of the throne glitter from around the corner. Two hulking minotaur guarded the cavern, sulking along the steps leading up to the throne. Zack recognised them as the minotaur from the museum.

“Just a few times. Rashali invites me around for tea.”

“Oh great, you’re best buds now, huh?”

“She’s nice.”

“You think everyone’s nice.”

“She tells me stories, ancient ones, histories.”

“Whoop-de-doo.” Iloa slapped him then, slapped him right across the face. Zack didn’t think Iloa had ever committed such violence before and was rather shocked. She stared at him through narrowed eyes. The minotaur stopped pacing. They had heard the slap. Hoof sounds were coming closer.

Zack padded his pockets. “Crap, no candy.”

“I have candy,” Iloa said as the minotaurs lowered their heads, ready to charge at the intruders. “I always have candy for snacks.” Iloa dug into her pockets and pulled out a fistful of tiny candy canes.

Zack snatched them and threw them into the air.

“Run!”

THE GENIE AND THE MONSTER

A ring of horses closed in on them, their hooves kicking up gravel. With fists clenched, Troll braced himself for a futile fight. One drop of poison, Roan had said — that was all it took, if the hooves didn't do the damage first. That was fine by Troll, anyhow; no sense in dying slowly, wasting everyone's time.

Troll counted ten mares. Ten! Jeese, they bred fast, and no doubt there were dozens more hidden in the shadows. Talon reached out a hand to pat the horse. Troll pulled him back before he could lose his hand and his life.

Two feet landed on either side of his cauliflower ears. Something was on his head. Spike gave a growl, and the mare backed away.

"Hah, stupid horse," Troll cackled. But his victory was short-lived. The horses tensed their flanks. They were going to charge. Troll spun to dive. But his feet slipped, and he ended up lying face down feet away from the gooey nest of eggs.

Spike dived from his head and into the eggs. The eggs! That was a brilliant idea. What mother is going to destroy their own offspring? These mares may have been downright nasty buggers, but they would not stomp on their own flesh and blood, right? He hoped the mares had better maternal instincts than they looked.

Troll burrowed into the egg clusters, a soup of unhatched eggs and some wriggling with their touch.

Where was Talon?

"Ouch! You bit me, you cheeky little thing." Great, he was playing with the horses. Troll, reluctantly, hauled himself out of the safety of the nest and found Talon not so far away, his entire right arm dangling from his body, his tattooed flesh sizzling as if it were roasting over coals.

"Hello Troll."

"Why aren't you dead?" Troll asked, hauling the delusional man into the eggs again. Spike was barking and growling, rolling in the pods, snarling at any mares that dared venture too close.

"Why? Should I be?"

"The venom…" But Troll remembered Bitey, how he had not died either, and just assumed it was because Bitey was a foal. Perhaps, not being a full-blooded Mare of Diomedes, the venom was diluted. However, this was no comfort to Talon, as the diluted mare venom disintegrated his right arm down to the bone.

"Why are you not screaming?" Troll asked. He knew Talon was, for want of a better word, *not all there,* but he would realise his entire hand was melting off his body.

"Why would I be screaming?" Troll asked as they began to walk slowly, creeping through the egg clusters, Troll covering himself in egg slime like it was moisturiser. The slime prickled like weak acid.

"Never mind." Troll figured pointing out Talon's missing hand wouldn't achieve very much at all. Spike guided them, bouncing from pod cluster to pod cluster as if deciding which one would be his next chew toy.

"I think this is where he has been spending most of his time," grumbled Troll, not that Talon was much by way of company.

They slunk and kept close to the walls; now and then they would hear a distant snort or grunt, but they encountered fewer mares than they expected, except for one that had taken a bite out of Talon. She was following as if waiting for her snack to drop dead so she could finish her meal.

"These horses aren't so scary, Spike," Troll made his own conversation. "I can't see how Rashali will destroy the world with them if they get scared of you."

But Troll's answer was revealed to them when they turned a corner and bounced off a silken force field. The mare that was following them recoiled and reared its front hooves with a repellent kick.

Troll looked between the mare, Talon's disintegrating bone and vacant expression, and Spike, who was already trying to swim through the silky force-field like it was a wall of jelly.

He figured that, unless he wanted to become horse dinner, he would take his chances with whatever was on the other side of that wall. So, he pushed Spike's rump through the rest of the way, grabbed Talon by his good arm and pulled him through after him.

#

"You want me to tell you what this cauldron is?" Denin said, arms folded, staring at Ava incredulously. "I'm pretty sure you are not meant to be here."

"Obviously not," Ava replied, standing beside the cauldron, which was seeping tendrils of grey mist into the surrounding stone.

"Mummy is keeping secrets from you again, is she?"

"Shut up. What is this? Tell me all you know, or I'll exchange your pant-suit for a birthday suit."

"Would be far more comfortable." Denin picked a wedgie from his ass crack as he spoke. Ava had made him complete the ensemble with a G-string, and it was getting on his nerves.

"Consider your wish granted, birthday boy." Ava clicked her fingers as if she were the genie, and now Denin was butt-naked.

"Thanks," Denin said wiry.

"Glad we can still have some fun." Ava gave a wink. Denin rolled his eyes as he approached the cauldron cautiously.

"Let's see; Proto-Greek symbols, evil mist … I would say this is Pandora's cauldron."

"You mean her box?"

"The woman had more than one object to put all this … stuff in." Denin waved a hand and stooped, narrowing his eyes at the ancient script along its rim.

"Mist of Achlys. Makes sense now." Denin said to himself with satisfaction, then locked eyes with Ava, enjoying the taunt of knowing knowledge she did not.

"Want me to find something more humiliating than a birthday suit?"

"On the contrary, I find this the best look so far."

"Tell me all you know."

"Oh, my dear Ava, your mother is dabbling in some ancient magic, old friends, one might say."

"Achlys?"

"She is known as the Mist of Death, but she is more than that. Just as, you may have noticed, your mother is a genie of the earth. Achlys is of the winds. However, just as one would trap a genie in a bottle, Pandora trapped Achlys in this." Denin flashed his hands over the cauldron as if he were showing an art project.

"Then why the horses? Why did she kill Mav?"

"Pandora was clever when she trapped Achlys. It broke her down to something … else, something more… instinctual, beastly. The horses tempt her back into this world. Only one part of her, part of her essence can escape."

"And Mav? Why did she sacrifice Mav?"

"Ah, she is clever," Denin muttered to himself.

"I command you to tell me whatever it is you just worked out."

"Mav is mortal. Rashali was instructing the mist to kill mortals, thus preventing the deaths of the creatures she is fighting to save."

"Rashali spoke as if they had met before, called her sister?"

"Rashali is more ancient that you or I could ever fathom, before the plates of the earth split apart. Before humans created their own myths, legends, and cultures, her kind travelled the earth. So yeah, even though a Greek cauldron traps her sister, I have no doubt they share a relation."

"Is that all this cauldron is? Some vessel for a deadly mist?"

"Go ahead and take a peek and see what else is in there, I guess," Denin shrugged. "Pandora put more than one thing in her box. Maybe she has more than one thing in this cauldron. Maybe some terrible, powerful magic could be yours."

"I think you should look first."

"You really want to risk your one and only source of magic?"

"I'll take my chances." Ava smiled sardonically. Denin cast a half-assed eye over the cauldron.

"Just some weird, hellish portal."

"That's not what I meant."

"Fine." Denin sucked in a breath, braced the sides of the cauldron and shoved his head into its centre. Ava braced herself, waiting for something to happen. Denin did not emerge, but he did not fall into oblivion's depths either. After what felt like forever, Denin finally raised his head, his face wind-swept and covered in coal dust.

"There … might be something useful," Denin spoke, not because he wanted to, but because it was part of his command. But before he could elaborate any further, they were interrupted.

"Oi, what the hell are you doin' here?"

Ava leaped back from the cauldron. Denin, apart from being stark naked, looked bored.

"Troll, fancy seeing you here," he said, then his eyes cast to Talon and Spike. "Brought some friends, did we?"

Talon waved cluelessly and asked, "My goodness, that man is naked? Do you think we are overdressed? Should I take my clothes off too?"

Denin's face lowered with a growl. "Someone put the Valsha curse on you, I see. Finally got your wish."

Troll neared, eyeing Ava who was stalking with equal caution. The room offered few weapons, only a collection of rocks and debris but Troll could throw a rock.

"We just want to collect Iloa," Troll warned. "That's all. Don't want to interfere with whatever … this is." He waved a hand at Denin's naked form. "What you do with him isn't any of my business."

"That's not what is going on here." Ava folded her arms angrily. "Now, if you just go back the way you came, we can forget you saw any of this and live to see the end of the world."

"Yeah, there's a bunch of angry mama horses out there that want to eat my flesh, and well, Talon's already lost a hand so we're going to stay right here, thank you very much."

"Would not advise that," Denin muttered under his breath. His eyes were on Talon, who had not said a word since Ava had spoken. Troll noticed it too.

"Maiya? Maiya is that you?" Talon rushed forward before falling to his knees.

"What are you talking about?" Ava stepped back, confused.

"You know how I said that you can't break a Valsha curse?" Denin muttered, edging towards Troll.

"Put some pants on," Troll grumbled back.

"No, no, it's you Maiya, I thought … I thought I had lost…" Talon stared sideways as if watching a lost memory.

"When confronted with the truth, the brain has no choice but to remember. And that goes one of two ways."

"Look, can you just show us the way out of here?"

"Roan, well, he became catatonic, but Talon, well, his brain is pretty messed up as it is. I think he has finally snapped and remembered."

"Get off me." Ava kicked the man as he tried to grovel.

"Maiya, no, don't say that, no."

"I am not Maiya."

"But you, you have to be. You look so much like her. You … I…" Talon looked towards Denin, who was still whispering to Troll.

"Killing the caster of the Valsha curse is the only safe way to remove it. Breaking it like this, well, I suggest we duck for cover."

"My daughter," Talon finished. "I killed Maiya. I killed…"

Now it was Ava's turn to realise who Talon truly was but before she could speak, Denin interrupted.

"Yes, yes, father meets daughter, great, family reunion, okay, let's get out of here." Denin tried to shove Troll out of the way, but the Troll, naturally, would not budge.

Ava glowered down at the man who had murdered her mother. The man who was now fighting against memories that were supposed to have vanished with the curse. His body was contorting and writhing again.

"Ava, might I suggest getting out of here."

"No," Ava snarled with just as much gravity as Talon, whose limbs were elongating, who was shoving his face in the dirt screaming, "Maiya!"

"I've waited so long to find the man who killed my mother."

"He did that!" Talon writhed and flung an accusatory finger at Denin.

"You ordered me to!" Denin screamed back.

"This is some pretty heavy shit," Troll muttered to Spike, who sat on his feet chewing a stolen foal egg.

"I don't care anymore, I don't." Ava spat on the floor in disgust as Talon began to thrash and heave as if every muscle was being electrified. "I'm going to rid myself of my disgusting mortal blood once and for all. I will be pure Mythica.

"My daughter, no!"

But it was too late; Ava plunged her arms into the cauldron.

Talon wailed, his body cracking, his one good arm reaching towards his daughter.

The skin along Ava's arms began to swell and split in cancerous bouts of pus. The cauldron changed; something was coming out of it, something rotten. It plumed to the surface in a bubbling, globular conformation. Ava's skin broke away, ripping, tearing, revealing bleeding muscle. The creature was pulling her skin, and Ava was pulling back. She pulled herself from the cauldron, but whatever held onto her followed.

"My daughter! No!" Talon lunged forward to protect her. But the mist surrounded them both; the swirl of grey steamed and distorted their bodies, as if the acid was melting them together.

"Achlys was ordered to destroy anything with mortal blood," Denin explained as Troll gawked from the sidelines in complete horror. "So it will."

Ava would not stop screaming; she gasped and cried as every fibre of tissue ripped. Then her skin was gone, and all that remained of Ava was her bones held together by connective tissue, which somehow kept her upright.

She was not dead. Magic was keeping her alive, but it was mutating her, fighting against Talon's grip. Talon was clawing at her, crying, the mist consuming him too, causing to lose whatever was left of his mortality, leaving only black ink and curses.

Black ink and curses that clutched onto the closest thing they could find: Ava.

Denin was so mesmerised by this scene of destruction that he did not hear the chink of metal at his feet. Ava was coming towards them, her bone contorting into some hulking thing that resembled the skull of a bull. Her bones kept cracking and contorting to form new features.

Spike growled and lunged forward, protecting Troll and Denin. But the Ava-monster, now twice the size of Troll, snatched up the chupacabra in one hand, bit his head off, and threw its twitching body across the cavern.

“Shit,” Denin said.

Troll, too angry for tears, too angry for words, he did only what Troll knew how to do. He swore, balled his fists and charged.

#

Silken curtains enclosed them, hiding them from the distracted minotaur.

“Zack, I don’t think we should do this. Rashali isn’t who you think she is. She’s actually really nice. And the twins, well, they are creepy, but they don’t mean any harm.”

“Iloa, you don’t know what you’re talking about.”

“I do, and you’re being a dick.”

“Fine, okay, I’m a dick, whatever. You can’t think it’s right for Rashali to just blow up the world as we know it.”

“She’s not trying to do that.”

They continued to argue as Zack searched the empty cavern. Shrouded in hanging red sheets, there was a low-lying bed. Beside that was a shelf of ancient pottery that was sealed with lines of gold, but this gold slithered and moved around the cracks, altering the shape of the pots and cups as if the clay was still trying to decide what exactly it wanted to be.

“I don’t know what you expect to find here,” Iloa said.

“Something that will stop what she is doing, something to stop the end of the world.”

“I don’t know how to stop it.” Iloa fell down on the nearest pillow, “Maybe it’s easier to go along with it because I know we don’t have a choice.”

"If you had a choice, Iloa, would you stop Rashali?" Iloa looked down at her elongated hands. Her mind went back to the twins' words. She was never meant to be this way, never meant to look like this, have these thoughts, never meant to have met Zack, or Troll or Roan. She liked them; she was glad she had met them.

But then, she thought of all of them in that dingy apartment: Roan, hacking his lungs out against Troll's cigar smoke. Roan almost gave his life to get back to his tribe; he sacrificed everything he had here, gave himself to Rashali, and if some part of Roan was prepared to sacrifice the rest of the world for Mythica, why shouldn't she?

"You don't get it," Zack interrupted. "You were never human. I was. Sure, we aren't perfect, hell, we are far from it, and humans do horrible, stupid shit all the time, they have for decades, and if I live long enough, they will probably do it for decades no, centuries more, but, Iloa, you can't … you just can't…"

"You didn't come down here just to save me, did you?"

"No."

"What if I said that I think Rashali may be right. Humans had their chance to do right by our kind, and they haven't."

"I would say that you've been brainwashed."

"How paternalistic, Zack. I can see the mortal blood is still strong in you." Rashali swept silently into the room.

"Rashali, stop this."

"Too late, it's already begun. The horses are released, the Mist of Achlys will follow, devouring everyone with mortal blood, which, is probably a good thing you are down here Zack, sometimes my sister is not as discriminatory as she should be when it comes to half breeds."

"So, we're trapped down here. Great."

"Can I offer you a cup of tea? Well, blood?" Rashali waved a hand, and a dainty teacup of blood appeared. Beside it was an equally dainty cup of warm honey-water.

Iloa slipped down on a pillow and held her teacup solemnly in her hands. Zack hesitantly did the same.

"Iloa, do you remember the Great Gods I told you about?"

"Off by heart," Iloa replied proudly.

"Well, I will tell you one more story. Do you remember the God of Earth?"

"Yes. The god made of rock."

"God of Earth grew lonely, because the Sky God was so far away. She had chosen the Sun God over him. He gazed at the rock that formed him and sighed. And his breath reached the Wind Gods, who took pity on him. The wind breathed life into the mud until the mud began to breathe itself. Life was created, and man was made. But man was mortal and died, and the Earth God was lonely once more. Again and again, the Wind God breathed, but still humans died without knowing the Earth God was even there.

"And so, one night the Earth dreamt of magic, and this magic grew and it wove itself into something more. He took molecule after molecule and the very first bits of dust from the world to create a companion. She was his daughter, and they travelled the world together. And from then on, the Earth was not lonely anymore."

"You were Earth's companion," Zack confirmed, he had not taken a sip of his teacup, tense and ready to run.

"I still am. Just as the Mist of Achlys is the Wind's companion, made from the final breaths of all that have died." Rashali showed her inked wrists.

"What is that?" Zack asked, as if Rashali was trying to tell him something without saying a word.

"It is the unfortunate curse of a genie, Zack, that they are often in servitude to another."

It was then Zack realised Rashali might not be the one commanding the end of the world.

"You cannot stop a god's wishes, Zack, you can only stay out of the way."

Zack sipped his teacup of blood in silence.

The silence lingered until it broke with a growl and a grunt and, "Why you have candy? Where my candy? Ra-ra!" A troll barged through, getting caught in the silk sheets that seemed to wrap around her, stopping her from coming any further.

"Kit? What is it?"

"Bad troll and yucky man. Chased them into horse pit. Stole my hat. Want it back."

"Troll!" Zack leapt to his feet. "We have to get him."

"I want candy. Bully bull got candy, where's mine?"

Rashali summoned a pile full of candy at the troll's feet.

"Come on, let's go fetch your friend," Rashali sighed, "or rather what is left of him."

THE CAULDRON AND THE SACRIFICE

Troll scrambled around heavy rocks. The Ava-monster swiped and clawed, ripping his arms open. The mares, behind the glutinous wall of protection, gathered, bloodthirsty and impatient, just waiting for that barrier to break.

"Troll, we have to get out of here." Denin, still naked, screamed, hiding behind the billowing cauldron.

"Bitch … killed," Troll threw a right hook, then a left hook, "Spike."

"And she will kill you next, come on." Then Denin saw it on the ground, something he had not noticed before. The bangle that had bound him to Ava had fallen off; he was no longer a captured genie. So, naturally, the first thing Denin did was fashion himself his favourite suit and cravat. The second thing he did was a dive for the bangle, which just happened to be right in the Ava monster's current path.

A hand the size of a horse's head came down at him, hitting him where he smacked against the rock wall beside the force field. With his head ringing, he swore he could feel the hot breath of those creatures who were growing more and more eager for every fresh drop of blood spilt. Denin was not going anywhere without that bangle, but with his body limp and head spinning, he could not harness threads of magic, let alone pull that bangle towards him.

"What the hell is that?" Denin flopped his head sideways to see Zack gawk alongside Rashali, Iloa, and Kit the troll.

"It's what you get when your daughter betrays you," Rashali growled.

The Ava-monster was a ripple of flesh trying to rebuild itself as the mist tried to tear her down. Talon's curses flooded her limbs with magic, which made her a hideous sight of rippling flesh that withered like maggots.

The Ava-monster turned at the sound of Rashali's voice and forgot all about Troll. Denin scrambled out of the way just in time before Ava skidded into the horse barrier. The magic glued itself to her, Talon's curses seeping into the force field and pulling it cleanly off the rock.

"Crap," Denin breathed as the horses charged forward. Bangle or not, he was getting out of here. But before he could click his fingers and wrangle whatever magic was in the air, his eyes caught on Zack, who was holding the bangle in his hand. Like hell he was going to let that dweeby vampire have the key to his capture.

In hindsight, it was a stupid thing to do. He should have just flashed himself out of there, but instead, he lunged and scrambled towards Zack.

"Give me that!"

"And let you leave?" Zack fought against Denin's wrangling grip. Around them the horses swarmed. The Ava-monster was swinging her elongated arms around, smashing the horses against the rock walls, which only made them angrier.

Troll was screaming somewhere in the distance, raging as the horses surrounded him. Iloa, somewhere close by, screamed and ran. If Zack had noticed, he would have stopped her, but he needed that genie in his power if they were going to have any chance of escaping this.

In their fight, Zack kicked Denin in the kneecap, and as he fell to the ground. Zack grabbed his arm; Zack slapped the bangle around his wrist. Invisible needles dug into his flesh and bound his magic to that god-awful vampire.

Crap, Denin thought, he should have just got the hell out of here.

"Save her," Zack's first command.

"Who?"

"Iloa!" The two men looked up now at the manic scream surrounding them. The Ava-monster tossed horses into walls, some biting her, melting her flesh while she unhinged her jaws in retaliation and bit a smaller one in the neck. Rashali was forcing the mares away from her, screaming at what remained of her daughter, trying to protect the cauldron.

But Iloa?

"There?"

They both stared at Iloa; she was scrambling over the rubble and the rocks and had collapsed over Troll's immobile form. Something was happening to her. Denin could feel it. He could sense the magic moving.

"Iloa, watch out!" A mare reared above her. Iloa did not move. Its hooves kicked her away from Troll. Denin could see it now. Whether or not Iloa knew what she was doing, Denin knew. He watched as Zack scrambled forward; he watched as Iloa scrambled too, her feathers were falling from her head like a trail. She flew herself back over Troll's body, protecting him with every ounce of magic that she had. Denin did as he had been commanded and sent a pulse of magic towards an oncoming mare. By the time Denin reached Iloa, she was slumped over Troll's torn body, her magic billowing from her like its own mist.

"Iloa, stop," Denin warned, seeing what was happening.

"Save her, get her out of here, what kind of shit, useless genie are you?" Zack was screaming at him.

Of all his captors, Zack was the easiest to resist, perhaps because his commands were more desperate than commanding, or perhaps because Denin was unsure how to perform what Zack was asking of him.

"Go away!" Iloa shrieked as Troll gurgled blood. Her magic flowed and flowed heavily. Denin could not access the magic; it belonged solely to her. She directed the torrent of magic, drenching the troll and healing his injuries.

"Iloa, stop." Denin saw how weak she was growing, how this swarm of magic was uncontrollable, like a child driving a car too fast and unable to reach the brakes.

Troll began to twitch and clench his fists. He sat up. Iloa slumped into his lap.

"Bring her here, Troll." Denin reached forward, but was knocked back by the Ava monster. He tried to pulse magic through the air, but it did nothing but bounce off and ricochet against a hoard of mares. As the Ava-monster turned, a long had swung and threw Iloa across the cavern, where she slumped, unconscious.

"Magic won't work," Rashali called, but Denin had already realised that. But what did they have? The Ava-monster was devouring the mares now; whatever venom or magic they had in them was making her larger, engorging her, until she was breaking through the rock ceiling of the cavern. Rashali threw herself towards Denin. Zack tumbled towards Iloa as the ground shook and walls crumbled.

"I'll need your help," Rashali screamed at him, placing something small and cold in his hand.

A bullet.

Rashali gripped Denin's shoulder as the surrounding earth gave way. Sunlight and dust fell around them. The Ava-monster was about to escape, hauling herself up out of the earth. Buildings were creaking, threatening to topple; cars were nosediving. They did not hear people screaming; no, in fact, they did not see a single mortal daring to look at the scene. Zack could feel the creak of metal and the crash of cement in his bones.

"Not the sort of *end of the world* you were imagining."

"Never have children, Denin; they are such a disappointment." As the Ava-monster hauled herself up out of the rubble, Rashali and Denin used what remaining magic they had to raise the bullet in the air. Would they have enough to accelerate it? Would it be enough to stop the Ava monster? They had to try.

The two genies, arm in arm, their feet tremoring and crumbling ground. They raised the bullet in the air.

Then a horse came.

The mare bucked and bellowed toward them, breaking their magic. Denin and Rashali rolled in different directions. The mare whinnied and trampled over Rashali, who fought back with what little magic she had left, sending it blasting across the cavern. Behind her the cauldron rang out as if in distress; small tendrils of mist remained and shrouded Rashali as if protecting her, no, not protecting her, dragging her back into the cauldron.

"I need you," Denin cried. He didn't have enough magic; he could barely make their bullet hover. Then, he looked over to Iloa, trying to rise to her feet. Denin couldn't break his command, could he? But if he didn't kill the Ava-monster, it could attack Iloa. He needed to kill it to save her, right?

Denin tumbled closer to Iloa.

"Denin, get her out of here."

"Order me to kill Ava," Denin screamed back, the bullet hidden, clutched in his fist.

"What! Yes, of course, if you can do it, kill the bitch," Zack screamed back, throwing a gun from his back pocket. Where did Zack get a gun from? Would it fit the bullet? Would the extra bit of gun powder spare Iloa's life? Denin loaded the gun, Zack's command was all Denin needed.

Denin took in a breath, sucking in whatever shreds of magic Iloa had left, raised the gun, and with all his magic and Iloa's combined, pulled the trigger at the scratching Ava-monster just as she was raising herself up onto the streets. The bullet hit its mark at the back of her head. The monster did not move for a moment, its body seized, claws gripping the rubble. Then, with another shoot of magic, just for good measure, Denin sent the bullet zooming back into Ava again, and again, just as the earth orbits the sun, the bullet shot through the Ava-monster as she fell, collapsing back down into the cavern.

The Ava-monster was dead.

Sunlight dampened, and Denin soon realised why. The mist. It was everywhere, cascading down into the pit.

Denin turned back to the cauldron. Rashali was cradling it. The mares were devouring the limp remains of the Ava monster. The mist, in turn, devoured them. Iloa was lifeless. Zack was screaming. Then he noticed someone else hiding. At first, he thought it was Troll; no, it was a different troll, yes; he had seen her around before; Kit.

"Kit, help them, I can't." Denin rose, choosing to rescue the seemingly inert cauldron first. Kit, more damaged by the falling rocks than anything else, obeyed. She hauled Iloa over one shoulder and snatched Troll by the ankle and dragged him forward. Zack followed urgently as the mist swirled towards his mortal blood curiously. They slipped between rock crevices.

"Kit, I don't have enough magic. Could you?" Kit grunted and with a boot, kicked the precarious rocks until they crumbled, securing them back into refuge. The mist did not follow.

"Guess this is home for a while," Denin grumbled. Clasping a bitter hand on Zack's shoulder. "I suggest you find something other than mortal blood to drink in case that mist mistakes you for food."

"Thanks for the tip," Zack grumbled.

"Aren't we just going to have a wonderful eternity together?" Denin replied bitterly, somehow, the bangle on his wrist, felt just a little less daunting than when Ava had placed it on him.

#

Iloa did not wake. They had carried everyone back into Rashali's chambers, where the silk curtains turned to stone behind them. "Use your *fucking* magic, Denin!" Zack sobbed weakly, falling down beside Iloa's body where Kit had dropped her upon the coffee table. It was strange seeing her, bald, her skin paper-thin as if losing magic had sucked her dry.

"Bad…to…swear," Troll's broken voice rasped before he coughed out blood.

"I don't have any magic left," Denin panted, "Used it all on … that… bitch." Denin narrowed his eyes at Rashali, who looked just as drained as he did. She said nothing; instead, she fell to her knees as she stared at the fading henna on her forearms.

"Iloa, Iloa, please. Please give her magic back. Come on, Iloa," Zack screamed.

"Kit," Rashali said eventually, "go find the Vetali twins. They will be somewhere in the Refuge. If anyone can save her, it will be them."

Kit did as she was told, but not before jabbing a finger at Troll and saying, "Don't die."

"I hope you're happy now," Zack growled across Iloa's body at Rashali. "You got what you wanted."

"I am," Rashali replied, the henna across her arms now completely disappeared. She flexed them as if seeing her limbs for the first time.

Only Denin seemed to realise what was going on. He stared down at his own arm, now bound by the magic that Rashali was free of.

"The earth had released me." Rashali looked to Denin, her golden eyes wide, almost lost. She crawled towards Iloa's form. Zack screamed, "Get away from her."

Zack stood over Iloa, not wanting to get close, half believing this was not Iloa, that Iloa was somewhere else.

"She has a heartbeat," Denin spoke. "I shouldn't be near her; I'm taking her magic."

"It doesn't matter anymore," Rashali grunted. "Half of her is gone."

"That's not true!" Zack bellowed like a desperate man.

"It is true," Kayne said from the stone entrance. Beside him stood his sister.

"We should never have left her side."

"I'll sacrifice more years, anything, take them," Zack begged as the twins approached. The twins looked at one another with pity.

"That won't be necessary."

"She is already dead."

"Not quite."

"As dead as the re-born can be."

"She is fighting it."

"She doesn't want to pass."

"She knows…"

"Knows? Knows what?"

The twins did not speak.

"Denin," Zack growled, not caring to wait for an answer, "hit him." And of course, Denin obliged with a right hook to Kayn's face. Lath gasped as if her brother's pain was her own too.

"They're telling the truth!" Rashali said, trying to soothe them, stroking Iloa's bare head. Zack slapped her hand away.

"She won't die because she doesn't want to," Rashali explained. "Because she knows that when she is reborn, she won't remember any of this."

"She won't be Iloa anymore," Lath agreed.

"Not as you know her."

"She doesn't want that," Zack said. "If she wanted that, then she would have died and been reborn already. She wants to stay as Iloa."

It's impossible for her to do that.

"She will find a way." Zack clasped her hand, "I know she will."

What remained of their small, mismatched crew stared at one another.

Troll hauled himself up by Zack's side and clasped a bloodied, broken hand onto his shoulder.

"Margo's dead, Troll," Zack sniffed. "I think you should know that."

"Selfish old bat." Troll wiped blood (or was it a tear?) from his cheek.

There was no mercy in the real world, no happy ending, no cure, or deus ex machina. Iloa remained in the state between life and death; she would stay like that, corpse-like and sallow.

Zack was only one man, one boy, a seventy-three-year-old teenager who seemed little more than a child right now. Because when you're faced with something like this, you realise how vulnerable you are.

Not even a genie, not even all the magic in the world could make a stubborn bird-girl accept death.

And so, Zack nested beside Iloa, remembering a time when she was alive, his memories fractured by the screams of the dying above his head. The mist was attacking New York.

"We're stuck down here, aren't we?" Denin asked.

"Until the mist returns." Rashali stroked the cauldron.

"She's in there, isn't she?"

"Achlys? Yes."

"She can't escape."

"No."

"Why?"

"She has not been granted permission. Even I needed to be granted permission to stand above ground. Only her mist, an extension of her consciousness, her most primal consciousness, was permitted to escape."

"And now?"

"I've earned freedom … until the Earth demands something of me again."

"But Achlys?"

"Different master. I don't make the rules."

"I'm not looking so bad now, am I?" Zack said bitterly to Denin, mustering some sort of dry humour.

"Yes, well, I'm assuming all you desire of me is to bring your girlfriend back from the dead. Not an impossible task at all," Denin replied with equal bitterness.

"How about this: you bring her back, and I'll let you free?"

"She needs to die and be reborn into her true form."

"No, she doesn't want that. Why would she care what she used to be when she never got to be who she is now?"

"That is life," Lath said.

"And death."

"Death is unsympathetic to what you want."

"I don't care what death wants either," Zack growled.

"So…"

"Mortal of you."

They stared down at the bird-girl made of magic. Her pallid skin glowing, fighting against a ripple of embers deep inside her. No, Iloa did not want to die; she did not want rebirth. She wanted sunlight and sugar packets and music.

And hell, Zack would not give up on that.

THE APOCALYPSE

Five months later,

The apocalypse had lasted three months. In that time, the horses reigned, and the Mist of Achlys devoured them in waves and waves. The mist took humans just as it had been commanded to do. Many remained inside, locked their doors and their windows, but they all had to come out eventually, and when they did, Achlys was waiting.

In the weeks that followed, Zack had remained in Refuge. He visited the surface only once he had fed off the blood of Troll (which tasted god-awful, by the way). It was an excursion he regretted. Humans, the stragglers, were still around. He watched a small toddler being ripped to pieces. The boy had been crying in the street for his mother. Zack had seen him from a distance and was about to approach when the mist came.

The mist spared no one.

From then on, Zack could not bear to resurface.

Eventually, Zack agreed to keep Iloa's body with the Vetali twins. They kept her body safe at the mortuary.

The world was an alien planet now. The elves had claimed New York as their own, releasing the stored bonsai trees upon the city where they had twisted and grown with unearthly speed. All Mythica agreed this was a welcome change. The sun filtered through canopies of emerald green and iron; the underground cracked open by their roots, creating earthy caverns and tunnels where moss and lichen thrived.

Many of the Mythica had deserted man-made areas to live as they would naturally. Some remained to scavenge what they could. Zack didn't know what was going to happen; he doubted they would set up a government; there wouldn't be any sort of law. It would be every Mythica for itself. Of course, Mythica would form alliances and trade, but Zack wondered how long they would last. These creatures had been bound by a common enemy. Now that the enemy was dead, what was holding them together? Troll journeyed out with Kit and reported back to Zack.

One day, when the humans had almost completely disappeared, Troll said, "You can't stay here for eternity."

"Yes, it is rather depressing. May as well be in a coffin," Denin always lingered around, waiting for an order. Usually, it was *make Troll's blood taste better*. Occasionally Denin could convince an elf to donate, but that would make Zack's head spin as if he were high. Zack did not like it, but Denin said it made him more pleasant.

"We can visit Iloa?" Troll offered. He was being unusually kind. Usually Troll did not offer; he would just grab Zack by the scruff of his neck and drag the vampire to the Vetali twins.

"I don't want to. No point."

Iloa rested in what remained of the mortuary. She lay in a too-small wooden coffin. Lifeless, still fighting to return to life, guarded by those creepy-ass twins. Zack couldn't bear to be around her but could not bear to be away. So he lay for hours in the room she had lived in at Refuge, slumped on a dusty beanbag.

"You are right, no point." Troll's oversized hand ripped him from his beanbag of self-pity. He saw now that a duffel bag was packed and Kit and Denin were also standing, waiting.

"You forgot about your horse," Troll said, shaking Zack, his feet still off the ground. "We are going to find him."

"Denin, can you take them to where ever Roan is."

"Nope, no magic. You need a good walk."

"Do I have to come?" Denin whined.

"Yes, family holiday." Troll had become oddly sentimental since Spike had been ripped to shreds, not to mention the loss of Margo. Zack still wasn't sure which one Troll missed more.

"Fine," Zack sighed.

The airports were down, and Zack doubted a plane would fly again. But boats still existed. Kit had found a group of trolls who had taken to the sea. They stole military submarines and warships. The entire ship stank of rotting fish. It was a miserable time. Perhaps in another time he might have enjoyed meeting new Mythica, learning and exploring. But Zack was in no mood to make friends; he just wanted his old ones back.

The journey took a little over four weeks. Denin suspected the trolls got lost but refused to take his advice on celestial navigation.

Once they made it to England, locating centaur tribes was the simplest part of their journey. Everyone knew them. They had just about taken over England, culling the horses that Achlys couldn't devour. The centaurs were the peacekeepers, and when they were around, no one fought. They were a species that demanded a sort of reverence. Not even the fey dared cross them.

Zack could see them now in the distance, racing across the moors. Wind whipped at Zack, chilling him to the bone. The centaurs were galloping shapes in the distance, un-phased by the typical English weather. Zack huddled his laptop bag close to his chest and staggered down the gentle slope of the hill towards these creatures.

They were so different from what Zack understood a centaur to be. In all his life, he had never appreciated what Roan was. To him, Roan was always just a grumpy old fart of a horse who complained his joints hurt from lack of exercise.

Now he saw these beasts leap off the ground as if there were repulsive magnets under their hooves propelling them forward. One shot an arrow from his bow while in the air. It pierced a rabbit twenty meters away. Zack had to squint a little to realise that the centaur who had sprung the arrow was Roan. Zack's heart sprung like an arrow, and he raced down the last part of the hill, his arms clutching his overloaded bag.

"Roan!" Zack waved. The centaur stood there, stunned a little until Roan recognised his old friend.

"Zack!" Roan galloped forward, signalling to his tribe that Zack was no threat. Zack realised now that there were so many of them and still more racing up the horizon. Roan slung his bow back as he approached. "What are you doing here?" Roan's hair had grown long and was tied with a vine. He had not looked this young in years; in fact, Zack had never seen him look this young at all.

"Didn't have anywhere else to go." There was something in Zack's voice that told Roan they needed to talk. And so, he gestured for Zack to walk alongside him. His tribe stayed where they were.

"I see Rashali won then."

"It's … more complicated than that." And Zack explained how Ava double-crossed Rashali, how she had become a monster. How Margo had died. How their mission had failed and how Iloa had paid the price for it. Roan listened patiently; his silence was almost comforting. He felt like a ghost beside Zack, a guiding spirit. Once Zack had finished, they had reached the dead rabbit. Roan took it and tossed it into his pack, replacing the arrow in its quiver. Zack waited for Roan to speak.

"Do you think it was worth it?" Zack asked when Roan remained silent. "All that death? Could there have been a better way?"

"There could have been thousands of ways," Roan replied, "but this was the way we chose."

"I watched children die."

"So did I," Roan's voice was rigid when he spoke.

"Maybe it's harder for me because, well, I used to be human."

"Perhaps. Or perhaps you feel more guilt because you had some freedoms with being a vampire. But my tribe, we speak of the human reign as a nightmare finally come to pass. We have revived so much of our old lives that we don't ponder the innocent deaths."

Zack didn't know what to say. Everything had turned out perfectly for Roan. His tribe had accepted him; he found his brother. He returned to England to do what he had dreamed of doing since his exile all those years ago. He even had a mate, Eila. There were many foals too in the tribe, those that humans had bred for servitude. They were being taught the old ways, the old language and traditions, or rather, whatever remained of it.

"Zack…" Roan was thinking long and hard; Zack could see it on his face. It was as if he had aged centuries again. Those croaks and furrows and thin lips. Eventually, he spoke, "Remember back at the museum when I stole that cuff?"

"Yes."

"Do you want to know why I did it?"

"Because you're a crazy ass horse who was trying to get us both killed?" Roan gave a sideways grin. He looked so different without his fedora.

"Because in that moment I glimpsed back at my past, I saw it as it was and how it is now, and I wanted it so bad, so I took it. It belonged to me. Iloa belongs with you. Now I don't know how you can get her back, or even if you can. I would never have imagined I would be here like this now, but some things you can't imagine, some things you can't predict, Zack."

Zack managed a grin. The centaur was always too deep and meaningful to be understood.

“Our lives are shaped by a cluster of whims and poor choices, not to mention poor advice, and well, my advice would be to find the right sort of magic to revive her. There is a world of Mythica now, a wealth of knowledge that an ex-mortal has no clue about.”

“Ex-mortal,” Zack scoffed to think about it. How different his life could have been. He would have been what? An eighty-something year old corpse by now?

Roan laughed a robust laugh, the sort of laugh that would have ended up with severe smoke inhalation in their old apartment.

“Oh, here.” Zack handed Roan his laptop case. “They’re your memoirs. I thought you would like them back.”

And so, these two old friends departed with words of hope and friendship, unsure what troubles their choices would bring them.

#

Earth orbited in a state of profound transformation. Cities that once were, crumbled to make way for leaf and root. Mythica rose and flourished like seeds in springtime. All except for one Mythica, who remained dormant.

There lay a bald bird-girl. She lay in a stagnant state of silence within the confines of a mahogany coffin. Those brilliant golden eyes were closed, flickering madly behind translucent eyelids.

Those eyes did not witness the purple-hued magical shield swarming above her. That shield was there to keep her safe, protect her from even the Vetali twins, which Zack still did not trust. That shield kept her confined, caged, trapped in a body that was not truly hers.

She did not see the twins’ concerned expressions that peered over her every day.

She did not see Zack’s face say goodbye to her before he left for England.

And she certainly did not see the bullet that sliced easily through that magic shield and plunge into her chest.

www.ingramcontent.com/pod-product-compliance
Lightning Source LLC
Chambersburg PA
CBHW022125050726
47590CB00002B/407

* 9 7 8 1 7 6 4 0 6 5 4 2 9 *